#BestYearEver

#BestYearEver

Karli Cook

MOUNTAIN ARBOR
PRESS

MOUNTAIN ARBOR
PRESS
Alpharetta, Ga

This is a work of fiction. Names, characters, businesses, places, and events are either the products of the author's imagination or are used in a fictitious manner. All persons and events are written in the interpretation and understanding of the author and do not claim to be absolute truth.

ISBN: 978-1-63183-812-5 - Paperback
eISBN: 978-1-63183-813-2 - ePub
eISBN: 978-1-63183-814-9 - mobi

Library of Congress Control Number: 2020906462

Printed in the United States of America   0 4 1 4 2 0

⊗ This paper meets the requirements of ANSI/NISO Z39.48-1992 (Permanence of Paper)

You don't have a right to the cards you believe you should have been dealt. You have an obligation to play the hell out of the ones you're holding.

—Cheryl Strayed

Chapter 1

Barely Survivin'
to Nothing but Thrivin'

"Jack, let's go to the potty."

"Jack, try to use your words to tell Momma what you want."

"Jack, please go back to sleep—it's three a.m. and Momma has a busy day tomorrow."

These are just a few sentences I've said numerous times on a daily basis over the past three years. My seven-year-old son is autistic, and falls into the severe category due to his significant lack of speech. Luckily, his behavior falls into the mild to moderate category, so it makes low-functioning autism a tad easier.

My name is Piper, and I am an autism mom.

I used to actually be more than just an autism mom, but I seem to have lost a lot of myself over the past four years while figuring out this thing I like to call "autismland." I have a master's degree in social work, so I used to be kind of social at one point in my life. I had friends, and would go out, and occasionally drink, and sometimes break out the cigarettes. My husband and I would have people over for dinner, or we would go to other friends' houses to eat, drink, and be merry. I used to take Jack on play dates with my friends' similar-aged children. My husband and I would also travel a lot. A LOT, a lot. Even after Jack was born, my parents would watch him while hubby and I played in many places across the pond, like Rome, Paris, and Amsterdam, just to name a few.

Then autism reared its ugly head into the household. It was very ugly in the beginning. Every day was spent driving to numerous therapy and doctor appointments, and buying only organic, gluten-free, casein free, sugar-free foods at Whole Foods, and putting at least twenty different vitamins and supplements into Jack's juice. And that just scratches the surface.

I think the worst part of our particular autism journey, which is different for everyone, was the sleep deprivation. Unfortunately, a large percentage of autistic children also have sleep disorders. And since I have always loved sleep more than anyone or anything in the world, it was no surprise that I was given the one child who could live on two hours of sleep . . . every night . . . sometimes for weeks at a time. I cried almost every day and night, because I was so mentally, physically, and spiritually exhausted. I wanted to curse those who told me, "God doesn't give us more than we can handle," because He did. He gave me way more than I could handle.

Those first two autism years are a blur, but not the same blur you have for the first three months after you bring your child home from the hospital. No, not that kind of blur. It was the kind of blur that only special-needs parents, or those with medically compromised children, can have. The kind of blur that when you are past the worst of it, you realize you blocked out the part where you woke up every morning wondering how you were going to make it one more day . . . how you would make it through one hour without crying . . . how you were going to muster up the energy and time for a shower, or at least brush your teeth.

Now imagine these daily struggles, and then imagine how much they can impact a marriage. To begin with, both you and your spouse try to figure out how this whole autism thing happened in the first place. The who and what that is responsible for it all. I didn't dwell on this issue as much, or as long as my husband did, therein starting the steady progression of marital unbliss. I wanted to put my energy into finding the "cure" instead of the "reason."

While my husband decided that his coping skill was to work too much and avoid being home, I was trying to help my son. At first, I was trying to help him so I could have that "normal" child everybody else around me had. But I soon realized he was slipping further and further away from all other kids his age, and it turned into survival of the fittest. I was simply trying to give him the tools to survive in this challenging world.

All the while, I was also trying to find my own tools to survive in the autism storm. And helping my marriage survive took a back seat to my son. I could barely get the energy to feed myself, let alone make food for my husband. I could barely keep my eyes open all day, let alone keep them open long enough to have sex. And I could barely have a thought process longer than thirty seconds that didn't involve autism, because Jack's quality of life depended on it.

And while the sleep deprivation was the hardest aspect of the whole autism process, it was also the hardest on the marriage. Just like most married couples, we always slept in the same bed. We had to have the monitor on all night, since Jack could wake up at any moment. Why couldn't we just keep sleeping while he stayed awake, you ask? Yeah, sounds easy enough. But not with a severely autistic child.

Jack was actually happy and content, for the most part, at 2:00 a.m. or 4:30 a.m., or whenever he decided he had already had enough sleep for the next twelve to twenty-four hours. He rarely left his room during these middle-of-the-night "parties," and his room was childproof. But nothing is really childproof from an autistic two-year-old. They don't understand the concept of safety at any level. Jack could easily climb out of his crib and decide the knobs on the dresser were the perfect size to help him climb to the top of the six-drawer dresser. Or that the bathtub was the perfect location to jump off the side and into the tub, pretending all the while there was water in there to soften the landing when there actually wasn't. Or the main safety hazard of thinking the bed was his trampoline while jumping up and down, then diving headfirst into the mattress. However, sometimes it might be the hard wood of the crib smacking his face instead of the soft, cushy mattress. And because I was a decent human who cared about my child, I couldn't just "sleep through" these endless possibilities of ending up at the ER in the middle of the night. Or worse.

When Jack transitioned to a big-boy bed from his crib, life was actually harder. He now liked to explore even more, like standing at the top of the second-floor banister to plot his escape by jumping off the thirteen-foot railing, not understanding at all that this would 99 percent end in his untimely death. And again, because I was a halfway competent mom, I couldn't take that risk.

So, my husband and I had to figure out a way to function on little to no sleep, and the logical solution was to sleep in separate beds and take turns with the monitor. Not the best solution to keep a marriage alive, but survival is the only mode necessary at these times.

The separate bedrooms were definitely helping the sleep deprivation, since only one of us had to suffer each night. But it definitely wasn't helping the intimacy. The problem with special-needs parenting is that we put ourselves last, and the marriage even after that. So, needless to say, sex did not happen very often. And honestly, when you are having such extreme emotions over a three-year period, and your only goal is to help your son and try to stay alive in the process, sex is the last thing on your mind.

A few years later, things in the autism world remained pretty much the same, but we felt we were better equipped to deal with that world by then. So, hubs and I started finding ways to enjoy our lives. And when I say "enjoy," I mean happiness from the little things like watching a movie together, to the big things like taking mini vacations while the nanny watched Jack. However, even when on vacation, one of our goals was catching up on sleep and life in general, so intimacy was still limited. And unfortunately, (or fortunately, however you want to look at it) most of these fun activities and vacations excluded Jack. Taking him anywhere was pretty much a nightmare, but not so much for us as it was for the strangers who couldn't handle his incessant stimming screams.

Sometime after Jack turned six in June 2016, I decided to take control of my happiness. I realized happiness is not something that lands in your life like a job opportunity, but rather something you create, like a strong friendship. It's something that takes time and energy, but is worth it in the end. Happiness, in my opinion, is what and how YOU make it.

Chapter 2

Oh, to Be Eighteen Again

I made a mental list of things and people and places that made me happy, and started putting a plan in action. Luckily we had the finances to be able to afford all of these happy things, so I created what I could. My husband decided that he would rather stay in his avoidant phase, but I was determined to embrace the challenges with a positive attitude.

First, I decided that I wanted to use all of the challenging autism experiences and be an advocate for those who did not have a voice. I set up a website to promote my services, and opened myself up for any one-on-one or group/organization that wanted information on autism. I also started writing a book about my last four years, and the autism roller coaster, since I felt that I was finally at a place that I could finish the book with a positive tone. A year before, my mood and thought process was so imbedded in the struggles that the book would've been 100 percent negative. At least now it would only be partly negative.

I started this new "happiness adventure" by going on my third New Kids on the Block cruise. Yes, you read that right. NKOTB, as they now like to be called, had been my source of infatuation and giddiness since I was fifteen. I had only been on one of their yearly cruises since they reunited, so I was ready for another one. My first New Kids cruise was in 1990, and even though it included all members of my family, it was still a pretty darn good time. But the best time of my life so far was the

NKOTB cruise in 2009, and I was always ready for the challenge of one-upping that trip.

I had five months to plan for my cruise. Obviously it doesn't take five months to plan a cruise, but I had to be on my A game. I started with the physical component, and began a new skin care regime. I was forty-two years old, but I wanted to look thirty-two. Even though all the members of NKOTB are older than forty-two, I still wanted to look good. Now keep in mind, I am not delusional enough to think that I would actually "hookup" with any of the guys. But hey, a girl can dream. And since all five of them were on my "hall pass," I didn't have to worry about my husband getting mad if the opportunity ever presented itself. One of the members was gay and married to another man, but I still kept him on the pass. You never know!

I had six guys on my hall pass list. Besides all five members of the New Kids on the Block, the sixth person was someone I always called the "love of my life." However, he was more of the "obsession," or "infatuation," of my life. When I think of what the phrase "love of my life" truly entails, I think of something mutual between two people. But it was never like that with Patrick and I.

Patrick had no idea that I even existed until I was eighteen years old, and he was twenty. However, I knew everything about him when I was sixteen, including his license plate number and all the names of his family members. I had the typical adolescent girl stalker-type mentality. I remember the very first time I ever laid eyes on Patrick. He was sitting in the bleachers at our high school football game. I was there doing my halftime dance routine with the high school pom-pom squad, and he was home from college visiting his alma mater. I know it sounds like I should be popular and pretty if I was on the pom-pom squad, but not exactly. I mean, I wasn't ugly, but I definitely wasn't anyone that Patrick Barnes would ever consider going out with. Patrick was the football star when he was in high school, and was also playing football in college at the time, so everyone seemed to know him. He looked like a celebrity to me . . . tall, blond, and handsome, and everybody stopped to talk to him. Everyone except me.

After staring for what seemed like five seconds, but was probably more like five minutes, I pulled my tongue off of the floor and asked my bestie who he was. When Dianna realized who I was pointing at, she looked at me and said, "You don't know who that is? That's Patrick Barnes, he was the football star last year. But I don't think he's a star in college." Dianna thought this was funny, and chuckled a bit. I have no idea how I never noticed him before, but Patrick was hands down the most beautiful thing I had ever seen. Dianna then said, "Come on, let me introduce you." As Dianna began pulling my arm to follow her, I yelled, "Hell No!" I was still in the awkward stage of trying to find myself, and trying to figure out how to put on makeup at the same time. I was not a girly-girl, and I was still sort of in love with the New Kids on the Block.

Jump ahead two years . . .

I just graduated from high school, and was going to enjoy the summer doing nothing before I left for college in the fall. I had a boyfriend who was actually a pretty great guy. He was so great that I decided he was the perfect one to take my virginity. We had sex for the first time a month before high school graduation. It wasn't his first time, but I never regretted losing my V-card to such a good guy. I knew he was crazy about me and, for the most part, the feeling was mutual. However, I am not going to lie . . . I had spent the last two years stalking Patrick any chance I got. I knew when the college breaks were, and would diligently scope out all parking lots for his bright red Mazda RX-7. And, luckily, it was kind of hard to miss.

My boyfriend had already moved to the University of Texas campus, so I spent most of the summer with my good friend, Cyndi. One night we decided to play tennis instead of going out. We sucked at tennis, but it was something to do in small town Texas. After sloppily hitting the ball, we decided that getting ice cream was so much easier and better. All the way to the ice cream shop I had to listen to Cyndi tell me about this guy, Derrick, that she had just met. She went into great detail about how awesome he was, how sweet he was, and how great of a kisser he was. Blah, blah, blah! I had tuned out the rest of the details until she looked at me and said, "Oh my gosh, I can't believe I forgot to tell you who Derrick's roommate is . . . Patrick Barnes!"

Right at that moment, all sanity left my body, and I was sixteen again. It was just like in the movies when the heavens open up, with the sound of the gospel choir singing dramatically in the background. All I could think about was finally getting my chance. Now he might actually want to touch me, since I didn't look like a prepubescent teenager anymore, with a bad perm, and an obsession with a cheesy boy band. Well, I was still obsessed with NKOTB, but now I hid it well. Okay, so I didn't hide it *that* well, but I wasn't ashamed.

So, this was it! Cyndi set up a double date for all four of us to go bowling. I know bowling does not sound too exciting, but remember, this is small town Texas with not a lot of options for those under twenty-one. I was very surprised at how "normal" I felt on the date. I hope I appeared normal to him, anyway. I was comfortable with Patrick, and that was a foreign feeling for me. It's really hard to keep it together when you feel like you are with a celebrity, but he made it easy. I completely forgot what actually happened during that game at the bowling alley. I just remember trying to stop myself from staring at him every second.

And what else did I forget that night? I forgot that I already had a boyfriend.

After the date, Patrick drove us to my parents' house to drop me off, since I had a very strict curfew. The story about why I had such a strict curfew is for another book. Cyndi and Derrick were busy in the back seat making out. I didn't think RX-7s had back seats, but they somehow made it work. However, I don't think those two hated the lack of space.

After staring at each other for a few seconds, likely thinking the same thing, Patrick leaned in to kiss me. I don't remember every detail, or how the actual kiss was, I just remember how happy I was. I truly felt, at that moment, that I had to be the luckiest girl on earth.

However, one thing I do remember *vividly* about the kiss was what Patrick said to me right after we made out for a few minutes. Thinking he was going to say something sweet and romantic, Patrick looked at me and said, "I felt like I was kissing myself."

Um, what? At first, I thought he meant it felt like he was kissing a friend, or even worse . . . his sister. I wasn't quite sure how to take it. And he must have sensed my confused look, because he then smiled his gorgeous smile and said, "I mean, you kiss just like I do." His smile, and his lean in for a second kiss made me realize it must have been a good thing.

After we said our goodbyes, I immediately went into my parents' house and called my boyfriend, to break up with him. I know it was kind of a shitty thing to do over the phone, but I felt it had to be done quick. The breakup was not because Patrick gave me the idea that he wanted to be mutually exclusive. Actually, quite the opposite. I knew all about his other girlfriends, and I was surprised that he even went out with me to begin with. I guess I just figured that if I could make out with another dude and have zero regrets, I probably didn't love my boyfriend the way he loved me, or at least the way that he deserved to be loved.

I moved into the dorms at the University of Texas in the fall of 1992 to start my freshman year, and Patrick was going to be returning there for his junior year. And believe it or not, I wasn't attending that college just because Patrick was there. Well, it may have been like the twelfth reason on that list, at best. I always planned on going to school at UT, even before I knew who Patrick Barnes was. However, Patrick was not playing football for the university anymore. I never got the story on his reason for leaving his football fame, but I'm assuming he lost a scholarship, or didn't make the cut one year. I don't really know how college sports work, and I never asked. I honestly didn't care that he was a popular football player. There was something so special about Patrick that I didn't care what he did, or how much money he had, or what he wanted to be when he grew up. I thought Patrick was perfect.

A few days before school started, as I was settling into the dorm, Patrick invited me over to his apartment. He was technically a junior, so he didn't have to stay on campus, and could have his own apartment. That night was the first time we had sex. You would think that I remembered every single detail about that night, but I don't. Patrick was only the second person that I had been intimate with, and I had lost my virginity just three months earlier. Instead of being able to enjoy every second of him, I'm guessing I was internally freaking out that my dream of over two years was finally coming true. Also, I was probably focusing on not looking like a completely inexperienced lover. I figured he had been with many girls, so I didn't want to disappoint.

Two days later, I decided that it would be fun to go over to Patrick's apartment and surprise him. However, on this particular afternoon, *I* was the one that was surprised when a girl answered the door. I remember she was not completely dressed, and she told me that Patrick was in the shower. The funny part was that she was giving ME the dirty look. Shouldn't I be the one doing that? Well, I guess not if Patrick was doing the same things with her as he was with me, which was likely the case.

I knew what was going on, and that she had obviously spent the night. I remained calm and I told her that I would just wait for him. I wanted to see his expression when he came around the corner and saw me sitting at his kitchen table. I have to say, the look WAS priceless! And as Patrick was trying his hardest to tell me that she was actually his friends' girlfriend, and that his friend had just left to get lunch, the girl crawled right back into Patrick's bed, making it more than obvious that she wasn't his friends' girlfriend after all.

I kept in occasional contact with Patrick for a couple more years in college, even after the "find girl in bed" incident. I was probably the only person in history that didn't get upset about seeing another girl in the bed of someone she just had sex with days before. Don't get me wrong, I was definitely pissed about it, but I never let Patrick know it. You can call it either stupidity or naïveté, but honestly, I didn't really have a right to be pissed. Patrick had never said anything about "being an item," or "mutually exclusive," or whatever the hell we called it back in 1992. And I already knew his reputation before I did anything with him. I wanted to be Patrick's girlfriend more than anything in the world, but I always figured I wasn't good enough for him. I was young, and far from the beautiful, confident-type that Patrick usually dated.

The summer before my senior year in college, I happened to run into Patrick at a popular bar on campus. And believe it or not, I actually wasn't stalking him this time. I had just met a guy that I was really diggin', so I wasn't planning on doing one of our usual booty calls. But, we definitely had fun talking at the bar all night. That's one thing I always enjoyed about Patrick . . . our silly banter and deep conversations. Yes, besides being the most beautiful man I had ever seen, I simply enjoyed his company tremendously.

About thirty minutes after I got home from the bar that night, Patrick knocked on my door. He had never been to my apartment, so I was very surprised to see him when I opened the door. He told me he called information and got my number and address. "Back in the old days," that was the only way to find anybody. You just dialed 411, and they could give you anybody's information. There was no social media, so that was the only way to be a stalker back in the day.

This ended up being THE NIGHT . . . the night to end all nights . . . the night I never ever thought would happen . . .

The. Night. I. Said. No. To. Patrick.

Yes, you read that right. I said no. From what I remember, I did kiss him a little bit. I mean, if this was going to be my last interaction with Patrick, I wanted to enjoy a little something. I stopped him midkiss, before any article of clothing came off. I knew that once anything was taken off, there was no way I could say no. There was just something about him that I always found irresistible. But for the first time, I resisted that night.

Not surprisingly, Patrick was very cool about it. It wasn't like he was crazy about me, so turning him down was simply just a busy signal to a booty call for him. I'm sure someone else would've answered his call that night.

After saying goodbye and shutting the door, I remember feeling very proud of myself. However, I don't think I slept that night. I kept wondering if I made the right decision, since that was likely my last chance with Patrick EVER. I honestly thought I would never be able to say no to him, but I did.

Unfortunately, it was not as easy to say no twenty years later.

Chapter 3

Only in My Dreams

So, my hall pass list consisted of all five members of the New Kids on the Block, and Patrick Barnes. And to actually use this hall pass on any six of these guys was about as unrealistic as getting my eighteen-year-old body back. Which translates to, "will never happen." The five members of NKOTB being unrealistic for obvious reasons, while Patrick was unrealistic because I didn't even know if he was still alive. We had mutual friends, but nobody I kept in close contact with. Last I had heard, he moved to California in 1995ish. That was over twenty years ago, and God knows how things can change in that time span.

About a week before the cruise, I was "busy" watching those stupid dog videos on Facebomb, as most of us do whether we admit it or not. I saw my "suggested friends" list out of the corner of my eye. At the top was a name that I never thought I would see on social media. Yes . . . Patrick Barnes.

At first, I had to make sure it was actually him. We had six mutual friends, so I figured it was. However, I know in the past, some of his friends liked to be pranksters, doing silly things like posting his picture on wanted signs all over the city. I thought maybe somebody had made up a profile for him as a joke. You know, saying that he was homeless, and jobless, and divorced four times with twelve kids. I clicked on it, OF COURSE, and realized after a few minutes that it was probably him. It said he lived in Newport Beach, California, but it didn't have any current pictures of him.

When I talked about my hall pass members, people would always ask me, "If you haven't seen Patrick for so many years, what if he's really ugly now, and gained three hundred pounds?" There was something about Patrick that I knew I would always find very attractive and endearing, no matter what his physical appearance. I mean, sure, the physical appearance was the starter for the whole obsession to begin with, but Patrick always made me laugh. He was always witty and silly and fun. He was so free-spirited and did everything on his terms, which I actually admired. For the most part, he was honest. I mean, of course he was sleeping with other girls when he was with me, but he never tried to tell me he wasn't.

On top of that, for some odd reason, Patrick always stayed in the back of my head. I say the back of my head because he would literally show up out of nowhere in my dreams. At random times too. For instance, I wouldn't think about him for years, and all of a sudden, he would show up in a dream, sitting at the bar smiling at me. Unfortunately, I am not one to have awesome sex dreams, so they were never too exciting, but he was always there. If any other one of my exes showed up in a dream, it was likely a nightmare. I would probably wake up in a confused and pissed off state, wondering how and why they showed up while I was asleep. But when Patrick popped up in my dreams, I would wake up and smile. Then I would search the internet and social media, hoping I could at least locate him. Even if I never spoke to him again, I wanted to know if he did happen to gain three hundred pounds after all.

I could not tell by the limited information on Facebomb whether Patrick had gotten ugly, or if he was married, or had kids. I just knew that I had to at least send him a friend request. He accepted it a few hours later, and that was that, for the time being.

The cruise was a blast. The last thing on my mind was autism, or Patrick, or stress from sleep deprivation. I mean, I was sleep deprived, but in a fun sleep deprived kind of way. I got to see my five hall passes every day, all day, up close and in person. What more could I ask for? Of course, I never got the opportunity to take advantage of the hall pass. But, hey, there was always next year.

When I got home from the cruise, I was on a high for a few days. I was extremely exhausted, but I didn't care. Then that "what do I have to look forward to now?" feeling came over me. I reminded myself that 2017 was going to be my year of fun, so I had to start planning more trips.

While thinking of my next adventure, I was scrolling Facebomb again, this time watching the cats and cucumbers videos (which are hilarious, I might add). I came across a picture that Patrick posted of him and his dog. I'm assuming it was his dog, anyway. I thought to myself, *This might be a good sign . . . if he's only in pictures with a dog, he might be single.* Not that it mattered, because I wasn't single, but fantasies were much more fun when there was a touch of realism.

What was the most important thing about that picture of Patrick, you ask? Well, he was still beautiful! He had definitely aged a bit, but he had that same face, just now with more wrinkles and expression lines. But what the hell was I judging? We have all aged in the last twenty years, whether we wanted to or not. I was no spring chicken myself. He looked a bit heavier, but not in a "fat" kind of way, just a "limited exercise regimen" kind of way. But again, what the hell was I comparing . . . apples to apples in this case. I also had the "not fat but limited exercise" body.

I looked at the picture for a long time, studying every inch of his face. I suddenly remembered his lips, kissing me soft, then hard, and then his hands all over my body.

Whoa! I needed to stop, STAT! Where the hell was this coming from?

I knew I would always have a soft spot for Patrick. But, Jesus, I didn't have any of these feelings with other exes' pictures. With any other ex I would either have the "what the hell was I thinking?" reaction to seeing them after so many years, or the "not bad, but at least I look better than you" kind of feeling. But not with Patrick's picture! However, I didn't know why and where these sudden sexual thoughts were coming from.

I had not fantasized about anyone outside of my marriage before. Besides imagining that my husband was Donnie Wahlberg occasionally during sex, I never took my thoughts or actions of a sexual nature outside of my husband. I know we were not able to think much about sex since the whole autism stress started, but I definitely didn't think I would ever have these feelings for anyone again. After fifteen years with the same man, I had never let my mind go to this extreme. And looking at that picture of Patrick, I had never wanted anyone more.

I forced myself to go to bed, hoping that in the morning I would look at myself in the mirror and realize that I was just having a "moment." My hormones were probably out of whack, and maybe that time of the month was bringing on more estrogen and progesterone, or whatever the hell periods are supposed to do. I slept like a baby, finally catching up on the sleep I lost on the cruise. The only problem was that my first thought upon waking up the next morning was Patrick.

How was I going to get him out of my mind? I thought of psychological exposure therapy, where excessive repetition of the phobia causes you to become immune to the fear. Okay, so this would be kind of the opposite. But, would repeated exposure to his picture make me stop obsessing about him? Not sure if that was going to work. Or maybe trying the similar aversion therapy, where you expose yourself to a stimulus while simultaneously being subjected to some form of discomfort. Looking at his picture was giving me the opposite of discomfort, but the thoughts of cheating on my husband were a tad bit discomforting. My therapist brain was already trying to therapize myself, to figure out where these strong physical and sexual urges were coming from, and what the hell to do about them.

So, of course, that morning I went straight to his Facebomb profile. To my happy surprise, he had actually posted a bunch of pictures the night before, so my attempt at exposure therapy was in full effect. I still didn't see any pictures with women or kids, so that was good. There was one picture where you could see part of a woman sitting next to him on the couch, but all you saw in the picture was her hair and her leg. Let's just assume it was his sister. That made me feel better.

The more I looked at all of the pictures of him with dogs, or him with male friends, or him with his family, I started to wonder if he was gay. I was in love with the only gay member of NKOTB when I was a teenager, so I wouldn't have been surprised if Patrick was gay too. Not that there's anything wrong with that, because I would still keep him on my hall pass.

I know I sound like a total stalker. And to be honest, I was. I felt sixteen again, except this time I had more access at my fingertips to be a grade-A stalker. Luckily, 2016 was a much easier time to be obsessed with someone, since everybody's life was vomited on social media all day every day. I didn't have to drive around looking for his car anymore, which was kind of hard anyway since he lived two thousand miles away.

From zooming in on every picture, and reading all the captions and hashtags on them, the only thing I came up with was that I was still crazy about him. That, and the fact that I think he worked at a YMCA. I was a little confused about that, since I couldn't see a forty-six-year-old educated man working at the YMCA, but things are sometimes hard to put together based solely on pictures and captions. I didn't really care where the hell he worked, he was still fuckable in my opinion. Not that I was going to be fucking him but, you know, a girl can dream.

And dream is exactly what I did. Except most of my dreams were daydreams. Or, I would wake up in the middle of the night, unable to fall back to sleep, thinking about his lips on mine, and his body on top of me. Remember, I didn't have sex dreams unfortunately, so I had to rely on making things up while I was awake. I would design stories in my head about seeing him again, and him telling me how beautiful I had gotten, and how much he thought about me over the last twenty years. Obviously this would never happen, since I was about thirty-five pounds lighter the last time he saw me naked, but hey, I was dreaming. I can make anything happen in my fantasy head.

Every day, at least once a day, I would look at his profile and examine his pictures. But, one drastically horrible day, I couldn't find him. Patrick and his profile were completely gone. GONE! Nowhere to be found! It was like he never existed. Needless to say, I was devastated.

I tried looking him up repeatedly on Facebomb, and couldn't find him anywhere. My initial thought was, *Oh shit—he must have been able to tell I was stalking him and blocked me.* But when I had one of my good friends look him up, he was still nowhere to be found. It made me feel a little better knowing that it was likely not *me* being the reason he decided to deactivate his profile, but how was I going to look at his beautiful face every day?

I used this Patrick-free time to take a good look at my marriage, and what I truly wanted. I owed it to my husband to focus on "us" as much as I could, and figure out what this deviation in my sanity meant. I concluded that the main reason for my Patrick obsession was simple . . . it was an escape. Escape from autism, escape from a consistently absent husband, escape from my mundane schedule of driving to therapy appointments every day, and escape from life. But was it more? I always wondered if I loved Patrick. I had a hard time feeling love when it came to him, because love is mutual in my opinion. I don't feel like you can have a true love without it being reciprocated. And if I was right, this had to be simple infatuation. But why did I allow him to set up camp in my head?

I reminded myself that 2017 was going to be MY year. I had to start planning my fun in order to make it my best year ever. We ended 2016 celebrating my parents fiftieth wedding anniversary, and had a great time with family. I tried to tell myself how lucky I was to have such a wonderful, supportive family, including my husband. Life was actually pretty good, but I wanted it to be just a little bit better.

The new year started off just like any year . . . cold and miserable. But I knew things would get better once it got warmer. I hate fall and winter, and I especially hate holidays. I'm not a Jehovah's Witness or anything, but holidays aren't the same anymore with a severely autistic child. Christmas is supposed to be full of peace and hope, and our household usually has none of that around the holidays. Jack has absolutely no interest in opening presents, nor does he even get that it's Christmas. He knows nothing of St. Nick and Santa Claus. My husband works almost every holiday. So, Jack and I are stuck in the house, thanks to winter, without getting exercise or fresh air. And this time of the year also brings with it numerous infections and illnesses like strep throat, pink eye, and the flu. Fun fucking times!

As spring approached, my mood improved, as usual. I was still having thoughts of Patrick almost daily, but the play-by-play in my head was starting to dissipate, thank God. One day I was on Facebomb again, this time watching some autistic kid sing the national anthem, which was pretty good, by the way. As I started to scroll my FB feed, a picture quickly caught my eye, which was posted by one of my good friends, Brad. In the picture, Brad and Patrick were standing together. It looked like it was taken from Brad's house, which is in our hometown in Texas. I then noticed that Patrick was tagged in the photo, which confused me, since I didn't think anybody could be tagged in a picture if they didn't have an account. I clicked on Patrick's name, which was in bold, and his profile popped right up. The same one that he had deleted last year.

Not only was I excited to see that he was back on social media, I was more excited to see a picture of him with one of our friends that I still had occasional contact with. I realized that this could be my chance, now that I could easily get his phone number from Brad. I had to start planning something!

So, planning I did. One of my favorite places in the world is Los Angeles, which just happens to be about an hour from Newport Beach. And, LA also happens to be the home of one of my favorite people in the world. My friend, Heather. Heather and I met at a social work conference in Tennessee about ten years ago, and had kept in contact ever since. I tried to make it out to LA every year or two to visit her, so I started planning my trip for May 2017.

Patrick or not, I knew my trip was going to be a blast. It always was with Heather. I called Heather to let her know when I would be coming, and casually mentioned Newport Beach. I was trying to get a feel of whether a quick trip to NB would be an option, and whether she would be willing to drive my crazy ass all the way there just to see someone that I hadn't seen in over twenty years. I don't know why I thought this scenario was even a realistic possibility. First of all, the likelihood of actually getting in contact with Patrick was low. Not only was I probably too chicken-shit to call or text him, I wasn't even sure if Brad had his number. I also wasn't sure Patrick would even remember me, or want to respond to me if I did touch base with him. Plus, he also might be gay.

All of these doubtful thoughts constantly ran through my mind, until one day when I reminded myself again that 2017 was going to be MY year after all. And in order for it to be my year, I might have to do some things that were a bit out of character for me, or things that could leave me vulnerable. But isn't that how you achieve the unachievable? Isn't that how to get out of your comfort zone? My main motivator was simple . . . what the hell did I have to lose?

Well, I did have my husband to lose, for one. But I hadn't done anything, so I didn't have anything to worry about. Yet, anyway. But I had to ask myself numerous times over the last seven months why I was constantly thinking about somebody else. Why was there another man in my thoughts when I should have been focusing on my life at home? Especially since these thought processes and behaviors were a large deviation of character for me.

I started thinking that there must be a "reason" for all of this. I'm not a religious person, nor am I highly spiritual, but I do always go with the belief that every single thing in life happens for a reason. I'm fine if you don't have that same mentality, but it really helped me get through a lot of shit. I believe that you might not see the reason immediately, or you may not even see it in your lifetime. But you will see it at some point, maybe even in heaven. I remember being devastated years earlier after getting fired from a job when I did absolutely nothing wrong. They said that they legally didn't have to give me a reason, just that I was not a "good fit." I was so upset at first, not because I loved my job, but because it hurt to not fit in. I realized later in life that it was a blessing in disguise. Knowing the loyal me, I would still be at that job after fifteen years, miserable, with only cats to go home to. Not that there's anything wrong with cats, but the firing forced me to move to Atlanta and start my life over, which I have never regretted.

The job scenario might be a bad example of "everything happens for a reason," but I was still trying to find the "why" with my newfound obsession. I have been obsessed with Patrick since I was sixteen, but Jesus, I was sixteen. I'm forty-three years old now, I should know better. So, what's the "reason"? Is it a force bigger than me that's trying to tell me to take a good, hard look at myself? Is it a sign that I need to focus on myself more, and take care of myself, since I had neglected some of that over the last five years of autism? Is it a midlife crisis? Is it a trigger to force me to get out of my depressing, monotonous life? Or, is it simply that Patrick is the love of my life, and I'm supposed to live happily ever after with him? Okay, so that one's kind of extreme, but I was desperately trying to figure out why my mind could not switch off Patrick no matter how hard I tried.

I was leaving for LA in two weeks, and I still hadn't contacted Brad to find out if he had Patrick's number. I actually wasn't sure if I was going to. I kept going back and forth on the possible pros and cons with reaching out to Patrick. There seemed to be more pros, but I still had lots of possible cons in there too. As I lay in bed unable to sleep, thinking about that pro/con list, my mind would also drift into fantasy-land. I would conjure up these unrealistic, but absolutely fantastic, scenarios in my head. These, of course, pushed the pro-list higher, even if they were unrealistic.

One "story" that I conjured up in my crazy head was so fun to play out . . . over and over and over again! In this particular fantasy, I texted Patrick, he quickly and excitedly responded, and we lived happily ever after. Just kidding! But close.

In this "dream," Patrick told me to meet him at a local bar in Newport Beach. Heather and I walked in to meet him, and he greeted me like a long-lost best friend, with a sweet, tight hug. That part might be realistic, but even that was stretching it. Following the hug, we talked for hours about life, and how much he had thought about me over the years. Okay, so that part was likely not going to be the case, but still fun to pretend. He then told me in this "dream" that he was single, and had never been married, and that he wished we had stayed together forever. Yeah, so it gets more and more unrealistic, so what! Then, at the end of the night, our chemistry was so strong that we embraced in a long, hot kiss. And after the kiss, he told me that he remembered telling me twenty-five years ago that I kissed just like he did. Okay, I know . . . too much fantasy, and not enough realism.

Each night I would add more to the fantasy in my head. Sometimes it included more dialogue between us, and sometimes it included more sex. But each night seemed to stretch the scenario further and further away from reality. Hell, by the time my trip came, we had gotten married and were already past the honeymoon phase, and into the trenches of the hard part of marriage. That's how far I let this fantasy go. Which was actually a good thing, because I could see that being with Patrick in the end was not my happily ever after, but that my husband was. My hubby is who I wanted to grow old with. Even if I couldn't stop dreaming of someone else.

This new epiphany of wanting to be with my husband made me reevaluate some things. I was going to go to LA, and have a blast, regardless. But I still wasn't sure if I wanted to contact Patrick. Since I thought Brad may not even have his number, I figured these crazy scenarios may just be a moot point. One thing I did know is even if I reached Patrick and met up with him, I looked nothing like I did when I was twenty. I mean, I looked like the same person, and nothing majorly different, just older. And everything that comes along with "older," like graying hair, and a fat gut that had not been going anywhere since my C-section, and my gallbladder surgery. And the cellulite! Lord, did I have cellulite! Also wrinkles, and hair in places that I didn't know could grow hair, and sagging skin that I didn't know could sag. So, the fact that I was imagining him finding me attractive was in and of itself a stretch.

Chapter 4

I Love LA

I got to the airport two hours before my flight, like I always do. As I was standing in the really long security line, I had my phone out just like everyone else. I decided to send Brad a message. I had something else I wanted to tell him about, so at least I wasn't only reaching out for Patrick's number. Brad and I didn't communicate back and forth often, but I'm sure if I just contacted him for Patrick's number, he would have some suspicions.

I was pleasantly surprised when about forty-five minutes later, my phone dinged, and it was a message from Brad. I didn't even read what it said before seeing a phone number listed at the bottom of his text. OMG! I had Patrick's number. I've never had Patrick's cell phone number. There were no cell phones when I dated Patrick way back when. In fact, I think all he had was my parents number, and my sorority house's main phone number, which is crazy to think about in this day and age. I honestly don't even know how people dated back in the "old days" without cell phones, but somehow we figured it out.

I received Brads message right as I was walking onto the airplane, so that was the longest four hour flight to LA that you could ever imagine. When I sat in my seat, I actually read the message, but the only line I remember was the last one . . . "I'm sure Patrick would love to hear from you."

Was I reading too much into this message from Brad? Probably, but it sort of sounded like he knew that Patrick would want to hear from me, and how would he know this? No, I was definitely reading too much into it. Brad's a nice guy, so he was probably just assuming it would be nice for old friends to see each other again.

The whole flight I was on cloud nine. I was already excited because I was flying first class, which always makes me happy. I was also super excited about spending the next few days with my fun friend, Heather. But now every single fantasy I had ever imagined with Patrick was at my fingertips . . . literally.

Heather picked me up from the airport, and I'm pretty sure she thought I was on drugs. I was completely manic. It was the type of mania that a bipolar person has when they haven't slept for a week. That's actually how I felt too. Not that I know exactly how a bipolar person feels, but having worked with bipolar people in an inpatient hospital setting for fourteen years, I had a pretty good idea. And now I could totally relate to my patients.

We went straight to a Mexican restaurant in the valley, and I was finally able to process everything. It's hard to talk to people about sexual fantasies, and cheating on your husband. Not everybody is cool with that. I know if the situation was reversed, I would have a hard time hearing my friend talk about cheating on her husband. I really didn't want to put anybody in that situation. Luckily, Heather did not know my husband, nor had she met him, so it was probably a little easier for her to focus just on me and my issues without judgement. Not that I was realistically going to cheat, but the desires were there, and it was nice to finally get those desires off my chest and out of my mouth.

I was so excited that I could barely eat. Partly because I was in my favorite city in the world, but also because I had Patrick Barnes' phone number. I could die a happy girl now. But hopefully I wasn't going to be dying anytime soon, I had a fantasy to fulfill.

Heather helped me decide what exactly to text. I had decided to text instead of call. I imagined him answering the phone and being like, "Who?," when I told him who was calling. I thought if I texted and explained who I was, he would have some time to process, and actually remember me. I didn't know if it was hard to remember all of your past sexual partners when you've had so many. I didn't have that problem, so I wouldn't know.

Me:
May 18 4:04 p.m.
Hey Patrick! This is Piper Collins—long time, no see, I know. I got your number from Brad Fuller and he told me you were still in Newport Beach. I just flew into LA for a couple of days and may be taking a day/night trip to NB either tomorrow or Saturday with my girlfriend and was wondering if you had any suggestions of fun places to go or things to see? You're more than welcome to join if you're available, but any suggestions would be appreciated. Hope you are doing well!

Before hitting send, I read the entire text at least three times in varying voices and nuances to make sure it did not sound weird. I mean, if I received a text from somebody that I had not talked to or seen for over twenty years, there's a certain level of expectation and assumption to be made no matter who you were and what you meant to me. And to be honest, my biggest fear was that he wouldn't even remember who I was. And my next biggest fear was that he wouldn't text me back at all. Therefore, I had to make sure the text wasn't too bizarre so that when either one of these negative outcomes happened, I wouldn't kick myself too hard, and wish I had said something else.

I looked at Heather, and then I hit send.

I shoved my phone back into my purse and told Heather to not let me look at it for at least an hour. She knew that would be extremely difficult for me, so she decided that our next two stops were going to be ice cream, and a psychic reading. Heather knew me well . . . two of my favorite things! She said that the reader down the street was one of the best she had ever been to, and I figured it could not be a better time for someone to tell me what my future looked like.

The ice cream was the most odd, yet tasteful ice cream I have ever had. It was one of those quirky ice cream stores that never have just vanilla or chocolate. They have flavors like honey lavender, pear and blue cheese, and coava coffee and cocanu craque. I had something with the word "flowers" in it, and it surprisingly tasted a lot like eating flowers, if flowers tasted good. But, luckily it was in a much creamier and yummier form than a flower petal.

We got into the car to drive to the psychic, and right as we were pulling into the parking spot, I heard my text alert. I figured it was probably my husband. I texted him earlier and hadn't heard back from him, but my heart still jumped. What if . . . what if it was actually Patrick texting me back? I looked at Heather and couldn't even pull my phone out of my purse. It was like I somehow knew it was him, and I was straight-up sixteen years old again. Except we didn't have cell phones or texts when I was sixteen, so it was slightly different. After sending Patrick the text earlier, I put his name attached to the phone number, so that his name would pop up if he actually texted me back. I thought that would be more exciting than seeing a random Newport Beach phone number. And when I pulled the phone out to look, sure enough, it was from Patrick.

I actually started shaking, and handed the phone to Heather. I told her I couldn't read it. I don't think I would've been able to process anything that I read, so I had to calm down first. And if the text said something bad, I would probably revert back to my eighteen-year-old self who came face-to-face with a girl after knocking on Patrick's apartment door. I had to remind myself that I was a forty-three-year-old grown-ass woman, and that a negative text from a boy was not going to break me.

Heather read the text, but not out loud, and I just studied her face while she read it. I was anticipating a bad "oh shit" look, but instead she had a "pleasantly surprised" smile. The only thing she said when she handed me the phone was, "It has the word love in it."

What? What did she mean, he said the word "love"? Of course

this made me look directly at the text, and I quickly read it to find out what the fuck she was talking about.

Patrick:
May 18, 4:43 p.m.
What's up, Piper? Great to hear from you. Would love to hang with y'all. Nothing too exciting here but I'll give you a few suggestions. I'm going to a concert on Saturday and I can get more tickets if you want to join. If you come to NB please let me know. Have fun!!

Ok, so he remembered who I was, and he actually wanted to "hang." At least, I'm assuming he remembered me. There's always that possibility that he was just going along with the text, all the while trying to remember what the hell I looked like.

Regardless of whether he remembered me or not, this absolutely could not be happening! Shit like this doesn't fall into place for Piper, it just doesn't. What's the catch? Maybe I'll show up and he will introduce me to his wife, or maybe even his husband. Or, maybe he will tell me to meet him somewhere, make me wait for hours, and never show up or even call. That's the kind of shit I was used to happening in my life, and especially my history with Patrick. That's totally something he would have done back then, and my dumbass would have just said, "No problem," while secretly feeling depressed about it. Luckily, I'm not that type of person anymore. My stomach started to hurt just thinking about the "old" me, and how different I would be if something like that happened now. He would wish he never responded to my text.

I asked Heather . . . well, more like begged her, to drive me to Newport Beach at some point in the next two days. She told me we would have to do it tomorrow, because she had an event all day Saturday that she had to work. I knew a wrinkle in the plan would happen soon. I really wanted to go on Saturday so I would have plenty of time to catch up with Patrick. But what the hell was I bitching about?! Heather was willing to feed into my almost life-long fantasy, and drive me to Patrick. Hell, at that point I would have rented a goddamn car just to see him. I could feel it, so close but yet so far. Every single thing I had been hoping and dreaming about for the last seven months were coming true. Okay, maybe not the sex part, but I was going to actually see Patrick Barnes after twenty-two years.

"What the hell am I going to wear?" I said out loud, and Heather looked at me weird. She said, "Let's go get your psychic reading first, and maybe you can ask her." Oh yeah, I had forgotten about the reading, but the timing could not be any better. I wanted her to tell me what was going to happen tomorrow!

The psychic should actually change her profession to teacher, because she was way more into telling me what to do, instead of telling me what would happen. I told her the entire scenario, from my son's autism, to my rocky marriage, to my history with Patrick, in a little under ten minutes. Instead of telling me what was going to happen with Patrick, she told me that whatever is supposed to happen will happen. Gee, thanks, psychic! She then told me that if I chose to cheat, I was smart enough to know what the consequences would entail, so I had to think about those possibilities beforehand. Gee, thanks again, because I hadn't thought about that at all (eyeroll).

There was one scenario that she "predicted." She told me that my marriage was definitely able to be saved, with a lot of hard work. I believed this to be true, and was glad she said it. It sounded more realistic coming out of her mouth than mine. I really did want to work things out with hubby, but I could not stop thinking about tomorrow, and just Patrick in general.

I left even more confused than when I went in, but she was a good listener, at least. I needed to get a lot of that shit out. I felt like a tick on a dog, about to explode. Regardless of her "psychic ability," she did provide some hope for me. Plus, getting shit off of your chest to someone who doesn't know you is actually a really good feeling. That's why I became a therapist. I wanted to provide that ear that others never gave me.

I checked into my hotel in Beverly Hills, and could not think about anything else besides tomorrow. I couldn't stay with Heather because she was currently in a one-bedroom apartment with a hopelessly aspiring actress-friend sleeping on her couch. Plus, I need my alone time as much as possible when on vacation. I tried on all three of the different outfits that I brought. I was only going to be in California for three days, but a girl can never pack too much, especially when one of the biggest days of her life was about to happen. I decided on a black three-quarter-sleeve romper. The shorts weren't too short, so he hopefully wouldn't notice the increased thickness in thighs since he last saw me naked, or the obnoxious amount of cellulite that I had accumulated over the years. The shorts also luckily covered the unfortunate spider veins that I inherited from my grandmother.

Once Heather and I decided our game plan for the next day, I texted Patrick to give him an update. I was so worried he would not text me back, for some reason. He always seemed to put that kind of insecurity in my head. I was not an insecure person, but I was so freakin' vulnerable with Patrick. Something I never understood myself. He still made me feel like that sixteen-year-old pom-pom girl, obsessed with NKOTB, with my ugly permed hair, and timid demeanor. The one that would never be good enough.

Me:
May 18, 8:08 p.m.
Hey! Still making final plans, but it's looking like we may come down tomorrow. We will probably be there all day and possibly stay the night, so let me know if/when you can meet up. Looking forward to catching up!

Our plan was to sleep in, and slowly get ready before leaving around noon. Well, it wouldn't be so much slowly getting ready for me as it was intently getting ready. I had to make sure my lotion was in the right spots to cover up the cellulite, the eyeliner was not too thick and not too thin, the hair was curled just right, my contour and highlight were perfection on the cheeks, and my legs were shaved. I know most guys don't even notice makeup and hair, but I couldn't take any chances. I had to be the best version of myself, appearance-wise, at least.

I don't think I slept more than two hours that night, and that was even with melatonin. The melatonin helped me fall asleep, but even then, it took at least two hours to kick in. Besides the excitement about the following day, I was also anticipating a return text from Patrick. Did he want to see me, or was he just trying to be nice? Was he going to decide not to reply and forget about me all together, like he would back in the day?

After waking up from what felt like a good, solid four hours of sleep, I looked at my phone. I told myself not to look, but the anticipation was killing me. One of three options were possible when looking at my phone after my bathroom trip, and all three were negative outcomes:

#1 possible outcome . . . When I saw what time it was, I would think about how little sleep I'd had so far, therefore causing anxiety about my eyes being puffy the next day from lack of sleep.

#2 possible outcome . . . If there was no return text from Patrick yet, it would send me into a tailspin, worried he was blowing me off.

#3 possible outcome . . . If there was a text from Patrick, I would fixate on the text, reading it over and over again, excited about what tomorrow had in store.

Regardless, any of those outcomes would likely stop me from going back to sleep, so I decided to look. I should have just shut the damn thing off completely, but I was obviously not in my usual, practical mindset.

Unfortunately (or fortunately), both the #1 and #3 outcomes were the result. Now there was no way I was going back to sleep. It was 2:05 a.m., and I had only slept a little less than two hours, assuming I had gone to sleep when I thought I did. And, Patrick had texted me back . . .

Patrick:
May 19, 12:30 a.m.
I'm off all day so holler when heading this way.
Got a few fun spots to show y'all. U guys are

gonna love it here if you've never been ... also
have sweet hook ups at hotels so wait to see
which one u want. Could have gave me 1,000,000
guesses who I would talk to today ... glad you
called Brad. Be careful driving and let me know
if you need help.

Yay, he was glad I called Brad! But what did he mean by that? Of course, my limited sleep and utter excitement made me think back to all of my fantasies. Maybe he has had the same fantasies about me? Okay, so that's a stretch, but he at least remembered me, and acted as though he wanted to see me. The way he worded the 1,000,000 guesses comment made me feel like he was surprised, and I was hoping pleasantly surprised.

Chapter 5

And, I Love NB

I tossed and turned until about 6:30 a.m., which was really about 9:30 my time, so I was ready for breakfast. I went to the diner that was attached to the hotel and ordered an American breakfast. I ended up eating about three bites of the whole meal. I can't eat or sleep when I'm happily excited. Too bad I'm not always happily excited, I would only be about a hundred pounds if that was the case. As I sat there not eating my breakfast, I decided to text Patrick with our ETA.

Me:
May 19, 8:30 a.m.
Sounds great! I'm eating breakfast at Swingers right now. My girl said she's picking me up at 11-ish. Will likely be ready to drink so you just tell us where to go and we will be there. I'll text you when we actually leave, and she said it'll take about 1hr to get there.

I went back to the room and jumped in the shower. I might as well start my three-hour process to get sexy, or as sexy as I could possibly get, which wasn't that sexy, but anyway.

I heard a couple of texts beep on my phone while I was in the shower, but I didn't look at them because I was too busy shaving everything and everywhere. Yeah, I know it's a little presumptuous to make sure I was clean-shaven in all the right (and wrong) areas, but a woman has to always be prepared. Plus, it made me feel sexier and younger, and I needed all the help I could get. When I got out of the shower, there were two texts—one from Patrick and one from my husband. Suddenly the guilt kicked in, but then I had to remind myself that I had nothing to feel guilty about, besides the fantasies in my head. But, yeah, I was omitting information, which was kind of lying, so I started second guessing what I was doing. But I quickly got out of the second guessing mindset, because I trusted myself and my husband trusted me, and Patrick wouldn't want me anyway, so it didn't really matter.

Patrick:
May 19, 10:12 a.m.
Perfect . . . have you been to the Newport
Pier before?

Me:
May 19, 10:26 a.m.
Nope. Never been to that area at all.

Patrick:
May 19, 10:42 a.m.
You're gonna love it, but watch out . . . you'll blink
and spend 21 years here. See ya soon! Gonna
be fun.

Me:
May 19, 10:58 a.m.
Can't wait!

Heather was a bit late, so I used that extra time to re-pack my entire suitcase. I didn't have an overnight bag, and in case we stayed in a hotel somewhere, I wanted to have everything. So I brought the entire packed suitcase with me. I figured it was also a good deterrent. If Patrick even mentioned staying with him, I would be too embarrassed to be like, "Here's a few things I brought," while handing him my forty-nine-pound suitcase. Okay, so it was more like thirty-nine pounds, but still an embarrassing amount of pounds for three days.

As soon as we got in the car, Heather put a general Newport

Beach address into the GPS, just to get us to that particular area before we got an actual meeting address. Heather hit "GO" and a second later, she threw me a weird look. It was kind of like a "you are not going to like me" look. I looked back at her and said, "Oh shit, what?" She said, "Well, it looks like there's a little bit of traffic, so it will likely take us over two hours to get there."

Crap! We were already running about an hour later than what I told Patrick. Not only was I so eager and excited to see Patrick, I was being impatient, and I didn't want to have to wait two more hours. I had it in my head that I would be looking at those gorgeous blue eyes in one hour, not two. But my main worry was that he was going to stand me up. I was anticipating that text from him saying, "Well, two hours is way too long, so maybe next time." You know how he always put that insecurity in me.

I immediately texted Patrick to let him know the ETA, and crossed my fingers.

Me:
May 19, 12:53 p.m.
Getting a slightly late start and traffic is a bitch so it'll probably be closer to 3:00 or later. Hope that's cool. Give me an address when you can.

I hit send and held my breath. I put the air conditioner full blast on my face, and waited. Heather said a few things about the traffic, but I didn't really hear her. She was talking about one highway being closed for some reason, but it went in one ear and out the other.

Then I got a response. Thank God he didn't make me wait too long, I was about to pass out from unconsciously holding my breath.

Patrick:
May 19, 1:03 p.m.
No sweat darlin. Just be careful. Traffic is a bitch on Fridays. Will be at beach when u get here. I'll send u address for Billy's Brews.

Whew! He was willing to wait. Well, two hours, at least. Let's hope we didn't run into even more traffic. I don't think I could wait any more than that.

I was never big on cigarettes, but when Heather toked up, I had to join her. I will occasionally smoke when around others that do, but since I'm rarely around others that do, I very rarely smoke. I have not bought a pack of cigarettes in years, but it was fun to cave on occasion, especially when I didn't have to spend the ungodly amount of money on a pack. And, luckily, the cigarette did seem to help calm me down a little bit. I figured I didn't have to worry about stinky smoke breath, since the odds of making out with Patrick were slim to none. Okay, fine . . . none to none.

Two hours later, we were still not there. We ran into even more traffic, which I guess is pretty normal for any big city on Friday at 3:00 p.m. I tried to have meaningful conversations with Heather during those two hours, but I could not focus on anything else but my excitement in seeing someone that I had only been dreaming of seeing for many years, and literally dreaming of for the last seven months.

I looked up the address for Billy's Brews so that Heather would have an exact address to put in the GPS, and we would have a better ETA. It said it was going to be another thirty minutes (UGHH!), so I texted that info to Patrick. We didn't have cell phones when I dated him back in the day, and we didn't even have texting when I was dating my husband. So, I enjoyed the fun and flirty text exchange between us for that last hour in the car. It was something new for me. I felt like a teenager again, but a modern-day version.

About ten minutes after Patrick's last text, he sent me another one. This time my heart was pounding as I was hoping and praying he wasn't backing out, since that's the kind of shit that usually happens to me. Actually, getting into a car accident, while on the way to one of the most important days of my life, is more like the shit that happens to me. So, him backing out was a slightly better horrible outcome, but I was prepared for the worst. That's always been my motto—prepare for the worst and hope for the best. Most people call that being "negative," but I call it being "realistic." Call it whatever the fuck you want, but they should change Murphy's Law to Piper's Law. Sounds better anyway.

So far, no indication of backing out, and he seemed to still have his great sense of humor. That was the big thing I always loved about Patrick, his constant ability to make me laugh. Sometimes it was laughing at him, but mostly it was with him. He didn't mind making fun of himself, which is also attractive in my book.

I still didn't know if he was alone, or with a friend, or even a girlfriend. I prepared myself for any and all possible scenarios. Maybe it would squelch my sexual desires if I showed up and he introduced me to his girlfriend, or a spouse of any gender for that matter. I had no idea what I would be walking into. I also prepared myself to walk into the bar with Patrick sitting at a long table with about ten of his closest friends. That would be fine too, but I was kind of hoping he was there alone.

Patrick texted a picture of himself. The picture appeared to be taken right before he sent it, and in the pic he was holding a double gulp cup containing what looked like pink lemonade. That made me wonder if it consisted of alcohol. Shit, I thought, maybe he doesn't even drink anymore, and here I was talking about needing alcohol in one of my texts that I sent to him earlier. No, I highly doubted he was in recovery, or completely sober. It had to be filled with something besides pink lemonade.

The picture also had part of his beautiful face. Only half of it, but it was enough to get me even MORE excited to see him. And, it was another one of those, "OMG, Patrick has never texted me a picture of himself before," firsts.

I was planning on drinking, A LOT, before seeing him for the first time. Our original plan was to go to a bar halfway, get me tipsy while the designated driver stayed sober, and I could get a little loosened up. My nerves were shot! It was the good kind of nerves, but they were still making me slightly light-headed and nauseous. I knew we wouldn't be able to stop and drink before meeting him, since we were running so late already. But, luckily I had barely eaten anything, so the odds of me puking all over Patrick were slim.

Along with the pink lemonade picture, he wrote:

Patrick:
May 19, 3:45 p.m.
Watermelon & champagne xtra dry ... delicious.

Whew! He was drinking something that consisted of alcohol. Thank God. I didn't want him to think that I had turned into some kind of alcoholic lush, in case he was a born again Christian or a recovering alcoholic. The truth is, I actually didn't drink much. I like to drink socially and limit myself to about two drinks, usually wine or some kind of vodka drink. I wasn't a big beer or whisky fan, and I didn't care for any other alcohol besides vodka and gin. And, I never drank at home. I worked with alcoholics and drug addicts, so I guess seeing the extreme negative effects of drinking too much was a big repellent.

We continued some back-and-forth texts until we got to the area.

Me:
May 19, 3:47 p.m.
I want what you're having but a dirty martini, extra dirty, would be highly preferred.

Dirty martinis were my favorite! I did like that taste of extra olive brine, but I had to throw in the "extra dirty" as a kind of sexual innuendo. At this point, I would take anything that contained alcohol.

Patrick:
May 19, 3:49 p.m.
U guys staying tonight?? I can dial u up a nice place to stay for $0 if you want.

Well, he wasn't inviting us to stay at his place, which was probably a good thing. I hadn't even seen him yet, and I still didn't know if I could control myself if left alone with him. I'm not sure if it was because I hadn't had sex in so long, but I couldn't stop fantasizing about Patrick. I mean, after being with the same man for over twelve years, even Brad Pitt would lose some of his sexiness over that amount of time.

I read Patrick's text about the hotel out loud to Heather, and she acted weird again, just like she did earlier when she didn't want to upset me about the time it would take to get there. "What?" I asked, "Did we lose even more time?"

"No," said Heather, "but I didn't want to tell you that I have to get back to LA tonight. I have an event that I have to work tomorrow much earlier than I originally thought, and I want to be rested up."

My first thought was disappointment. I didn't want to be rushed for one of the most exciting nights of my life. But then, I kept myself in check. I realized that I was super lucky just to have a friend cool enough to drive me over two hours to meet my fantasy boyfriend. And, that I had a husband cool and rich enough to allow me to vacation to meet my fantasy boyfriend. And, that my husband trusted me enough to be with my fantasy boyfriend, even if he didn't know I was going to see my fantasy boyfriend in the first place. So, it was a good thing that I now didn't have to be tempted no matter what.

Me:
May 19, 3:53 p.m.
Doubt it. Heather has to go to work in the early morning. We should be there in just a minute.

Patrick:
May 19, 3:53 p.m.
No sweat I'll see if can hold a room if needed. I'll have a martini waiting xtra dirty. We can go wherever you want after you get here—it's your vacation.

Again, this "nice" Patrick was not something I was used to. I don't think he had ever taken me out on an actual date, besides our bowling night back in 1992. He likely never took me out in fear of running into all of his other twenty girlfriends, but I could not recall him ever buying me a drink. I didn't drink much in college, but a soda would have been nice.

We found the parking lot for Billy's Brews, and paid the five dollar entry fee. Getting out of the car, I noticed my knees were a bit shaky. The combination of my out-of-whack nerves, plus the lack of food, was making me a little weak. All I kept saying to Heather was, "OMG, I can't believe what is going down right now!" Honestly, I was feeling quite overwhelmed. These things didn't happen to Piper. Better yet, Piper didn't usually make things like this happen. I mean, good stuff has happened to me a lot, but it's rarely by my doing. If it's something good, it's usually one of those things that fall in my lap, that I just luck out. I rarely put a plan in motion that actually follows through successfully. And so far, everything was going exactly as planned.

As we were walking down the sidewalk toward the open bar, so many thoughts began swirling in my head. Is he even going to recognize me? Will he think I'm fat and ugly? Where is he sitting, at the bar or a table? Am I going to recognize him? What do I do, hug him or not touch him at all? Is he going to be drunk?

But the main thing that kept swirling in my head was how much I wished that I had a little bit of alcohol in me. I didn't want to act or talk like a complete imbecile, and alcohol would actually help with that, in moderation, of course. As many times as I have met the New Kids on the Block, you would think I learned to shake some of those nerves, but no. Not at all. Every time I left a NKOTB meet and greet, I would focus on what stupid things I said, or did, in front of them. Those stupid statements always superseded the good stuff, like when Donnie told me I was "looking good," or when Joe told me that he loved my hat. I felt like a stupid teenager every single time I met them, and this moment was no different. I'm not comparing Patrick to the New Kids by any stretch of the imagination, but there were a lot of similarities. The common thread was the fact that I felt like my immature, infatuated, obsessed, and insecure teenage self all over again. But I was forty-three years old now. I had to stop this ridiculousness, and get my shit together.

I was glad that Patrick had sent that picture of himself earlier, so I at least knew to look for someone with a hat and Dallas Cowboys shirt. I also noticed in that picture, and also in some of his prior Facebomb pictures, he had much longer hair than he used to. Back in the day, it was pretty short. Not like a buzz cut, but definitely short. He wore hats in most of the recent pictures, but I could see some long blond curls sticking out. And, God, did I love those curls! I couldn't help but imagine grabbing those curls while he was . . . (insert fantasy here).

Anyway, I walked through the door.

Chapter 6

Dreams Really Do Come True

Call it cosmic energy, chakra alignment, sexual chemistry, or whatever the fuck you want to call it, but I saw him immediately when I walked into the restaurant. He was sitting at the bar by himself. I guess he noticed me immediately as well, which kind of surprised me. I know I haven't changed much in twenty-five years, but I actually thought he might've forgotten what I looked like. He immediately got off the stool, and began walking toward me. We both held out our arms at the same time and embraced in a nice, warm, long hug, exactly like in my dreams. It wasn't like in the movies, when the long-lost lovers run toward each other in slow motion while a Barry Manilow song plays in the background, but it was sweet, nonetheless.

I don't remember all of the pleasantries that were immediately exchanged, but I do remember that the word "gorgeous" was one of the first few words out of his mouth, and I'm pretty sure he was talking about me. The most important thing that was immediately obvious was that he was alone. No girlfriend, boyfriend, wife, or husband. I introduced Patrick to Heather, and was hopeful that we would be able to include her in all of our conversations. I know I hate being a third wheel, and I didn't want her to feel left out.

After the three of us took a seat at the bar, with Patrick in the middle, I happened to notice that there was not a dirty martini waiting for me. That kind of pissed me off, but hey, we are talking about Patrick here. I guess he hadn't changed much after all. He told me to tell the bartender what I wanted, so he obviously hadn't even ordered it yet. Did he think I wasn't coming? I mean, I was pretty late, which gave him plenty of time to order a damn martini. But I let that fly. I let a lot of shit fly with Patrick.

After ordering my goddamn martini, Patrick immediately broke out his phone and said that he had to tell me about his new work adventure. He was slightly hyperverbal, talking like one of my bipolar manic patients. Or in nonmedical terms, very hyper. He apologized that the discussion was going to be all about him for the first five minutes, but couldn't wait to tell someone. I didn't care that it was all about him, because I wasn't drunk yet, and I just wanted to stare at him anyway.

He began telling me about his clothing line, and how he had just gotten a new contract and was going to be making a lot of money soon. Patrick continued to keep the conversation all on him, and told me that he had been working as a director at a local YMCA for the last twelve years. As much as he enjoyed it, he was ready to move forward and immerse himself in this new business venture that was hopefully going to be quite lucrative. Some women might be like, "Oh my God, he's going to be rich! Maybe I want to leave my husband after all." But money has never been important to me. I get that everyone needs money, and I wanted a working man, but I didn't care how much he brought home. I made my own money, and I really only needed the necessities of life anyway. Plus, my husband made a lot of money, and the last thing I needed was another rich husband.

After showing me pictures of the various clothes and sports accessories that would soon be available through his company, he finally directed the conversation to me. I was starting to calm down a bit, and had a few sips of my cocktail by the time he was done with his bragging. He said, "Well, enough about me, what about you? Where do you live?" I began to tell him a brief synopsis about my life, son, husband, job etc. "Well, I've been in Atlanta for about fifteen years, I have a son who. . ." and before I could finish the sentence about my son, he chimed in, "Oh, you live in

Atlanta now?" As I shook my head yes, and started going into more detail about my life, he interrupted midsentence again, and uttered the most amazing five words I have ever heard.

"I'm moving there this summer."

Wait, did he just say he was moving to Atlanta? No, can't be, absolutely not! This was not part of my fantasy. I hadn't even thought about him living close to me as a possibility. But Jesus, that would have made the fantasies even better, and slightly more believable. I quickly saw my divorce flash before my eyes. I saw my fantasy world with Patrick and a mansion, and spending every minute together, and getting married. But wait . . . I had to keep my shit in check. What the fuck was I thinking? But more importantly, what the fuck was I going to do now? And even more importantly, what was I going to say next?

I looked at Heather to see her reaction and realized that she must have either not heard him, or was not listening, because she did not have any kind of dumbfounded look like I must have had. I was relying on her to say something while I tried to figure out where to go with my thoughts. I didn't know how to get any words out of my mouth, or at least words that consisted of anything besides, "Yay, I'll start looking for our dream house when I get back home, and we can live happily ever after."

"Did you hear that, Heather?" was the only thing I could come up with. While Heather continued to look at social media on her phone, or whatever she was too busy doing to listen to our conversation, she looked up and said, "No, what?" I then said, "Well, Patrick here just told me that he's moving to Atlanta this summer." While I said this, I was bugging my eyes out like a colossal squid, and looked at Heather like, *Help me!*

I don't even remember what she said next, but whatever it was didn't help me. Unfortunately, my next two sentences were something like, "Wow, so you are moving to Atlanta? You will be in the same city as me?" That's really all I could come up with. Then I said, "I gotta pee."

I went to the bathroom, but not to pee, just to look in the mirror and say out loud to myself, "Oh my God! This could be really bad." Just as I was talking to myself in the mirror, and trying to make deals with myself on how well I was going to keep it together for the rest of the night, my husband called. I was actually really glad, because that quickly brought me back to reality. He was just calling to tell me how great Jack was doing, and that made me even happier, if that was possible. Plus, it surprisingly made me miss my boys.

I returned to the bar and found Patrick and Heather in good conversation, laughing together. Even if they were laughing at me for whatever reason, I didn't care because Heather was having fun too. Not as much fun as I was having, but she appeared happy.

After my sweet conversation with my husband, I was ready to be a normal human being with normal conversations and thought processes . . . until Patrick made another surprising comment. While I was finishing my life synopsis, I mentioned something about my husband, when Patrick interrupted again and said, "Oh, you're married? Dammit. I mean . . . that's nice." He said this in a lighthearted and funny way, but the reality was the insinuation of him being disappointed that I was married. Even if he was kidding around, it was still flattering, and my sixteen-year-old self definitely approved.

The rest of the night is kind of a jumbled blur. With the combination of excitement, nervousness, and a little too much to drink with no food in my belly, the specifics are difficult to remember. But I will touch on the important points, and the topics that left me wanting more . . . and more . . . and more, unfortunately.

The bottom line was that Patrick was still funny, and was able to make me laugh harder than I had in a really long time. I felt like 2017, which I had dubbed my "best year ever," was just now starting. I was finally somewhere that autism was the last thing on my mind. No matter what happened that night, or didn't happen, I was just happy with the escape, even if just for a few hours.

Besides getting each other up-to-date on life for the past twenty-five years, there was an occasional reminiscence. We talked about specific songs that we used to listen to together, and his awesome car that we made out in. We also talked about our parents, since they still lived in the same hometown we grew up in. He openly discussed his brother's recent cancer scare, which made me see a softer, more vulnerable side of Patrick.

The more we drank, the more the topics tended to get a little PG-13, then turned a bit R-rated. The important details from that conversation was that Patrick was single, never been married, and had zero kids, just like I had assumed from the looks of his pictures on social media last year. I was still trying to assess the gay possibility, but I figured with the way he looked at me, he was probably still straight.

I'm pretty sure it was the alcohol talking, but we somehow began discussing the last time we had sex, and how it had been a very long time for both of us. I think he said it had been nineteen months for him, which kind of made me laugh that he remembered it right to the exact month. It hadn't been quite that long for me, but I was married, so that time frame was almost impossible. Well, maybe not for an unhappily married person, but that wasn't me exactly. Patrick then joked that he would have to turn all the lights off in the room before getting naked, since his physique had gone a little downhill over the past few years. When I concurred about myself, and stated that I would have to do the same thing, he quickly made a point to say that he thought I looked amazing. Then he said something else that made me freak a little . . . he said, "I had to call Brad when I got your text to make sure he wasn't playing a joke on me." I was confused as to why he would think that Brad using my name would be a joke, so he explained a recent scenario at Brad's house where my name was actually brought up. Patrick explained, "Well, about three months ago, us guys were doing the typical guy talk, and one of the questions that we bounced around the room was, 'Who would you want to have sex with again from your past?' and I immediately said your name, without hesitation."

For someone whose overall night was a little blurry, this statement was clear as day, and still is. I'm not quite sure why, but this was like music to my ears. This was probably the greatest thing I had heard in a really long time. I know some girls might think, *How horrible that you thought of me like a piece of meat, and just wanted to have sex with me.* But no, not me. This is Patrick Barnes we are talking about. Just the fact that my name came out of his mouth, and three months ago at that. Wait, three months ago? So, he was actually thinking about me three months ago? This is the same person that I wondered if he would even remember who I was, let alone how I was in bed. But, I also knew this was not just about sex. Reason being, Patrick was the second person that I ever had sex with, and everyone knows that an inexperienced lover can't be THAT memorable. So why me, out of the thousand girls that he had probably had sex with? Okay, maybe not a thousand, but likely a very large number. Why is he telling me this? He's probably outright lying just to get me in bed again, but I still fell for it . . . hook, line, and sinker.

And he kept going . . .

"Brad asked me if I had seen a recent picture of you, and said you were hotter now than you were in high school, and you were already hot then. I always remembered how much fun we had together, and I have thought about you a lot over the years."

I thought the word *STOP!* secretly in my head, but I didn't say it out loud. I seriously don't think I could have taken much more. Even though I loved every minute of it, I was about to combust from the air coming out of his mouth mixing with the fuel of emotions inside of me.

This was even more substance than the fantasies that kept me up at night. These ridiculously amazing things that were physically coming from Patrick's mouth was more than I could ever dream about.

Then he had to go even further. He said, "You know what I always loved about you? That you liked me for me, and never wanted me to be somebody I wasn't. You were always so sweet."

Wait . . . *sweet*? He obviously had me confused with someone else. I can't remember a time in my forty-three years of life where I was considered "*sweet*." Now it makes sense, he's thinking of someone else. But no, I think he meant me. I knew it had to be me, because he was actually correct. I did always like him for who he was, and still did. I didn't care if he owned his own company and was going to be rich or not, I would still be sitting there with him, enjoying the banter.

With the amount of alcohol in my system, and the constant comments and compliments that I thought could only be heard in my head, I was on cloud nine. I hadn't seen anything from this cloud in years, and I had forgotten how beautiful it was. Even if I never saw Patrick again, I was satiated on so many levels. There were other words and conversations that night, but I think my brain shut off the rest. I don't know how much more awesomeness I could take while staying sane in the process. Or at least appearing sane to Patrick.

It was getting late, and Heather was getting a little antsy to get back home to get some rest before work the next day. I figured the evening had definitely surpassed my expectations, so I was willing to call it a night. I wasn't quite sure how the goodbyes were going to go. Luckily, or unluckily, staying with Patrick was not looking like an option. That's when I knew the "*Moral Gods*," as I call them, were doing their thing.

Patrick walked us to Heather's car, and there was only a quick kiss on the cheek, and a big hug between us. I knew there wasn't much to read into it when he did the same thing to Heather. However, there was that odd anxiety that you sometimes feel on a first date when you don't know if you're supposed to kiss, or hug, or what. That's when I knew there was definitely still some chemistry there between us, but neither one of us acted on it, thank God.

I opened the passenger side door of Heather's car as Patrick was walking away, and then I heard him call my name. He was probably about fifteen feet away from me, so I didn't know if this was going to be one of those TV moments where we run back into each other's arms, and kiss like it was the last time we would ever see each other. But, luckily I didn't start running his direction to find out. When I turned toward him, Patrick reached into his pocket, and pulled out one of those cheap costume gold chains that you buy when you are going to be a pimp for Halloween. He tossed it my direction, and I caught it, right above my head. He winked at me and said, "Bye."

I'm sure it was just because of my infatuation with Patrick, but I thought this gesture was absolutely adorable. It was one of those things that made me like him even more than I already did . . . that silliness and randomness that always made me smile or laugh. I mean, who throws a fake gold chain at an ex-girlfriend, let alone has one quickly accessible in his pocket? It definitely made me want to see him again very soon, and giggle like a six-teen-year-old, forgetting all about my mundane life once again. God, it felt so good to laugh again.

The ride back to LA was quite a blur as well. Heather was jammin' to her '80s hits, and all I could do was stare blankly out the window. I was actually speechless, which was rare. I was waiting to wake up, because these kinds of things didn't happen to Piper in real life. I mean, everything that I dreamed about just happened. Every. Single. Thing. Minus the sex, which was probably a good thing. At least I didn't have to leave feeling guilty. Instead, I left feeling alive, sexy, and most of all, happy.

Heather told me that she wanted me to text Patrick to thank him for buying all of her drinks and food, and said she felt bad that she forgot to do that. So, when I got back to the hotel room, I thought I would send him a quick text to tell him thanks, and also let him know that I made it back to the hotel safely.

Me:
May 20, 12:12 a.m.
I forgot to thank you for buying all the drinks, and Heather wanted to make sure I told you thanks from her. I got back to my hotel. So glad I got to see you.

Patrick:
May 20, 12:16 a.m.
Are we breaking up?

Patrick:
May 20, 12:17 a.m.
Again?

THIS, Y'ALL! THIS was why I was so crazy about Patrick. His texts might appear somewhat childish, and in all honesty, they were. But, I loved his sense of humor. I'm not sure if it was the sense of humor part that I was in love with, or just the fact that someone was making me laugh. I hadn't felt that content and free in such a long time, and I loved every second of it. I would have been happy texting all night, just to giggle a little more, but I knew there was nothing but reality from here on out.

Me:
May 20, 12:19 a.m.
LOL Goodnight!

Patrick:
May 20, 12:23 a.m.
Thank you for making the effort to come say hi. Nobody does that. Hope to see u before another 25 yrs. Goodnite.

Chapter 7

Back to Life . . .

I got home late Sunday night and hugged my boys. Even though I had such an amazing time, I loved being home. It was comfortable, and reliable, and happy in its own way. I guess because we were in a type of routine that fit us all. Unfortunately, that's when you get stuck in your comfort zone, so I was proud that I forced myself out of it for a few days, and did something I never thought I would.

The fantasies continued even after I got home. Except now, they were even stronger, if that was possible. I'm assuming it was because I finally heard everything that I had ever wanted to hear from the only person I ever cared to hear it from. Before the trip, these daydreams and fantasies were just that . . . fantasies. And sometimes fantasies can actually be better than reality. You don't have the guilt, letdowns, and the expectations that come from having your dreams come true. I should have left it at that, but I didn't. I couldn't.

I thought about the fact that Patrick was moving to Atlanta, and that gave me so many different kinds of feels. I didn't know where his company was based, so hell, maybe he would be moving down the street from me. I had completely forgotten to ask about more details that night, since I was not able to conjure up any kind of normal words at the time he informed me of this move. And because I live off of the *everything happens for a reason* mentality, I couldn't shake trying to figure out why this was all happening. Why, after crushing on this man for almost twenty-seven years, were all these dreams falling into place? Why did everything I had only imagined, minus the sex, actually come true? Do you know how easily accessible he would be when he moved? Why? Were those *Moral Gods* just tempting me to see how far I would go, or was there a bigger reason? I couldn't stop trying to figure this out.

It had only been three days since I got home, and I couldn't stop thinking about Patrick. I wondered if my feelings were something crazy, like *love.* But, I quickly realized that it was more like loving the feeling I got when I was with him. There's a difference between loving someone, and loving who you are and what you feel when you are with that someone. I already loved my husband and my son, and I didn't think I had enough room in my tiny little heart to love someone else. But why on earth could I not stop thinking about him?

I was finally getting around to unpacking when I found the gold chain at the bottom of my suitcase. This made me giggle out loud, thinking about his childish grin when he threw it to me. I got a brilliant idea to put the necklace on, take a selfie, and text it to him. I hadn't heard from him since that night, and had been thinking of ways to reach out. It had only been a few days, and I was curious to see if he would text me back. But, for some reason, I was a bit hesitant to send a text at all. I know we were just friends, and we all randomly text our friends for no good reason sometimes, but we were the weird kind of friends. The kind of friends who were a little more than friends, but not. And the last thing I wanted to do was to text him and have him wonder why I was texting him so soon, and for no other reason but to be silly. So, I had to look fabulous in this selfie!

Luckily, I had a date night with hubby planned that night, so I was already going to spruce up a bit. I just spruced a bit more than usual, feeling guilty the whole time about the extra makeup being for another man. I wanted to make the picture somewhat humorous, so that he would be more likely to respond. Therefore, not only did I put on the gold chain, I also blinged it up a tad by throwing the West Coast gang sign with my right hand. I mean, if I was going to look pimp, I might as well go full-on gangsta. I knew this had to be the best way to get a response.

Along with the picture, I wrote:

Me:
May 24, 7:10 p.m.
Should I wear it out tonight or what?

Sure enough, about ten minutes after sending the text, I got a response. Not only did I get a response, I got a picture of him wearing a similar gold chain. It had obviously just been taken, since it was a similar pose to mine. Attached to his picture, he wrote:

Patrick:
May 24, 7:19 p.m.
Absolutely & I'll wear mine too. Be careful might get it snatched in Hotlanta.

I so wanted to respond, and text with him all night, but I was headed out to a dinner date with hubby and friends. I was just ecstatic that he texted back, and I left it at that . . . for two days at least.

Friday came around, and it had been exactly one week since I saw Patrick. I was hoping that by the end of the week, I would slow down on the obsessions, but no. He still consumed most of my thoughts and feelings, both awake and asleep. As much as I loved the mental escape, I hated it too. I was a rational person, for the most part, but my current thoughts and fantasies were far from rational. So, why was I doing this? Why was I allowing Patrick to take over my sanity? I had a wonderful husband who loved me dearly. Was that not enough? Hubs and I had definitely been struggling for a while, but never enough to look outside of the marriage, at least not for me. Or was this something else? Did I actually have extra-large feelings for Patrick, when all along I just thought of this as a fun escape from my "autism prison"?

As I was watching my son jump up and down on his small trampoline, while he watched his favorite Pixar DVD for the 976th time, I got the urge to text Patrick again. I couldn't think of what to text, but I wanted it to be something that would warrant a response from him. I was holding my phone, trying to figure out what to text, when Jack decided that he didn't like the taste of the dust bunny that he found on the floor, and puked all over the living room couch. While cleaning it up, I was reminded of how much fun I was having a week before, drinking martinis and enjoying the company of Heather and Patrick. So, I texted just that.

Me:
May 26, 7:57 p.m.
As I clean puke off the floor, I'm reminded of how much more fun I was having a week ago right now.

I went back to finishing the clean-up on aisle autism, and about ten minutes later, I got a response.

Patrick:
May 26, 8:10 p.m.
I just picked up dog shit n threw up so puke happens. Send me the gold chain pic again.
Too cute.

Okay, so he didn't admit to having more fun last week as well, but he did want a picture of me. That was pretty cool. I guess he either never saves pictures, or he deletes texts. This made me think he probably had a girlfriend or, at the very least, someone he didn't want to see his texts and pictures. Anyway, I sent the gold chain picture again, and was pleasantly surprised at his response.

Patrick:
May 26, 8:45 p.m.
Ur man is so lucky to get those back rubs.
You're gorgeous Piper.

Patrick told me I was gorgeous a couple of times in California, but now I had proof on paper, or the phone in this case. This comment from him got me thinking about how amazing it would be to give him one of those back rubs. That was kind of our signature back in the day. Every time I went over to his apartment, I would always give him a back massage. I wouldn't mind because it was usually the precursor to other things. After reading the text a second time, I was overjoyed that he remembered I did that. He also must have enjoyed the rubs, or at least enjoyed what came after.

Me:
May 26, 9:12 p.m.
Thanks, Patrick! And I'm sorry you missed the
Piper massage special last week.

I forced myself to avoid texting Patrick at all costs for at least a week. I focused on my life, and how it wasn't too bad after all, but it definitely had a hole somewhere. A hole that felt like, at the time, could only be filled by one person. The one person I couldn't have. But did I actually WANT Patrick? And in what form did I want him, if I did? I knew I could never marry him, that wasn't even a possibility. We would kill each other at some point, I'm sure of it. Did I just want one night? And if I got that one night, would it be enough? Would the fantasies and obsessions stop? Or, would I just want more? Would I fall in love, or was I already in love? I figured I would let the universe take it where it was supposed to go.

Exactly one week and one day later, I actually got a text from Patrick. If only I knew then that this text was going to be one of the few that *he* initiated . . .

Patrick:
June 3, 9:08 p.m.
I'm in Texas currently . . . I miss it. How's
everything in the ATL?

I was in the middle of putting Jack to bed when I received the text. Since Jack is nonverbal, he is very perceptive of other people's feelings and emotions. Even if we are not outwardly acting the same emotion that we are feeling, like laughing when sad, he can still feel the intensity. I was so elated about the text, and Jack kept looking at me like I was crazy. If he could speak he would say, "What is wrong with you, Mom? You are acting weird." I went from my normal, content self, to superduper excited. Jack sensed it, but luckily didn't know why.

Me:
June 3, 9:45 p.m.
Everything good here. What's new in the hometown? Visiting Parents?

Patrick:
June 3, 9:55 p.m.
Tipping cows

Attached to his last text was a picture of a beautiful, green pasture with three cows. I had no idea if the picture was his parents' house, or if it was just a picture he found on the internet when searching "cows in pasture." But, regardless, it was beautiful. At that very moment, I wanted to be teleported right to where that picture was, especially if Patrick was there too.

Me:
June 3, 9:58 p.m.
Did you just take that? And where?

I never got a response. It was that night that I realized Patrick was the one to end text exchanges, and I would have to get used to it. But, because I am the type to respond to everyone, even if it's just a thumbs-up emoji, I was okay with that. You're either *that* person, or you're not. Some need to have the last word, and others want to keep 'em guessing. One of my girlfriends is just like me, so sometimes our texts never end. They go on through the next day, because we have to reply regardless. Does this mean that we are control freaks? Or does it just make us good people, showing others that we hear you, and we care about you? But, I digress. I was just happy that Patrick thought about me long enough to text me that night.

Chapter 8

Take Me Away

While these thoughts of Patrick continued to swirl in all directions in my head, my marriage was still suffering. Hubs and I decided to go to couples counseling. I was a little worried what might come out in the sessions, though. I knew I had never cheated, but I was having an emotional affair. Even if Patrick didn't know it, I was thinking about him way more than I should. I knew that the only way couples therapy would work is if you are honest with each other, and the therapist. I couldn't be honest, though. I wasn't ready to end my marriage, and I knew if I was COMPLETELY honest, it would end abruptly. I really did want to try to make it work.

We went to a few sessions, and it was mostly a waste of our time. Probably because we were both lying to ourselves, and each other. I refused to address anything in the sexual part of our relationship, and mainly focused on the parts that I felt I resented in my husband, like him being a workaholic and traveling way too much. Since he was in IT, he could technically work as much, or as little, as he wanted. And because we had numerous Jack expenses that equaled approximately $5,000/month out of pocket, he didn't have a choice but to work as many jobs as he could get. So, this meant many days and nights with hubby away from home, which equaled no help with Jack. I would get exhausted and overwhelmed by doing it all myself, and hubs would get exhausted and overwhelmed from working and traveling too much, so this combination was a killer on the household. And when hubby got stressed, he would either yell, or not say anything at all, sometimes for days at a time. I usually got the silent treatment while Jack got the yelling, simply because his anger was rooted in the autism struggles. I could take hubby's silent treatment, but I couldn't take it when Jack got the brunt of his anger. I kept trying to emphasize that it was not Jack's fault, and we had to be the strong ones to help him through this process, which also had to be difficult for Jack as well.

I thought for sure this would spark something in the therapist to explore his anger, but instead it somehow got turned around to me being the bad guy. But because I was already feeling guilty with the Patrick fantasies, I took it all in stride. She told me that I was just being a caring mom, and that it was normal for a mom to be very protective of her child. She also said that I should work on my frustration toward hubs when he gets home from a business trip, so that he doesn't get angry, and take it out on Jack. All this did was piss me off even more, resulting in pulling away even further from my husband. Where is the accountability in that? She's getting on me for pissing him off, but not getting on him for taking his frustrations out on an innocent child? This not only caused me to pull further away from my husband, it also pushed me into my reality escape tactics, which at the time was everything Patrick. I needed something to get my mind off the constant stress at home. These occasional playful texts were not doing the job. I needed to see him. I needed to feel him. I needed to touch him. I needed him to "take me away," just like the water softener.

It had only been four days since our last text exchange, but I made up my mind. I was going to see Patrick again soon, come hell or high water. I had recently divulged every last detail about Patrick, past and present, to my best friend in Atlanta. I had to. Being a therapist myself, I know how hard it is to keep that kind of shit inside. It's sometimes necessary to process your thoughts and feelings with someone you trust, and who understands why you are having these crazy feelings. And lucky for me, Elizabeth seemed to completely understand. And, I trusted her. Not that she was in love with the fact that my current greatest desire was to commit adultery, but she knew the struggles I faced on a daily basis. And just like a best friend should, she was on board for whatever was going to make me happy again. Even if that meant keeping a big secret. Luckily there wasn't an actual secret to keep . . . yet, anyway.

One afternoon, Elizabeth called to see if I wanted to join her in a night on the town in the ATL the last weekend in June. She already had a hotel room reserved for us before I even said I could go. Her husband was planning on supervising a house full of eight-year-old boys for a sleepover, and since girls weren't invited, she wanted to take full advantage. She also knew that Patrick was supposed to be moving to Atlanta at some point soon, and figured I could also benefit from a night away from home, and hopefully with Patrick. I couldn't remember when Patrick said he was moving, but I had to find out. Maybe this was going to be the opportunity I was impatiently waiting for.

Me:
June 7, 4:11 p.m.
When did you say you were moving?

Patrick:
June 7, 4:22 p.m.
I'll be out there July 12–20, then moving last week of August. How are you doing? I'm in Kansas for work right now.

Attached to the text was a picture, which I'm assuming he had just taken of himself. He was standing in what looked like a baseball stadium, which would make sense, since he sold athletic clothes. It was a nice, big close-up of his face. I was so happy that I had another picture to stare at all day, and possibly utilize in my private moments, if you know what I mean. I was hoping and praying that he wouldn't ask for a pic of me at the time, since I had the *autism-mom look* going on, with the messy bun and no makeup.

Me:
June 7, 4:50 p.m.
I was asking because I have some free time at
the end of the month, but you won't be here
yet, so that kinda sucks. Won't see you.

I didn't even know if I was going to be able to get away that weekend anyway, but I just wanted an excuse to find out exactly when Patrick was moving. I also wanted to make it very clear that I really wanted to see him again. And I couldn't help but giggle at the "typical Patrick" response.

Patrick:
June 7, 5:22 p.m.
Don't give up so easy . . .

Me:
June 7, 5:30 p.m.
Well, if I have the whole weekend off, you
never know where I might end up.

Shit, at this point I was willing to go wherever Patrick was going to be that weekend, but I knew going anywhere to see him was next to impossible. I just wanted to put the thought in his head to see what he would say. And luckily, I loved his response, even if he was joking.

Patrick:
June 7, 5:47 p.m.
NB maybe? Jk. Would love to see you
again soon.

Attached to this text was a picture of a beautiful sunset on the water, with a palm tree in the middle. I'm assuming it was the view from his place in Newport Beach. But, wherever it was, I wanted to be there. Yesterday! And the fact that he said he wanted to see me again soon was all I needed to hear to continue putting my plans in motion. Nothing was going to stop me now. And I figured if he could be a little vulnerable, so could I. So I responded.

Me:
June 7, 6:13 p.m.
You never know. I forgot how you always made me laugh. I haven't had much of that for a few years, so it felt nice. I have to live vicariously through your free spirit.

Patrick:
June 7, 7:02 p.m.
I understand. You're an angel & what you're doing is way more necessary than my pipe dream. I'm so glad we're friends again. Xo

I actually loved the fact that he called us friends. That's what I liked about Patrick most . . . his friendship. Of course I'm beyond attracted to him in every physical and sexual way, but I have always enjoyed his company the most. I was so happy that we were at a place where I knew I could text him anytime, and not feel weird about it. We were friends at the end of the day, and that's what I wanted more than anything. I was almost not wanting to take anything further, because I know how that can screw up a friendship. ALMOST being the operative word. The physical draw to him was still strong, though, no matter how hard I tried to focus on the friend part.

Chapter 9

Our Song

A month later, I was sitting in the ATL airport on my way to Chicago to play with some friends. I used to live there, so I was lucky enough to still have some fabulous friends in that area. And since this was going to be my *best year ever,* I had to include a trip to my old stomping grounds to play for a few days. I was eating lunch in an airport restaurant when a song came on. I had to listen really hard, because I couldn't believe what I was hearing. It was a song that Patrick and I used to listen to in college, but even more than that, it was one of the songs that we had talked about when I was in Newport Beach. I can't necessarily call it "our song," but I guess it was the closest as any song was. Patrick would constantly play the song in his car back in 1992, and when I brought up all of the music we used to listen to back in the day, this song was the first one he mentioned in NB. So, I knew it must have reminded him of me as well. I couldn't help but feel like this was another sign of some sort. I know it's just a freakin' song, but it's not like it was a super popular song, even back in 1992. So, the fact that it was playing in the airport in 2017, I felt like I had to text Patrick.

Me:
July 6, 1:09 p.m.
I'm sitting in an airport restaurant and our song just came on, so of course thought of you. How was your 4th?

Patrick:
July 6, 1:18 p.m.
Hi there! I worked my last 4th of July at the
YMCA EVER!! I have senioritis so bad. Ready
to get out of this place! You doing alright? Hope
to see you again soon. Xo

Me:
July 6, 1:24 p.m.
I'm alright—heading to Chicago right now for a
few days to relax with some old friends. Did you
say you were heading this way next week? If you
could squeeze some time to come to ATL, let me
know . . . would love to see you.

Patrick:
July 6, 1:29 p.m.
I am nxt Wednesday night. Then hitting Nashville
and Athens, but should be in ATL a couple nights
throughout the week. Will keep you posted and
have fun!

I had a blast in Chicago, but I still had a very hard time getting my mind off of Patrick the entire time. I figured if I was intoxicated for the majority of four days, while playing and partying with old friends, and still thought of him, I must have it bad. He said "next week" in his last text, but even on vacation, I didn't want to wait that long. I had my mind made up that if I was lucky enough to see him again soon, and if the timing was right, I was going to sleep with him.

At this point it was all I could think about. I was hoping that if I did do it, I would somehow get it "out of my system," so to speak, and the dreams and extreme urges would go away, or at least chill out a bit. Or maybe the sex would suck, and I would stop these fantasies. I was rationalizing all possible scenarios in my head, and all of them pointed to being with him. However, the part of me that has never cheated on anyone, or even thought about it, ever, was the angel on my shoulder. That angel was loud and strong too, but not strong enough. This was a desire that I don't think I have ever had. I didn't think of it as an opportunity as much as I did a necessity. An actual need to escape, and temporarily flee this autism life, which at times was pure hell. Yes, the escape is just an excuse, but I had never felt this way before, and I didn't know how else to stop the desires.

Then there was the possibility that he may not even want to sleep with me. I'm not one to walk around assuming that every guy wants want to fuck me. However, I felt some pretty crazy chemistry when I saw him, and I hoped he did too. But I was married. Maybe he was a born-again Christian, and didn't want to have sex again until marriage. Well, that probably wasn't the case, but he may not have it high on his priority list to have sex with a married woman. Most men are not all about that, so maybe I was being too presumptuous. But he did mention wanting to see me again. And he did put "Xo" on the end of a few texts, so I felt confident. Or was I reading too much into it? Or was I reading too much into reading too much into it?

Luckily, I had to work for a few days after my trip, so that kept me from staring at the phone all day, waiting for a text. One afternoon I was talking to a patient, and felt my phone vibrate, and just knew it was him.

Patrick:
July 16, 1:23 p.m.
How was the windy city?

Me:
July 16, 1:30 p.m.
It was fabulous! You still in the south?

Patrick:
July 16, 1:45 p.m.
Yep. Just got off 85 headed toward Athens.
Wanted to say hello. Been in Nashville for 4 days,
it was nuts. I know why you had such a great time
in Chitown . . . I have a memory like an elephant.
Naughty girl.

This honestly confused me. I had no idea what he was talking about. I know I was a bit intoxicated that night in Newport Beach, but I didn't remember any specific discussion of Chicago, or doing anything naughty.

Me:
July 16, 1:53 p.m.
Well, you must have a better memory than me bc I have no idea what you are talking about. But please refresh my memory if it was that good. Let me know if you are gonna be in the city.

Patrick:
July 16, 2:27 p.m.
We were talking about the last time we had amazing sex & Chicago was your answer.
I was just messing with you. Sorry, jk.

I was still confused, and didn't remember a discussion like that, but I was a little out of sorts on all levels when I saw him last. I sensed from his text that he must have assumed I had "amazing sex" while on vacation in Chicago. Which was so far from the truth. I had fun, but no sex or grooving happened in any way, shape, or form. But his text did make me think of the first time he and I kissed, and what he said to me. So I thought I would test his "elephant memory."

Me:
July 16, 2:36 p.m.
I guarantee there was none of that this time, and don't apologize. I can take it. And if you have such a good memory, what did you tell me the first time you kissed me? I bet money you don't remember.

I'm not a betting girl, but I would have bet a lot of money that he didn't remember what he told me after we kissed in his car back in 1992. I mean, I was kind of embarrassed to admit that *I* remembered. But come on, I was eighteen at the time, and had kissed less than five guys total, and only had sex with one. Plus, girls usually remember cheesy shit like that. I was a little hesitant to admit to him that I was the crazy girl that remembered everything about him. However, it helped that I was married, and could be a little more forward with my flirtation and interest, without fear of rejection. If he thought I was a little psycho for remembering something that probably didn't matter much to him, I was okay with that. But, luckily this wasn't the case.

> **Patrick:**
> July 16, 2:46 p.m.
> I said I have a trunk like an elephant too! Ha. I
> said you kiss just like me. Don't want money
> but will take some form of payment. Jk again. I
> shouldn't be this dirty on Sunday. I'll repent
> in the shower tonight.

O. M. G. He actually remembered! Not only did he remember, but he was pretty confident in his response. It wasn't like, "I think that's what I said." Instead, it was like, "BOOM, told you I have an excellent memory." So I had to wonder, was it his elephant-like memory skills, or was that kiss as meaningful to him as it was to me? Or, did he say the same thing to all the girls he kissed?

> **Me:**
> July 16, 2:59 p.m.
> Wow. You really do have quite the memory. I'm
> impressed. But I bet you tell all the girls that when
> you kiss them. : You could just skip the shower,
> come here, and collect on the bet. Jk, as
> you would say.

Hey, no holds barred at this point. I was pulling out the big guns. I was letting it be known that I was here, ready, and waiting. I know I put the "jk" in there, but we all know there is always a little truth to a "just kidding."

Patrick:
July 16, 3:01 p.m.
Not at all true. Don't cheapen it young lady.

Me:
July 16, 3:05 p.m.
JK

And that was that for the texts on Sunday. If I didn't know he had such a good sense of humor, I would worry that he was mad at me for the kiss comment. But, I figured out by now that Patrick liked to end texts whenever he felt like it, and that he was not angry. So at this point, he knew I was interested, and the ball was in his court. If he wanted to see me, he would let me know. I wasn't sure how long I was willing to wait before texting him, because I remembered he was leaving midweek, and I was getting desperate. Luckily, I only had to wait about twenty-four hours.

Patrick:
July 17, 4:46 p.m.
I'm in downtown ATL & I haven't seen a white person in an hour. Not that that is wrong but I'm a little surprised. Should have brought my grill.

Okay, so I was super excited he texted me, but he didn't say anything about seeing me. Was he playing hard to get? The fact that he texted when he was in my city was the ammo I needed to push the subject of seeing each other. The problem was, I didn't have a sitter, and my husband was out of town on business. But at this point, I couldn't even wait until "late." I needed to see him now. I was wishing he had said something in his texts yesterday about tonight, so I could have made plans and gotten a sitter.

I have to admit, I did not care for the "white person" comment in his text, but I also knew Patrick enough to know he was joking, and wasn't racist. Maybe a little prejudice, but that's unfortunately what happens when you are raised in a predominantly red state, whether you like it or not. I admit that I had that Texas mentality as well, until I moved to Chicago, and got to see for myself how fucking awesome all races and ethnic groups were. But until you are either raised in a nonprejudicial environment, or you learn on your own as an educated adult, you tend to keep the "backwoods mentality" if that's all you know.

Oh, and one more thing . . . I thought he was joking about the grill. He wasn't!

Me:
July 17, 4:57 p.m.
Welcome to Atlanta! : How long are you here?
And thanks for letting me know ahead of time :
I would've liked to have seen you.

Patrick:
July 17, 5:02 p.m.
No shit. Pictures aren't good enough. U look
beautiful.

Attached to his text was a picture of me, and it was my latest Facebomb profile picture. So, for someone who is "never on social media," which is what he told me numerous times in Newport Beach, it appeared as though he had taken the time to get on my page, and save my profile picture. That was quite surprising, very flattering, and exciting. I know I was also saving his pics, but I was the obsessed one. To know that he thought about me long enough to get on my page and save my picture just gave me more ammunition to do whatever I had to do to get to him. Tonight!

Me:
July 17, 5:05 p.m.
So, when can I see you?

Patrick:
July 17, 5:09 p.m.
When can u?

Come on already! I would like to think he was just being considerate, since I was the one that had to work around a kid and a babysitter, but this back-and-forth was a bit frustrating. Just tell me when the fuck I can see you, because it's going to happen, tonight! Tell me where to go, and I'll be there. I should've just texted that, because obviously he needs a little kick in the ass.

Me:
July 17, 5:15 p.m.
Let me see what I can work out and I'll let you know. Are you free tonight?

Yes, I was being the aggressive one. I prefer to call it "assertive." I wasn't going to wait until tomorrow before his flight, and continue to play this "whenever" game.

Patrick:
July 17, 5:25 p.m.
Yes, unless I meet a cute biker down here w/ big muscles. My mom said I could stay out later tonight. Finally.

I know, I know . . . you readers want me to quickly end this texting, and get to the hotel, and down to the nitty-gritty. But you're going to have to wait. I waited one and a half years for this particular moment. This exact evening, to be specific, so you can wait a couple of minutes. If you want to get technical, I have actually been waiting twenty-two years, since the night I kicked him out of my apartment back in 1995.

Me:
July 17, 5:32 p.m.
About time! I'm trying to find a sitter but I can't leave until 9 or later.

Patrick:
July 17, 5:44 p.m.
Anytime u can or want to see me is perfect

That's all I needed to hear. If he wasn't going to tell me when, then I was going to tell HIM when. During this text exchange, I was at the pool with my son, texting every babysitter I knew. I finally found one who was willing and able to get to my house in an hour. That gave me almost an hour to take a shower, shave my legs (and then some), put on loads of makeup, and do my hair. I have never done all of that in an hour, but tonight had to be the exception. He seemed to not care how late I was going to be, but I cared. And he probably didn't care what I looked like either, but I did.

Me:
July 17, 6:30 p.m.
I think I worked something out to be there a little earlier but I'm warning you, I look nothing like I do in the picture above. It's been a frazzled day.

Patrick:
July 17, 6:39 p.m.
Well, I don't like spending time w/ you because of the way you look . . . I love being around you because I can be myself 100% all the time and don't feel I have to pretend to be someone I'm not to make you like me. Being hot as shit doesn't hurt though.

This was probably the most beautiful text that Patrick had ever sent me. I know how important it is to be able to be yourself around someone, and he knew I liked him for him. Always have, and always will. It's just a bonus to hear that the man of your dreams thinks you are hot as shit.

Me:
July 17, 7:02 p.m.
So glad you know that about me! Tell me what hotel and I'll be there in about an hour. And please have a dirty martini waiting for me this time.

I had to put that in there. Can you tell I'm still bitter about the previously absent martini?

Patrick:
July 17, 7:22 p.m.
Sure will. I'll be at the bar. Hammond Buckhead.
No rush, just so glad you're coming to see me.

I threw Jack's corn dog in the microwave as I dried my hair and put on makeup. Because Jack is nonverbal, he has to rely on his other senses to navigate his world. As I mentioned before, with this sensory system comes an extreme ability to feel others' emotions. This can be bad at times, like when other kids cry at school, he cries too. He can feel that strong emotion, positive or negative, and it can sometimes be too overwhelming for him. But it can also be very helpful for me, like in this particular instance. I was so fucking excited, and Jack could sense it. I tried to remain calm, but he could feel my energy. It was positive energy, but it was a strong force of positivity. Since Jack is usually very needy and demanding of my attention due to his inability to perform daily tasks, plus his bad habit of putting every non-food item in his mouth, he must've sensed that I needed this hour to get ready without interruption. He sat quietly and watched his show, while I ran around like a chicken with my head cut off. I kissed Jack and quickly flew out of the house the second the babysitter got there, and then texted Patrick to let him know I was on my way.

I was pissed that my car was low on gas, and the extra five minutes that it was going to take to fill up was five minutes too long. I didn't have time to go to the gas station that I usually go to, so I went to one in the "not so great" part of town, since it was on my way. While I was pumping gas, wishing it would come out faster, a tall, young African American male came from behind the gas station and began walking toward me. As he began to say something, I raised my hand to stop him, looked at him with the biggest smile on my face and said, "Sorry, I'm on my way to what is hopefully one of the best nights of my life, so I'm in a hurry. Good luck to you." He actually turned around and walked away with a smile on his face too. I have no idea what he was going to say or ask, and I felt kind of bad, but I was on a mission! And I think he was actually rooting for me a little bit too.

During the twenty-five minute drive, many thoughts were swirling in my head. Surprisingly though, the biggest thing I was saying to myself was, *What is wrong with you, Piper? You are not going to have sex with anyone tonight. First of all, you are stupid to cheat on your husband. You never have, and never wanted to before. Second of all, Patrick will most likely not want to have sex with you, so it's a nonissue.* And I was okay with these thoughts. I was honestly just excited to see Patrick again, and laugh, and reminisce, and feel sexy. That's what he did, he made me feel sexy again. I haven't felt like that in a very long time, and that's what I believe was at the root of all of this attraction. It was the way he made me feel when I was with him.

But then there was the devil on my shoulder, reminding me that I had lost about ten pounds since the last time I saw Patrick. That devil was saying, better yet, he was screaming, "Why not just go for it! If the opportunity presents itself, do it, or you will regret it." I wasn't sure how I had lost so much weight over the last two months, but I had been lacking an appetite since before LA, for no particular reason. At first I thought it was just the excitement of my trip to California, but my normally ferocious appetite never came back after the trip. It was almost like the universe knew that I had an upcoming opportunity where I had to be my best self, so it was preparing me and my body. I appreciate the universe sometimes, and this was one of those times.

And the last thought I had while driving was one that I actually hadn't thought about yet, up to this point. As I said before, Patrick was on my "hall pass list." This is a list that is supposed to give you "permission" from your spouse to sleep with a particular individual, or group of people, if you like that sort of thing. But, doesn't your spouse have to know who is on the list, and what the rules and regulations are with the list? I just realized that my husband never knew who was on my hall pass, and likely didn't even know what a hall pass was, so I guess it wasn't actually a hall pass after all. At this point, I felt like I needed something like a permission slip to take to the principal, instead of a hall pass. This wasn't a pass to leave class to go to the bathroom. This was more like a permission slip that needed to be signed by your parent, or husband in this case, and taken straight to the principal's office. And to make matters worse, hubby didn't even know I was going out, or who I was going out with. I knew he was in Boston and too busy with work, so there was no reason to make him worry or wonder, even though he was probably too busy to do either, as usual. Looking back, I should have called him while I was driving to inform him that I was on my way to visit a hall pass member, and that I might need to utilize one of those passes, but it's probably good I didn't.

These thoughts of hubby made the guilt start kicking in. As much as I was ready for anything, I was also human, and a married human at that. A human with actual feelings, and who honestly loved her husband. That feeling had never gone away. Resentment and anger toward him had taken over me in the last four years, but I still loved him. And just because he was struggling a little more than I was with this autism life, it didn't give me permission to do whatever the fuck I wanted to do, and to possibly hurt him in the process. Or did it? I tell all of my patients that they have to put themselves first, to make THEM happy, before anyone else. I also need to practice what I preach. If being with Patrick tonight was going to make me happy, then I had to do that for myself. Yes, this is a very selfish viewpoint. But there are times in life where you have to be selfish, and I learned that early on when my ex-husband left me. I quickly realized that it wasn't about me, and that I would never want someone to sacrifice their happiness on account of me. So again, I had to follow my heart. I was not an impulsive person. Never have been, never will be. If I was going to have sex with Patrick, it would be a well thought out, nonregretful move on my part.

Chapter 10

So . . . That Was It?

As I pulled up to the hotel valet, I realized that I never got a return text from Patrick after I told him I was on my way. When he doesn't respond, I quickly turn into my teenage self, and start wondering if he is going to blow me off. After I got my valet ticket, I began walking into the hotel when I heard Patrick say my name from behind me. I turned around as he was putting out his cigarette. We embraced in another nice, warm hug, similar to the one in California. What I found so cute was that Patrick seemed nervous, but in a "I like you" way, kinda like a first date. I thought it was sweet that he seemed like the insecure one this time, like the tables were turned.

As we walked inside, I realized he must have been sitting outside smoking, and not at the bar, which also meant I didn't have a dirty martini waiting for me. AGAIN! This is where men, and people in general, disappoint me. I don't ask for a lot. So, the little I do ask for, I have a bad habit of expecting. But here's the thing . . . I got over it quickly because it was Patrick. If this was anyone besides Patrick, they would have gotten my wrath. But Patrick was so freakin' cute, I let everything slide.

We sat at the bar and ordered drinks, and at least he paid for them. I'm not one to expect men to pay, but if you don't have my drink waiting like I asked, TWICE, the least you can do is pay. I hadn't eaten much that day, so the one martini kicked in really fast. I ordered a second, since I knew I would likely be there a while, and I needed to get loosened up a bit. I knew I wouldn't let myself get wasted, because I was going to remember this night, and everything that came with it, no pun intended. I wanted to treat it like it was the last time I was going to see Patrick for a while, if not ever. Because it might be.

I guess I was tipsy for the "conversation" part of the evening, because I don't really remember a lot of what we talked about, only the important parts. I do remember our usual fun banter, mixed with a little sexual energy. But, what I will always remember is how I felt when I was with him, even just talking to him. He always appeared to listen to everything I said, which was something my husband hadn't done in years. He also looked at me like I was the most beautiful person in the world. I doubt he really thought that, but his eyes looked like they said it. His smile was so amazing, I could just stare at it all day. Those are the parts I remember most about that night. In the bar, anyway.

There was, however, a moment that night, which will be branded in my memory forever. Patrick looked at me and shook his head, then said, "Man, I'm so mad that I let you get away. I can't believe I didn't see how amazing you were, and still are." Now, he was likely just trying to butter me up, and it worked. However, my response was, "No, we would probably have two kids and be divorced by now." I know I probably ruined the mood, and he was hopefully being honest, but I was being honest too. Ever since I "found" Patrick again, he struck me as someone who would have difficulty in relationships, always putting himself first. And, maybe not a very responsible father figure as well. I knew he had it in him to be an excellent father, I just never thought he would be able to tap into it, especially this late in life after being single for forty-six years. He has always been great with kids, but when I thought about him being step-dad to a severely autistic son, I couldn't see it. Not that I thought about marrying him, but I did have to process those scenarios in my head, while trying to figure out what the hell was going on with my own feelings and emotions. But in his defense, step-parent is a difficult role for anyone, and adding severe autism to the mix takes a certain special individual. Not very many people on this planet would be up for that challenge, so I'm not singling him out. Point being, as much as I wanted to spend every minute with him, I knew we would never work as a couple. And there was my reality-based mindset rearing its ugly head. Sometimes it gets me in trouble, but I think in this scenario, it saved me from years of hurt. I hope, anyway.

One other conversation that sticks out from that evening was when Patrick told me about a particular ex-girlfriend. He casually mentioned that she physically abused him on a daily basis. I'm not sure if it was the alcohol, or if I thought he was joking, but I laughed a little after he told me that. Looking back, I know I shouldn't have done that. Abuse of any kind is not right, man or woman. But the thing that stuck out in this conversation was how low his self-esteem and self-worth must have been. This characteristic is normally very unattractive to me. I like a confident but not conceited man, and someone being abused on a daily basis for two years is likely not confident. This seemed so far from the Patrick I thought I knew. In fact, this was the complete opposite. But for some reason, this made him more endearing, and real to me. Maybe that was his plan, and maybe that's why he told me.

I also remember calling him out on it. I told him that he must not care about himself enough to see that he deserves better. I told him that he was capable of loving, and being loved, by a much better person. Whether I loved him or not, I know I'm not necessarily a better person, but I'm definitely not abusive. I just wanted him to know that he was worthy of love. In return, he told me that he felt there wasn't any good women out there, or single ones anyway. The way he negatively talked about women was not the Patrick I knew. You could tell he had been hurt on all levels over the last few years, and was still quite bitter.

After talking about the ex-girlfriend, he came out and told me the whole truth of his current relationship. I knew there had to be more to the story. He admitted that he had been dating a girl for over two years, but was very unhappy. He also said they currently lived together, but hadn't slept in the same bed for over a year. We obviously bonded over this, since I could more than relate. He said he had been trying to break up for a while, but felt he had to move to a whole different state to sever all ties. I reminded him that he didn't have to move in order to break up, but he told me that he was ready to start over somewhere else anyway, and be closer to his family.

Right when the second martini kicked in, Patrick said he wanted me to come up to his room, so he could show me some of his company's new products. Finally, the part you have all been waiting for. Well, not the products, obviously, but the "alone in the hotel room" part of the story.

We got to his room, and I swear it was fifty degrees in there. Anyone who knows me well knows that being cold is probably the thing I hate most in this world. Patrick told me that he didn't know how to adjust the thermostat, and must have messed it up earlier, because it got even colder. And because of my hatred for all things cold, I have a pretty good relationship with most thermostats. I immediately adjusted it to the right temperature, and he looked at me and shook his head, obviously a little embarrassed that I made it look easy. He handed me a robe to wear until it warmed up.

After showing me all of his new products that he was going to be presenting in the meeting the next day, Patrick took his shoes off, and lay down on the bed. There was only one bed, and thank God it was king-sized. I sat on the other side, to the far end of the bed. As much as I wanted him, I'm never one to make the first move. However, I also wasn't going to leave that room without something. I just didn't know what or how yet.

Patrick was lying on some pillows on his side of the bed, and respectfully kept his distance. I continued to sit at the end of the bed, wrapped up in the robe he gave me, while we watched one of those Investigation Discovery shows. Even though I was dressed in short shorts and a tank top, I was not showing even one inch of skin, thanks to the robe. Heat will always come before sex for me, any day of the week.

During the true crime ID show, we were still talking and laughing about life, while intermittently paying attention to the TV. But we continued to keep our distance. After about forty-five minutes, Patrick looked at me and said, "You can lie down on the bed, I promise I won't bite." At which point, I gave the only appropriate response which was, "Well, maybe I want you to." Because in all honesty, I really wanted him to. I just wanted his touch, from any part of his body. Even teeth, if on the right body part. He made a small grunting noise that if made into words would be something like, *Jesus, please don't tell me that, or I will jump on you, and bite all over your naked body.* Even though he didn't say that, I'm pretty sure that's what he meant by the guttural sound, and I was more than okay with that.

I finally took off my shoes, but kept all articles of clothing on, including the robe. I know, not very sexy, but I was fucking cold. I lay down next to him on the bed, while still keeping a safe distance. We continued to intermittently discuss the crime drama, and talked about other random stuff for another half an hour. We could always talk, about anything, and I loved that about him. We also laughed, nonstop, and I loved that too. Before Newport Beach, I hadn't laughed so hard all night in maybe, I don't know, forever?

At one point, he mentioned how hot I was in my profile picture on Facebomb. I knew things were starting to get a little flirty when he then said something about how he utilized that picture. If I remember correctly, I think his words were something like, "I may or may not have touched myself when I looked at it." I then felt it necessary to admit that I also utilized his pictures many times over the last two months. If I was telling the whole truth and nothing but the truth, I had actually been utilizing his pictures for nine months, since the day he posted his first picture on Facebomb. But I didn't want to admit that I had been planning out this exact night for almost a year.

As for another practical use of my profile picture, Patrick said that one of his partners in his company had texted him earlier in the evening to ask if he was coming to his house to stay for the night, so he didn't have to rent a hotel room. Patrick said he responded with, "Nope, and here is why," and attached my profile picture. This was another one of those flattering moments that I could listen to all day. Just the fact that Patrick wanted to *show me off* was the biggest compliment I had received in years.

I knew at that point I could easily go in for the kill, but I prefer being the prey instead of the predator. However, the main hesitation of jumping his bones was the sheer truth that I was married. Plus, I had never cheated on my husband, or anyone for that matter. I had no idea what I would feel after, so I was still trying to decide what outcome I was hoping to achieve.

We seemed to get physically closer to each other on the bed as the night progressed. At one point, me and my robe-covered body was almost touching his not-so-covered body. He said, "Lay your head right here and let's just cuddle," while placing his hand on his chest. I didn't know exactly what to do, so I just looked up at him and gave him a sly smile as if to say, "Okay, but you better keep your hands to yourself," then slowly put my head where he instructed. I was trying to look like I was playing a little hard to get, at the same time letting him know he would get me if he worked hard.

Once I put my head on his chest, a very weird but wonderful feeling came over me. The weird part was because it had been so long since I did something as simple as a little cuddle. It had probably been a good seven years, believe it or not. Even though I wasn't sure exactly how long it *had* been, I just knew this moment felt perfect. I felt like I could fall asleep on his chest. It felt comfortable, and right. This scared me a little, but not enough to get off his chest. It was like I deserved to feel comforted. I had been comforting an autistic child for over six years, and it was time I was comforted too. I had been the strong mom, the one who didn't need reciprocated love, because I was too busy loving and caring for someone who couldn't do anything for himself. I was giving every ounce of love and affection to a helpless little six-year-old, so I deserved this.

He put his arm around my shoulders as I lay on him, and lightly rubbed my arm. Just his touch alone had me getting a bit wet in an area I hadn't been wet in a long time. I had forgotten that my female anatomy could react to a touch like that. Well, I couldn't remember EVER having that quick of a reaction before, so this was almost brand new for me. As he rubbed my arm, I smiled on his chest, because the feeling for me was that of utter contentment. I couldn't believe that I was only imagining this in my fantasies for the last eight months, and it was now actually happening. I didn't even care if we did nothing else that night, because this one single moment made me so happy. Okay, well, that's sort of a lie. I did want to take things further, but I was just enjoying the moment while it lasted.

As we continued to talk, my head still on his chest, I would occasionally lift my head to make eye contact with him. Our mouths were so close, and I could tell we both wanted to kiss, but I felt *his* hesitation along with my own. My hesitation was simple . . . I was married. And I'm assuming his hesitation was for the same reason. I know he was trying to be respectful, but I could tell he wanted it too. Finally, I looked up and thought to myself, *Just a kiss won't hurt. It's not really cheating if it's just a kiss, right?* He must have known what I was thinking because we both paused, looked into each other's eyes, then he kissed me.

I wasn't sure what my married instinct was going to do when and if anything actually happened between us. I suddenly remembered stopping Patrick midkiss back in 1995 because I had just met a guy I liked. But this wasn't just a guy I liked, this was ten years married to my husband. I assumed guilt would immediately take over me, since I'm one of those weirdos who like to follow rules, and tend to be loyal to a fault. I mean, I was still going on New Kids on the Block cruises after obsessing over them for almost thirty years. That's loyalty right there! I've been at the same job for over fourteen years. That's loyalty too. All I know is in *that* moment, loyalty was not important to me, and I wasn't married. I was Patrick's. Even if just for a brief moment, I was happy and free.

Patrick kept kissing me, and I never wanted him to stop. I had forgotten how much I loved kissing him. Well, of course I forgot, because it had been over twenty years since my lips had touched his. I knew it was already very late at night, but I remember thinking how much I wanted time to stop, so I didn't have to go back to my reality. I could have kissed him for hours.

According to a Happy Worker article that I read online, "a long-lasting kiss quickens the pulse, and heightens levels of hormones in human's blood so much that it shortens the lifespan by almost a minute." If this is true, I will die soon, especially after this particular night. I was so hot, both physically from the robe, and emotionally from his kiss, that my hormones were doing stuff they had never done before. I can honestly say that in all of my intimate encounters this one was, by far, my favorite. I know we haven't even gotten to the good stuff yet, but this is what good stuff was made of right here . . . making out with your childhood crush twenty-five years later.

And just like passionate kisses tend to do, the kiss turned into a lot more. I had taken off the robe at some point while kissing him. I was not only getting hot, I wanted to feel his body touch mine. We were both lying on our sides, and also still fully clothed. Since I didn't have a lot of clothes on to begin with, it was easy for him to explore. His hands began moving up my leg, and then toward my inner thigh. He could easily get his fingers inside my underwear, since I had on my sexy short-shorts. I thought about warning him of how wet I was, but I couldn't even conjure up the words. I swear, I have never been that wet in my life. I always assumed that men liked it, and thought the wetter the better. You know, more lubrication and all. But I was almost embarrassed by how wet I was. I was surprised that it wasn't dripping down my leg. I don't know if it was because it had been so long since I had sex, or because it was Patrick, or because I had been dreaming about this moment for so long, or the combination of all three of those, but I had never been that turned on.

As I worried if I was actually TOO wet, I still let Patrick explore my clitoris. I sensed he must have liked how wet I was, since I could feel his erection as his body pressed against mine. At this moment, my urge to take off every article of clothing was something fierce. However, my urge to stop before it got any further was more fierce. I softly pulled away, and told him to wait. That goddamn guilt kicked in the minute I felt extreme pleasure. I knew it was going to win at some point tonight. It was like my brain was saying, *Nope, not today*, but my body was screaming, *HELL YES, PLEASE!* Patrick was respectful about it, and got up to get a drink. He said he understood, but joked that it wasn't really cheating if we had done it before. Yes, it had been about twenty-three years, and we had done it before. Quite a few times, actually. But to me, it felt like I was having him for the first time.

When Patrick returned to the bed, we began kissing again immediately. It was like a magnet. We couldn't stop. He pulled up my shirt, and began kissing my breasts, while lightly sucking and biting my nipples. And that was it! There was no way in hell I was leaving that night without feeling him inside me. All I had to say was, "I want you," and all of our clothes were off before I could get the words "inside me" out of my mouth. And immediately, that's where he went. For that brief moment, I had never felt so amazing.

As Patrick went in and out, it was as if my thought processes were in conflict with each other. My loyal and honest side, which is a very strong part of me in general, was shaking its head. I knew that what I was doing was wrong. But nothing, and I mean nothing, had ever felt so right. I also knew that as wrong as it was, I would have been way more angry with myself if I left without feeling him inside me. It was as if I had to have him, in some weird way. It wasn't like an option as much as it was a need. I needed to feel sexy and wanted again, I needed to feel pleasure again, I needed to feel free and happy again. And I felt all of those things, for about two minutes.

Until I didn't.

After wallowing in the indescribable happiness I was feeling, I realized I wasn't feeling him. Literally. I thought it was my guilt that wasn't allowing me to feel the pleasure, until I realized he had lost his erection. He immediately pulled out, and went down on me. But here's the weird thing . . . the whole time he was down there, I couldn't wait for him to come back up and get inside of me again. I mean, of course it felt good. There's very few women who don't enjoy a little oral pleasure every once in a while, but I only had the desire for him to make love to me. Or fuck me. Or have sex with me . . . whatever you want to call it. I couldn't allow myself to relax enough to orgasm because I didn't want his lips and tongue down there, I wanted his dick down there.

When it dawned on me that I wasn't going to get what I wanted, I was disappointed, to say the least. He came up for air and began kissing my stomach, and then my breasts. But it wasn't in the way it was before, like when things started heating up. This time it was slow, light kisses, as if to say, *Okay, that was nice, we are done now.* It was obvious to me that this was the "cool down" part of the night, unfortunately.

So . . . that was it? Don't get me wrong, it was amazing on numerous levels, but I just cheated on my husband for that?

We kissed lightly for a minute, and then he got up and got dressed, and handed me my clothes. Okay, I guess that's that! I actually did have to leave because it was about 1:30 a.m. at this point, and I didn't tell the babysitter I would be late, and I didn't want her worrying. But I also wanted to stay with him, be held by him, and to keep kissing him. We walked to the elevator holding hands, not saying much, but with smiles on our faces. Yes, it wasn't the intended outcome, but it was still pretty fucking awesome in my opinion.

On the drive home, I began to process the entire night. I knew enough about sex, impotence, and performance anxiety to know that the misfire, for lack of a better word, had nothing to do with me. I know that drugs and alcohol also play a role, and God knows how much he drank before I even got there. But no matter how much you know, any normal human in that scenario tends to feel like they did something wrong. Maybe I wasn't sexy enough? Maybe I wasn't wet enough? Well, I know that wasn't the case, so maybe I was too wet. Is that possible? *I'll look it up when I get home*, I thought. Maybe he didn't tell me the whole truth about his girlfriend, and maybe she's at home waiting for him, and he felt guilty. I know guilt can make your body do subconsciously crazy things too.

I had no idea what the fuck happened, but I did know one thing for sure before I pulled into my driveway. I wasn't done. I was going to get what I wanted, somehow, someday, someway. I figured I had manifested the shit out of tonight, and everything I ever wanted happened. Well, besides the orgasm, and the actual intercourse I had been hoping for. But I was determined to finish this out. I made it happen, after all. Piper fucking Collins actually planned a fantasy that, for the most part, came true.

Chapter 11

Your Friend Is Hot

The next morning, the continued thoughts of completing my mission were still strong. I remembered Patrick said he had a meeting at 10:00 a.m., and it was about 11:00 a.m. when I decided to text him.

Me:
July 18, 11:06 a.m.
I hope your meeting went well. What are you doing until your flight?

Patrick:
July 18, 11:27 a.m.
Went awesome, took maybe 2 minutes for the CEO to say . . . Wow, those are so cool. Now I have a full presentation in midAugust. Do you give do-overs ever?

My immediate thought was, *Yay, maybe I can make it happen in August.* Obviously I still had sex on my mind, and already excited to see him again. But that still wasn't good enough. I wanted to see him TODAY! My biggest concern was that Patrick would think I was disappointed in him for his performance, or lack thereof, and was worried that he would think I wasn't interested in attempting anything of a sexual nature again. But that could not be further from the truth. I actually wanted him more now, if that was even possible. He was like a drug to me at this point.

Me:
July 18, 11:40 a.m.
That's great! I do give do-overs LOL I'm going
to be in Decatur later while Jack is in therapy and
I have a free hour or so. Not necessarily for a
do-over, but to say goodbye, if you are free.

As much as I wanted the do-over, I figured that Patrick checked out of his hotel. Plus, I only had about an hour, which was not enough time to go to a hotel, or to my house. I just wanted to see him to reassure him that I still wanted him, and that I don't give up that easy.

Patrick:
July 18, 11:49 a.m.
Yep. Let's go somewhere really close to where
you need to be. Just tell me where and I will be
there.

I was very happy and surprised at his eagerness to see me. He had all day to do whatever he wanted, and he chose to spend some of it with me, even after the awkward evening. I texted him the address for Jack's therapy office, and told him to meet me there at 3:00 p.m. I knew it might be a little weird, since he would be meeting Jack, but it's not like he didn't already know I had an autistic son.

As always, I worried that he wouldn't show up. There was no reason for him to back out, but I couldn't help but feel like he might. He didn't even blow me off back in the day, so I don't know where my negative thought process was coming from. I guess I just couldn't believe my literal dreams were coming true, especially since that kind of shit never happened to me. Plus, I hadn't made plans to meet a guy I liked in about twelve years, so there's that. And, the last time I dated, there was no such thing as texting, so there's that too.

Patrick was there when I arrived, and right on time, which was pretty impressive for someone who didn't know anything about

Atlanta traffic. I briefly introduced Patrick to Jack and his therapist, then I kissed Jack goodbye, and hopped in Patrick's rental car. I knew of a bar in the area that was totally up Patrick's alley, so I instructed him where to go. It was a perfect spot because it was midafternoon, and nobody was there. We had the bar almost to ourselves. I also knew that the odds of running into anyone I knew were pretty slim, since I didn't live in that area.

We ordered a couple of appetizers and beers. It was a little weird at first because it sort of felt like a date, and I wasn't used to dates anymore. It also felt weird because I couldn't remember going to a restaurant with Patrick, like, ever. Yes, we sort of dated way back when, but it was college dating, which rarely meant dinner. Especially since our particular relationship was probably more "booty-call-time" than "dinner-time." It felt good to feel like Patrick's girlfriend, even if just for an hour.

We did our usual talking and laughing, and he told me a crazy story about getting kidnapped in Mexico, and how he was naked when they found him. I thought he was joking or exaggerating, but I soon realized the details were both too specific *and* too ridiculous to be made up. I couldn't help but laugh, because Patrick always put a funny spin on everything, even though it was quite an intense and scary story. We talked about where we have traveled, and where we still want to go. And, we talked about his upcoming move to Georgia, which the timing was now up in the air. He told me more about his brother's illness, and his desire to live closer to his family because of it.

But one thing we didn't talk about was the elephant in the room . . . the inability to complete the mission the night before. However, he did mention some things about his insecurities, which I believe was his way of telling me why he couldn't do the deed. He told me that he was a very confident person when it came to business, but lacked a lot of self-esteem when it came to his looks and appearance. This really confused me, because I personally thought that Patrick was the most beautiful person on the planet. I know looks are primarily a matter of opinion, and I could see how not everyone would think the same thing I did, but I assumed he would realize that he was quite attractive in general. The old Patrick I knew was the complete opposite of insecure. He was more along the lines of conceited, maybe even to a fault. The ex-girlfriend who abused him in his recent past started to make a little more sense. Sometimes, people who think they don't deserve anything good will attract those who treat them bad. I almost felt sorry for him.

I'm not one to stroke anyone's ego, not even Patrick's. But I did tell him that I have always thought he was very attractive, and still do. What he told me next continued to confuse me. He said that I gave him hope, and I made him realize that maybe he could get a hot girl after all, even one with a good head on her shoulders, like me. He said he felt flattered that I was attracted to him, and said I was "way too hot for him." I'm not sure if he was just fishing for compliments, but I kept most of them at bay. He already knew I liked him.

There was a small part of me that wanted him to tell me, right then and there, that he wished he could have *me* and not just a replica of me. I *almost* wanted him to say that he wanted me to leave my husband so we could be together. Luckily, it was only a very small part of me that wanted this. My realistic side is a much bigger part of me, and this part was clearly happy he didn't say anything of the sort. I guess I just wanted to hear Patrick tell me that he wanted me and only me, for the first time in my life. Those are words I longed to hear from his mouth for the past twenty-seven years, but I guess I had to be happy with a "I want someone just like you," instead.

Right about the time that I was trying to convince Patrick of his hotness, a text beeped on my phone from Jack's therapist, Alexis. She texted to let me know how the session went, and at the end of the text she wrote, "Btw—your friend is hot," along with a few fire emojis. Alexis was divorced with two kids and currently single, so horny was probably an understatement. I turned to Patrick and said, "See, even the therapist that you just met thinks you're hot." He looked at me like I was feeding him the biggest line of bull, and truly thought I just made that up to make him feel better. I hesitated to show him the text, because I wanted to stop stroking his ego, but I needed him to know I wasn't lying. He blushed a little when I showed him, and seemed to believe that maybe, just maybe, he was attractive after all.

When we walked back to the car together, Patrick put his arm around my shoulder, so I put mine around his waist. After a few steps, I looked up at him, then he turned to me and smiled. He didn't have to say anything. I'm pretty sure I knew what he was thinking, and I smiled back to let him know that I felt it too. I don't know why, but it seemed as though the smile said a few different things, such as, *Thank you for making me feel better about myself*, and *It feels good to walk with our arms around each other*, and *I respect you, Piper*. But most of all it seemed to say, *I'm going to miss you*. He didn't verbalize any of this. But for some odd reason, I felt as though I knew Patrick pretty well, and maybe he wasn't able to put his thoughts into words, so I did it for him. Or maybe it was just because I was thinking all of that, but I kept it in my head too.

Patrick dropped me off at my car, and we just gave each other a small hug, and a peck on the cheek. We kept it minimal, mainly because Jack and his therapist could have easily seen. But also, why make more out of something we have no idea what to make of in the first place?

Driving on the long ride home with Jack, so many thoughts were swirling in my head. Luckily, since my son is nonverbal, I can actually say a lot of things out loud, and not have to worry about him repeating any of it. Once I had a friend ask me if I was worried that Jack would start repeating the words to all of the gangster rap songs that were constantly played in my car, but I told her *absolutely not*. I said that if I ever heard Jack say anything from a song, curse word or not, I would throw the biggest fucking party ever! I would love for Jack to say anything, even if it was something about dicks and pussies. But don't worry, I wasn't saying anything like that now. However, I did ask Jack if he liked

Patrick, and told him he was my boyfriend. Of course, Jack didn't answer, and I know Patrick wasn't my boyfriend. But it's fun to say stuff like that out loud to see what it sounds like, and I didn't have to worry about Jack saying anything.

Chapter 12

911

The next couple of months were busy, both good and bad, on my end. Mainly Jack issues. With autism comes a lot of comorbid conditions, such as seizures, mental health problems, and the previously mentioned sleep disorders. Luckily, Jack had never had a seizure, even though about 25 percent of autistics suffer from the disorder. However, one night in August, we received a frantic phone call from Jack's regular babysitter, Laurie. She has been with Jack since he was two years old, so she falls into the "family member" category for us, and knows Jack well. When Laurie first started working for us, I called her the Jack whisperer. She could get him to try any food on his plate, which was a huge challenge for us. And she could also get him to go to sleep without his pacifier, which we never could have achieved without her.

We were extremely worried when Laurie called us while we were out eating with some friends one night. She never calls, only an occasional text, so when I saw her number on the caller ID, I knew immediately there was a problem. Her voice sounded different, and I could hear her telling Jack to "wake up" while trying her best to calmly tell me that something was wrong with him. I kept asking what it was, but she couldn't say exactly. She said he had vomited a lot after dinner, which was definitely weird for him, but not unheard of. She then said something about him turning gray, so I hung up the phone, grabbed my husband, and ran out of the restaurant. I handed him the phone as I was running, and told him to call 911. Then I sped home as fast as I could, which was not the smartest thing to do, but luckily we made it home safe.

When we got into the house, Laurie had Jack laying on the couch, and I could see vomit all over the kitchen floor. I ran over to the couch and found Jack barely conscious, with his eyes half open. He was responding, but it was like trying to wake a heavily medicated person. He wasn't taking any new medicine, so I knew that wasn't the problem. Just then I heard the ambulance pull up in our driveway, so I went to open the door while hubby inspected the vomit, since Laurie mentioned that she thought she saw some blood when he threw up.

I didn't really know what to tell the paramedics, because I could see how Jack just looked like a "tired kid" to the EMTs. But they didn't realize that Jack was NEVER tired. He went from Energizer bunny to fast asleep, with no in-between. They were asking questions like, "Did he eat or drink something he wasn't supposed to?" And, "Has he had a fever or illness lately?" The answers were all no. Then they asked if he ate anything before he vomited, and Laurie told them that he ate his entire dinner. So, now I'm thinking that Jack just appeared to be a kid who ate too much, and wanted to go to sleep, and now the paramedics would think we were crazy for being concerned about nothing. But I knew that in Jack's six short years, I'd never seen him like that, so I was very concerned.

Since I am not a huge fan of vomit, I had my husband check it out. He told me it looked normal, and that he couldn't see any blood. The paramedics put Jack in the ambulance, and I rode in the back with him. When they began inserting his IV, Jack bolted up and screamed. I told them not to worry about the IV until they had to. I knew what Jack could handle, and what he couldn't, so I'm glad they listened to me. I figured that if he was coherent and alert enough to cry when a needle was inserted into him, he was likely not on the verge of death. So, that was sign enough for me to hold off on any kind of torture that I didn't find necessary. The most important thing to note when parenting an autistic child is to always pick your battles. In this case, it would be much more traumatic to Jack for an IV to be stuck in his arm, annoying and hurting him so much that he would most definitely pull that fucker out with all his might. And trust me when I tell you that autistics are some mighty strong peeps. Unless his vitals plummeted to the edge of death, I was going to avoid anything and everything unnecessary, and I was so glad they obliged.

Right as we pulled into the emergency room, Jack was completely back to his baseline. He was sitting up and looking around like, "Where the hell am I?" If he could talk, I'm pretty sure that's what he would've said. The doctors and nurses did their thing, but now we kind of looked like a crazy couple who was worried about absolutely nothing. To them, it looked like there was no emergency whatsoever, and luckily by this time, there really wasn't.

Hubs was worried that it was some kind of seizure. After looking up absence seizures and petit mal seizures, I was worried too. However, the doctors said he must have a bug of some sort. I wasn't quite sure how a bug would make someone turn gray and pass out, but I wasn't a doctor, and I only cared that Jack was fine, for now. They did give us a referral to a neurologist, so that we could rule out any seizure activity.

As for the "good" moments for the rest of the summer, I was able to do a couple more girls trips, and had a blast! One trip was a party weekend in New Orleans with two girlfriends from high school, whom I hadn't seen for a few years. You know those friendships where you don't talk, or see each other for a long time, but it doesn't matter because you quickly bond like you did when you were young. It was like that, and I couldn't love them anymore. Ironically, these two friends were with me through the early Patrick days, so I couldn't say anything about him. They would not only know exactly who I was talking about, but would probably rip me a new asshole because I was wasting my time with him once again. And I couldn't blame them. They knew how obsessed I was back then, and the last thing I wanted was for them to know I not only cheated on my husband, who they love, but did it with the only person on the planet that I shouldn't have done it with.

I also went to Florida with my friend, Elizabeth, and stayed at her aunt's condo. It was just me and her, and we had a blast. Luckily, Elizabeth knew about Patrick, so I could talk a little about him on this trip. But I guess it was more like a *lot* of talking about him, because I couldn't stop thinking about him. I was grateful that I had Elizabeth to talk to about everything. Not only because she knew every juicy detail, but because she didn't judge me for it. She knew I needed a release, for lack of a better word. She was very aware of how hard my life had been with Jack, and all his "autismness," and I think she was worried I was going to explode if I didn't get some form of escape.

No matter how much fun I was having on my girls trips, or how much trauma with Jack I was experiencing in my day-to-day life, Patrick was still in the forefront of most of my thoughts. I was grateful for the escape that Patrick had provided for me, at least up to this point, but it wasn't enough. I needed more escape. The distractions did help, but I was still waiting for the orgasm. No, but seriously, it wasn't exactly the orgasm I was anxiously waiting for, although I would've loved one. I was anxiously anticipating when I could lay in his arms again, and to kiss his lips again. I don't know what I was going to do to make it happen, but I knew our story wasn't done. It may sound cheesy, but I still thought there was a reason for all of this, and I had to figure it out. Because again, why would someone with a very good head on her shoulders be pining away for a man she couldn't have? I was a confident woman who had a good family already, so why was I going after someone who was not good for me? He was a player with more issues than a *National Geographic*, so what the hell was the attraction?

Patrick told me that night at the hotel that he was a "different person now," and how much he had "changed for the better." But how much do people actually change at the end of the day? I could definitely tell he was different, but how much different for the better, I didn't know. I still focused on the fact that I couldn't see him as a life partner, especially one to help take care of a disabled child. And that thought process helped me to snap out of my fantasies, and put me back to my realities. Yes, some of my fantasies did come true, but I couldn't see that one come true, simply for the fact that I didn't believe Patrick had it in him. As awesome as I thought he was, I couldn't see him succeed in the "special needs stepdad" role. And at the end of the day, that child is the utmost important thing in the world to me.

Chapter 13

Who's Jimmy?

During those two months of girls trips and Jack drama, I did have occasional text exchanges with Patrick. But it was always pretty low key, and me constantly texting first. I guess he was likely hesitant to text me because I was married, and he had said something about it at lunch that afternoon in Decatur. He jokingly mentioned how we should have code names in our phones, so nobody would know exactly who we were if someone else saw our texts. He said his name was going to be Jimmy, since he was nothing like a Jimmy, and I didn't know of a Jimmy that was in my phone already. I told him I wanted to be Jasmine, since I always loved Princess Jasmine from Aladdin, and there wasn't anyone with that name in his phone either.

In a nutshell, the texts from Patrick were mainly me asking how he was doing, and him telling me about his upcoming work trips. He mentioned that his last day in Newport Beach was going to be August 23, and then he was moving to Texas until his work slowed down a bit. He wasn't kidding around when he said he was traveling a lot. He was going to be in three different countries, just in one month alone.

I was super bummed that he never said anything about moving to Atlanta, but he did say everything was up in the air at this point. Plus, I was *kind of* glad he wasn't going to be moving to Georgia, because I didn't know how I would feel with him being so close in proximity to me. It would be really hard not to constantly want to see him, and as much as I wanted that, I knew I couldn't. But it was nice to hear that he was moving back to our hometown, since I did go there every once in a while to visit family and friends, and my parents still lived there for half the year.

One night when my sister-in-law was in town, her and I had a girls night out. Of course I didn't tell her anything about Patrick, since I'm married to her brother, and all. As we were waiting for our food, a text beeped on my phone with an unknown Texas number. Every one of my friends and family in Texas were already programmed in my phone, so I was a bit confused when I saw an unidentified 254 area code number show up . . .

254/555-0157
August 28, 8:14 p.m.
Hey Piper, it's your old friend, PJ. How r u?

I honestly didn't know who it was for a minute. I looked at my phone like I was trying to figure out a trivia question. I could tell my sister-in-law was also confused by the odd look on my face, but I couldn't say anything because I thought it might be Patrick. Some of Patrick's friends used to call him PJ, because his name is Patrick James Barnes, but I hadn't heard that in forever. Patrick had said nothing about getting a new number, but I did know he was probably moving to Texas temporarily.

I think another reason for the strange look on my face was because I was pleasantly surprised that if it *was* Patrick, he was texting me first. I guess he just wanted me to have his number, so that made me happy to know that I made the cut. At least I wasn't the reason for him getting a new number anyway. I couldn't respond until I got home, for obvious reasons, and I wanted to make sure it was him.

Me:
August 28, 9:29 p.m.
The Texas number threw me off for a second.
Are you there now? Do I change Jimmy's phone
number and replace it with this #?

I figured if it wasn't Patrick, they would text back something insinuating they had no idea who the hell Jimmy was. And if it was him, he would respond accordingly. I went ahead and assigned the number to "Jimmy" in my contacts, since I had a pretty good idea who it was. Sure enough, five minutes later . . .

Jimmy:
August 28, 9:35 p.m.
Yes, please. Thanks Jasmine.

Good, it was him.

The following weekend, my husband was out of town for a conference, and Elizabeth and I were finally getting our downtown Atlanta girls getaway, except we didn't. We had the hotel already booked, but Elizabeth had to back out at the last minute, something about a sick kid. So, I kept the hotel room, since I already had the sitter lined up for overnight, and planned to get some work done instead. I had a big presentation on autism coming up, so I figured I would work on it, instead of drinking and partying. It's good to be responsible sometimes.

The presentation was for a hospital, so I already knew everything I was going to present, but I'm kind of obsessive when it comes to stuff like that. I want to give people what they need to know, and present it how they can learn it best. Even though I could probably do it all with my eyes closed, it was next to impossible to do anything when Jack was in close proximity. I'm sure it's difficult when even a neurotypical child is around while trying to work on a project, but I'm assuming an autistic child makes it even harder. I have to check on Jack every two or three minutes, if I don't hear him. I have to get up and physically look for him all over the house to make sure he is not trying to escape out the back door, or put a snake in his mouth, which he has actually done before and inside the house, nonetheless. So, I figured I should take advantage of the Jack-free hotel time and get everything done.

While I was sitting in my hotel room, I was envisioning how fucking awesome it would be to have Patrick there with me. Then it hit me that there would be a slight chance he MIGHT be in Atlanta, and I would kick myself in the ass if he was here and I didn't check. I mean, if there was any way he could join me in the hotel, that would pretty much fulfill my recent fantasies. Regardless of sex, I wanted his body next to mine. I wanted to kiss him. And, of course, the sex would be a plus.

I ordered room service, since I was on a role with my presentation and didn't want to stop my flow to get something to eat outside the hotel. I decided on a turkey sandwich, which happens to be Patrick's favorite food, so I had to text him.

Me:
September 9, 6:49 p.m.
I just ordered a turkey sandwich from room service, since I am by myself in a hotel, and I'm wondering if you are in China and going through turkey sandwich withdrawals.

I had to throw in the "by myself in a hotel," just in case he was in the area. I hadn't gotten very far into my presentation when he texted right back, and quickly squelched all possible excitement.

Jimmy:
September 9, 6:57 p.m.
No I'm in Okla till Monday, Athens til Wed, Minn til Friday, ATL til Sat morning, China till the 25th, Mass til 29th, Austin til Oct 5th, Okla til Oct 12th, Chicago til Oct 18th, Austin again til Oct 25th, Japan til Nov 2nd . . . then I'm crawling in a hole for a week to sleep. Why are you in a hotel by yourself?

WOW was my first thought. That is more traveling than I had ever seen anyone physically be able to do. And I wasn't happy to see that when he *was* going to be in my area, it wasn't even long enough to squeeze in some time for me. But, I was pleasantly surprised that he cared why I was in a hotel by myself. I didn't really think about it sounding a little cryptic. I just wanted him to know in case he was in the area, and could hang for the night. I didn't immediately respond because my sandwich came, and I was enjoying it while catching up on *Friends* reruns, which appeared to be the only thing on television. About ten minutes later, he texted again.

Jimmy:
September 9, 7:03 p.m.
R u Ok?

I was surprised and touched by this. I wasn't used to him caring about my well-being. I wasn't really used to anyone caring about my well-being, to be honest. I was a very strong, independent woman, so even my husband rarely worried about me. I like to take care of shit myself, and let people know I can do it. And because I wasn't used to being worried about, I immediately texted back to let him know all was good. I didn't bother with the "hubby out of town" details, since he couldn't join me anyway.

Me:
September 9, 7:07 p.m.
Yeah, it's all good, just working on a project.
Sweet of you to ask though. But I AM sad
that I won't be able to see you until next year
at this rate of traveling. WOW!

I still didn't give him details as to why I was there alone, and I'm not sure why. I don't know if it just felt good to have someone worry about me, or if I was being minimal with my information so he knows what it feels like when he does it. Or, maybe I wanted him to think hubby and I were having problems. But that's kind of game-playing, and I wasn't much into that. I didn't have to play games with Patrick because I wasn't trying to date him. I was really just trying to get in his pants. I felt like a man when I had that thought, but that's what it kind of was, without sounding too sexist. For some odd reason, I believed that if I could have a great night of sex with Patrick, my urges and desires would cease. I felt like I would then be able to go on with my life, as it is, and that would be it. I'm not sure why I actually thought that would work, but I did. It was like tunnel vision. I was not even able to think about what would happen after. Would I want more? Would he want more? Would my husband find out? And if he did find out, what would happen? Was that all Patrick wanted too, just one night with me? Or did he not want me at all? I didn't have the answer to any of these questions, but I knew I had to get at least one night with Patrick. I'm not sure if I ever wanted anything more in my life.

Jimmy:
September 9, 7:38 p.m.
Well some days could change for sure. That's just a projection. U sure ur Ok?

Again, completely surprised at his continued concern for me, so this time I texted him back quickly. I didn't want him to worry since there wasn't anything to worry about.

Me:
September 9, 7:40 p.m.
Seriously, I'm fine. The good thing is I'm getting a bunch of stuff done for my presentation. I hope to see you before next year tho.

I attached a picture of my notes spread out all over the hotel floor. I wanted him to know I was okay, and that I really was just working on a project. I also felt it was important for him to know that I still wanted to see him. And in true Patrick fashion, I never heard from him again that night. Or for the next few weeks, for that matter. I realized I needed to get used to the limited texting and responses. But I appreciated the little I did get from Patrick, and I would take whatever I could get whenever I could get it.

When I lay in bed with a wide awake Jack at 3:00 a.m., thanks to autism, I would think about the last text from Patrick, and it would get me through the long night. Knowing that he was thinking about me in his excessive travels and work stress, I could get through the tough autism days. And let me tell you, there were a lot of tough autism days in our household. Autism-momming is hard, and I was happy to use Patrick as an escape.

Chapter 14

Karma Gods

Jimmy:
October 4, 1:35 p.m.
Hola, I will be in ATL both Sat & Sun night
downtown. One of my favorite bands is
playing at Victory Stage so if you can,
let's hang. I fly out Monday.

YES! FINALLY! Maybe this will be it! And the timing was almost too convenient. So, why? Why was this working out in my favor so far? My husband was going to be leaving for India on Saturday morning, and I already had an array of babysitters lined up so that I wouldn't go crazy caring for Jack nonstop by myself. I already had reservations at a restaurant downtown for Saturday night, since a friend from Chicago was going to be in town for a conference. What is the universe trying to tell me? The scenario could not be more perfect.

Me:
October 4, 2:26 p.m.
I'm meeting a friend who's in town for a
conference, so Sat is perfect since I will
already be there. Would I need to get
tickets for the show early?

The dinner reservations that I had for Jennifer and I were at a cool restaurant on the Beltline. Because I'm not super familiar with downtown, I looked online to see where Victory Stage was in relation to the restaurant, and low and behold, it was walking distance. Another one of those "Why is everything falling into place so perfectly?" moments. Seriously, why did it just happen to be when my husband was out of the country, and when I had babysitters the entire weekend, and when I could still see my friend, and walk to meet Patrick at the concert on the same night? Why? There had to be a reason why it was all working out. Why was the universe hell bent on letting this happen for me, when it was considered one of the seven deadly sins? It's actually two of the seven, to be technical. Lust and greed, all rolled into one huge desire. I was not only lusting after him, I was super greedy. But I felt somehow vindicated on that greed. I felt less greedy because I deserved this. I deserved to feel sexy, wanted, and desired. You would think that the universe would put any and all barriers up to forbid something like this from happening, but I truly think that the Karma Gods were like, "Girl, you need this bad! We will let this one slide because we know how much you deserve it!" I was very grateful to the Karma Gods that weekend.

Jimmy
October 4, 3:16 p.m.
Very cool. I got me +1 on the band list so if you want to, c'mon . . . if you can't, let's meet up for a drink before or whenever.

Me:
October 4, 3:54 p.m.
I can definitely come, and I'll see what my friend wants to do. I'll text you on Saturday.

Jimmy:
October 4, 4:00 p.m.
I'll be at a pool downtown all day til show.
Excited to see you.

I thought I would give him a taste of his own medicine, and let *him* be the last texter for the evening. He knew I was excited to see him, I didn't have to reiterate this. I could tell from his texts that he definitely wanted to see me. And to be invited to share his favorite band with him was such a good feeling. I knew that no matter what my friend wanted to do, I was going to squeeze Patrick in there somewhere.

I was super busy on Saturday, taking my husband to the airport, and getting my body ready for a magical night. Well, I was hoping it to be magical anyway. I was shaving in all the right and wrong places, and packing my "Down There" wipes in my purse, since you can never be too fresh. I got in a ride share to go downtown to meet my friend for dinner, and finally got a chance to text Patrick. I knew he was going to be at a pool drinking all day, so I was hoping he wasn't passed out somewhere.

Me:
October 7, 5:07 p.m.
Did you find your pool? Are you too drunk for the concert?

Jimmy:
October 7, 5:12 p.m.
I did! Can't be too drunk off
champagne and watermelon. Whatcha up to?

Me:
October 7, 5:17 p.m.
I would be wasted on champagne, but I'm a lightweight. In the taxi on the way to the restaurant for dinner.

Jimmy:
October 7, 5:22 p.m.
Whatcha guys doing after?

Me:
October 7, 5:24 p.m.
I'm coming to see you :

Jimmy:
October 7, 5:27 p.m.
Awesome!!!

Chapter 15

Manoj, Not Ménage

It looked like the Karma Gods were going to be busy breaking rules and making shit happen for me. Patrick wasn't too drunk to text, and he sounded excited to see me. Regardless of what was going to happen, I planned to make the most of it, and enjoy every minute of the evening.

Jennifer was running late, so I got to the restaurant and started drinking early by myself. When I have this type of excited energy, I have zero appetite. Which was actually a beautiful thing in this particular scenario. If, by any luck, I was going to be naked in front of anyone in the near future, I'd be grateful that I had eaten very little over the last two days. Another happy nod to the Karma Gods for helping a sister out.

I felt weird only eating a few chips after Jennifer got there, but I literally had no appetite whatsoever. I wanted to see Patrick, and kiss him, and do other things. But mostly, I just wanted to be in his presence. Being around him did something for me that's hard to explain. His energy was so dynamic, and I have never felt that particular way with anyone in my forty-three years. He made me forget that I was a worn-out, emotionally and spiritually beaten autism mom. I was young, beautiful, and free when I was with him, at least that's how he made me feel. And I was grateful for the privilege of those feelings, even if only for a night.

I couldn't give too many details about Patrick to Jennifer. She had never met my husband, but did know I was married, and I wasn't sure how she would judge me if I told her everything. I'm not one to care what others think, but I hadn't seen her in many years, and I wanted our short time together to be all good stuff. Not "I really hope I cheat on my husband tonight" kind of stuff. Plus, she talked a lot about her church, and how the congregation had helped her tremendously through her divorce. That was a big sign to stay away from all things non-Christian. However, Jennifer did know that I was going to be meeting a friend of mine after dinner, and that she was welcome to tag along if she didn't already have plans. She actually said she would love to, so I wanted to make sure with Patrick that it was okay. I also wanted to know if Patrick was by himself, or with friends, because that would determine the entire dynamic of the night. Plus, I was hoping that if he was with a friend, maybe the friend could hook up with my friend, and everyone would get a happy ending.

Me:
October 7, 7:19 p.m.
I'm waiting for the bill, and my friend wants to join us. Are you alone or with friends?

Jimmy:
October 7, 7:22 p.m.
I'm alone but u can bring anyone u like. It's definitely a sausage fest at the show.

Me:
October 7, 7:33 p.m.
Ok, how much are tickets and can she get them at the door?

Jimmy:
October 7, 7:36 p.m.
Everything's free girl! I'm just getting out of the shower. Meet me in an hour at the bar to the right of the venue . . . it has a blue neon sign.

My vagina started dancing a bit when I read the "getting out of the shower" part. He probably did that on purpose, but it worked. Jennifer and I slowly paid the bill, and started our ten-minute walk to the venue. The weather could not have been more perfect, which led to another one of those "Why is everything so fucking perfect?" moments.

While waiting at the bar for Patrick, Jennifer motioned to a guy walking in by himself, and asked if that was Patrick. The guy was dressed in black jeans, collar shirt, and boots. I knew immediately it wasn't him. I told Jennifer, "No, Patrick will be dressed in a T-shirt with some kind of emblem or band logo, khaki shorts, and flip-flops." It was kind of scary how much I felt like I knew him, and I really had only seen him twice over the past twenty years. And sure enough, I was right. Immediately after I told Jennifer what Patrick would be wearing, a guy with a Widespread Panic T-shirt, khaki shorts, and flip-flops walked in.

We did our usual greeting with a hug and a quick kiss. Patrick had one ticket in his hand, which I guess he had already gone to the venue to buy before walking into the bar. He handed it to Jennifer, and she thanked him for buying her a ticket. I knew he told me he was on the guest list and had a "plus one" for me, so I felt like a VIP. But I felt bad for those die-hard fans that had to buy their tickets, when I knew nothing about the group, and was included on the band list.

One thing I will never understand about Patrick is the number of people spread out across the world that he personally knows. I had lived in Atlanta for over fourteen years, and was pretty sure I would not be running into anyone that I knew at the show. But him, on the other hand, was already saying hi to numerous people there. And since they were saying, "Hi, Patrick" in response, I knew he wasn't just saying hi to strangers. How in the hell did he know so many people in a town that he never lived in?

We all enjoyed the concert, but Jennifer stated she had to get up early to fly back to Chicago, so she called it a night before the show ended. After she got in the ride share to head back to her hotel, Patrick turned to me and asked if we could leave early too. He then told me that he was at the same show the night before, which kind of explained the acquaintances. I didn't even hesitate before saying, "Yes, please." It's not that I wasn't enjoying myself, I just wanted to go somewhere quieter, and more private. He requested a ride share on his phone, but I still wasn't sure what the plan was, or where we were going. I trusted him, so I figured I would just go with the flow.

Patrick held up his phone to show me his ride share app so I could look out for the model/make of the car coming for us, and I noticed the drivers name was Manoj. I was pretty familiar with Indian-origin names, since my son was half Indian, and I did a lot of research on middle names for Jack when I was pregnant. I hopped in the car and said, "Hi, Manoj." Manoj turned around quickly to face me and said, "How do you know how to pronounce my name so well?" in his strong accent. I laughed, and told him that his name represented the God of Love, and that it meant "the one who understands others." Manoj's eyes opened even bigger, and he said, "How do you know that?" in an astonished, but happy voice. I explained in a brief nutshell that I was married to someone from India, and had done a lot of research when naming my son. He asked me if I had been to India, and I told him I had been there three times. He started asking me questions about my thoughts on India until Patrick looked at me like, *What the fuck?* and said out loud, "Are we going anytime soon?" I realized Manoj was so intent on talking to me that he was still parked at the curb.

Manoj began driving, but continued to ask my opinion on all things India. He seemed to focus on questions regarding my relationship with my husband, which I thought was odd. He finally explained that he recently dated a woman from Brazil, and the differences in their cultures is what ultimately broke them up. He seemed honestly interested in my feedback, so I did the best I could at answering. One thing I did say after a barrage of questions was, "Well, that's why he's in India and I'm here," insinuating that we couldn't have the best of relationships, since we were both in two different countries.

Patrick seemed to get slightly agitated as the conversation continued to focus on my husband. I kind of liked that he was getting a bit mad, because it made me feel like he was a little jealous, and to be a little jealous, you have to like someone first. Manoj must have seen the looks and attraction between Patrick and I in the back seat, and turned to us at a stoplight and asked, "Who are you?" while looking at Patrick. He didn't ask it in a rude way, just an Indian way, which in my experience can be misconstrued as rude to the general population of the United States. Blunt was probably a better explanation of how he asked it, which I was used to, and it didn't bother me anymore after twelve years of living with an Indian. So Patrick looked at me, and then back at Manoj and said, "I'm just her brother," while grabbing my hand to hold. I couldn't help but bust out laughing. With a combination of the alcohol, my excitement, and Patrick's overall sense of humor, I couldn't stop laughing. Then to make me laugh even harder, Patrick leaned over and kissed me on the cheek. I then told Manoj, "Yeah, we are very close for a brother and sister," and kept laughing. Luckily, Manoj took it all in stride, and just continued to smile and accept our ridiculous answers.

We pulled up in front of the Hammond Regency, and Patrick started getting out. I realized then that I was having so much fun, I didn't even wonder where we were going. Time seemed to stop every time I was with Patrick, and I loved it. He reached for my hand to help me out of the car, and kept holding it while waving goodbye to Manoj. I was still laughing hysterically, but kept hold of his hand. Even though we were joking around, I loved holding his hand. There was something about holding Patrick's hand that felt like home. Not "holding my brother's hand" kind of home, but home meaning comfortable and perfect.

Chapter 16

Hotel Hair Take Two

We walked hand in hand into the hotel, and headed straight to the elevators. We hadn't even talked about where we were going, and he hadn't asked me if I wanted to go to his hotel room. It was like he knew what I wanted, and he wanted it too. I was surprised at myself for not feeling concerned, walking hand in hand with Patrick inside a very busy Atlanta hotel. I know I should have worried about seeing someone I knew, but I didn't care.

We got in the elevator, and it took everything I had not to grab his face and start kissing him. I was looking at his lips all night, and I hoped he hadn't noticed. I couldn't wait for my mouth to be on his. I did contain myself, though, and was proud that I continued with that containment for at least another hour.

This is where it gets a little weird. I should be able to tell you everything we talked about in the hour after we got to his room, but I can't. I don't remember. It's not like a "I got roofied and don't remember," or "I was too wasted to remember" kind of forgetful. I think it was more of an out-of-body experience, without sounding like a crazy person. It was like an extreme state of euphoria. Patrick always made me laugh so hard, and it felt so good. He stimulated my mind in a weird way too. Not that he was brilliant or challenging, but he seemed to always talk about my interests, which also happened to be his interests as well. And he was insightful, and actually shared some crazy shit about himself, and didn't worry about me judging him. I liked that he trusted me with his thoughts and feelings. I don't really remember that part of him back in 1992, but we were so young that "insight" was not a word in my vocabulary yet.

I also can't tell you how we went from sitting on the bed fully clothed, to completely naked and having sex, but we did. I wish I could tell you all of the dirty details, but all I can remember is reveling in the amazing feeling of his naked body on top of mine, and his hard dick inside of me. And yes, this time it was hard. And it stayed hard. And it was amazing. I know I already said that, but I think "amazing" is pretty much all I can remember about that night. I do know that I was so into the sex, and how happy I was to have Patrick inside of me for a very decent amount of time that I really didn't care about anything else. Literally, nothing else that night. And did I say that it was amazing?

However, I do remember opening my eyes periodically while he was inside me, and looking into his eyes, just to make sure I wasn't dreaming. I also remember getting dressed, and having Patrick look over at me as I was pulling up my sexy undies, and say, "God, I love your body." It's probably sad that I remember *that* more than I remember the sex details, but hearing that from a man that I was terribly attracted to, for the first time in many years, was definitely memorable. And I was very happy that I had gone to Victoria Secret that week and picked out a little something sexy, which I also hadn't done in many years.

Unfortunately, I also remember wishing more than anything that I could stay in Patrick's arms all night, and into the next morning. But I couldn't. Laurie told me that she wanted me home by 2:00 a.m. because she had to be somewhere early the next morning. Because I loved her, and literally couldn't live without her and her support with Jack, she trumped Patrick. I noticed, as I was getting dressed, that it was 1:30 a.m., so I literally had to leave right then to get home in time. As we somewhat rushed to the elevators, Patrick asked what I was doing the next day. I said, "Spending it with you," partly joking, but hoping that he wouldn't refuse. His response . . . "Good."

Patrick was sweet to call me a ride share. As we waited for it, I told him what time the sitter was coming the next morning, and what times I was free. I was so glad that I had already scheduled a sitter to be there from 12 to 7 p.m. the next day. I didn't know if he wanted to spend that entire seven hours with me, but I wanted him to know he could. As I kissed him outside of the car, in front of numerous hotel guests coming and going from their late night shenanigans, I didn't care who saw. The odds of seeing anyone I knew at a hotel in downtown Atlanta at 1:45 a.m. were pretty slim, but you never know with "Piper kind of luck." The Karma Gods got another nod from me that night, since everything went according to plan.

In the ride share on the way home, the only thing I kept telling myself was, "Wow, you did it, Piper. You made all of those fantasies over the past year come true. Still no orgasm, but there's always tomorrow."

As I was paying Laurie, and apologizing for being a bit late, my phone beeped.

Jimmy:
October 8, 2:13 a.m.
Let me know when home safe.

I realized then that we hadn't said anything about touching base when I got home, but I was also not used to people worrying about me. His ride share app must have alerted him that his drive was complete, so he wanted to make sure I was home safe, which I thought was sweet. Even if I wasn't used to it.

Me:
October 8, 2:15 a.m.
Just got home. Alarm on. Jack asleep. See you
tomorrow.

In true Jack fashion, he was up and at 'em at 4:00 a.m. Which meant that I only got approximately one hour of sleep, since it took me a while to get to sleep due to my overwhelming excitement. But because I was on a Patrick high, as I will call it, I honestly did not care one iota. I still had enough energy and stamina to last at least another day on this happy adrenaline. I realized then that Patrick really was like a drug for me. I had never done illegal drugs a day in my life, but I had a feeling it was just like this. Now I could see why people got addicted. I was addicted to Patrick, but at least I was able to admit it, and accept it.

"Hi, my name is Piper, and I'm an addict." I had completed step one, and was able to say that I was "powerless over Patrick, and that my life may start to get unmanageable." I know I'm joking around, but I have worked with drug and alcohol patients for over fourteen years, and I fully respect and appreciate the twelve-step program. I am just being honest. If there was a PA group (Patrick anonymous), I would be its proud founding mother.

I was in the shower the next morning when I heard a text from Patrick. As usual, I feared that he was going to cancel on me, or say he could only see me for some of the day. There I was in my Patrick insecurities yet again. I didn't understand how and why he could do that to me . . . Every. Single. Time. Nobody else made me feel that way. So, was this love, or infatuation? I didn't really care what it was for the time being, I was too busy checking off boxes of my fantasies for the last eight months.

Jimmy:
October 8, 10:23 a.m.
You up for doing something fun today?

Wow! So not only was I wrong that he didn't want to see me, he was actually making plans, and asking if it was okay. This was something new and exciting for me. I was used to the typical marriage-type plans that only existed around the autism schedule. So this spontaneity was definitely new, but made me even more excited to see him.

Me:
October 8, 10:37 a.m.
I'm down for anything. I'm going on about 1 hour
of sleep tho, thanks to Jack. But coffee is helping.

Jimmy:
October 8, 11:15 a.m.
What's your ETA? Not rushing you, just checking when I should start putting on my make-up.

Me:
October 8, 11:25 a.m.
LOL. I should be able to leave right when Sasha gets here at 12. What did you have in mind?

Jimmy:
October 8, 11:42 a.m.
Might go to the Falcons game, if ok with you. If not, I understand. And take your time, don't care when we get there. R u hungry?

Me:
October 8, 12:08 p.m.
Kind of, I really just want a big fat Coke. taxi will be here in 4 minutes. You want me to meet you at the hotel? In the bar?

Jimmy:
October 8, 12:17 p.m.
How'd you guess? But I've kinda lost interest in going to the game. Rather just eat and relax with you. Is that ok?

Are you kidding? Okay? This was way more than okay with me. A whole day to eat and relax with Patrick sounded like heaven on earth.

Me:
October 8, 12:19 p.m.
Of course. See you in a few.

The ride share dropped me off at the hotel, and I walked in toward the bar. I could see the back of Patrick, and as I continued to get closer, my heart rate sped up. It's crazy how the back of his head not only got me excited, but got me horny. Just his aura was like a medicine to my psyche. I wish I could explain in words what he did to me, what he did to my mood, and how he made me feel every time I was with him. But I can only do my best to describe it.

I was going to grab him and try to startle him, but before I could, he turned around. He smiled at me, took me in his arms, and kissed my head. I knew this was going to be an amazing day.

We walked to a restaurant nearby that Patrick found on an app. We didn't talk a whole lot during lunch because we were both famished, and too busy shoving food into our mouths. Since the last two times we were together was mostly talk about *his* life, *his* exes, and *his* struggles, I thought I would share a little of mine. I talked about my divorce, which he sort of knew about already, since I was engaged the last time we saw each other at college. I said how devastating it was, but how much I learned and grew from it, and how it made me a much better and stronger person. Which I know all sounds cliché, but it's the truth. I talked about getting fired at my last job for something that I didn't do, and how hard that was to overcome. And how hard it was for me to trust people again.

I also talked a little about my husband, and how he allowed me be the strong and independent woman I am today, which was something I appreciated. I wasn't trying to talk too much about hubby, but I wanted him to know the good stuff, and never wanted to give him any kind of impression that I was going to leave my husband, or that I was unhappy and wanted a divorce. I was unhappy in a lot of ways, but I wasn't anywhere near a divorce. Plus, my son needed us both, so divorce was not even an option, at all, ever. I guess I also wanted Patrick to know that yes, I was somewhat using him as my escape, but he made it pretty clear to me that afternoon that I was doing the same, in a way, for him. He reiterated at the restaurant that he had lost a lot of self-esteem recently, especially after his most recent relationship. But I had been making him feel better about himself, and boosting his confidence. I liked hearing this because it sounded like he thought highly of me, and that always makes a person feel good. I know I was not doing very "think highly of me" things, but I'd like to think that Patrick knew me enough to know that I didn't just sleep around. After I spoke about my fear of him judging me for sleeping with him while I was married, he looked me right in the eyes and said, "Oh, don't worry, I know. You are not that kind of person." And I believed him.

When we got back to the hotel, it was as if we were a new couple, anxiously awaiting the moment to explore one another. He started taking off his shoes right when we got in the door, then took his pants off, and crawled under the covers. He still had his shirt and boxers on, so he wasn't being presumptuous. I followed suit, but kept my shirt and pants on, and joined him under the covers.

We talked a little, then started kissing right away, but not in an impatient way. We softly kissed and caressed each other, and it felt fabulous. We slowly and intimately took our clothes off, and he began to make love to me. I say "make love" hesitantly, because I always thought you had to love someone to make love. I was pretty sure he wasn't in love with me, and I had no idea whether I was in love with him. All I knew was in that very moment every single thing I had ever wanted for the last eight months was coming true.

I know we had already been intimate twice since we found each other again, but this was different. We had fucked before, and it was definitely nice. Not like "dirty porno"–type fucking, more like "bottled-up sexual repression"–type fucking. But it wasn't like that this time. I was completely sober, and I think he was too. He had a beer at the restaurant, but I don't know if he finished it. Plus, for someone who likely drinks some form of alcohol daily, a beer is pretty much equivalent to water at that point.

Afterward we just held each other, and I could feel that he was smiling. I was too. After a few minutes of quiet bliss he said, "I know this sounds weird, but I trust you. And I have a very hard time with trust. I haven't done this, or wanted to do this, in a long time, and I'm glad it's with you." I knew what he meant. He didn't necessarily mean trusting me with a secret, or believing words that I said. He meant trusting in me as a whole, and what I represented to him. He told me before that he hadn't had sex in over a year, despite the fact that he had been living with his girlfriend. Knowing that he trusted me, which was something he struggled with, meant a lot.

Oh, and no, I didn't have the "big O." I was disappointed, of course, but I knew that was next to impossible with my body, even if it was Patrick Barnes. And hey, now I had something to look forward to for next time. Hoping, praying, and wishing there was going to be a next time, maybe even in the next hour or two.

We started drifting off to sleep, so I rolled over and onto my other side, facing away from him. He rolled over to spoon me, but started lightly rubbing my arm, and continued to do so for almost ten minutes as I dozed in and out. I finally said, "Why are you being so sweet?" I don't know why this is the first thing I could think to say. I should have told him he *was* sweet, instead of asking as though I couldn't believe he was doing something so nice. But I actually couldn't believe he was doing something so nice. It's not that Patrick was mean, or an asshole, either now or when we dated as teenagers. But I'm used to that kind of caressing when you are serious with someone, and truly care for them. I sometimes forget that men have a different mentality than women when it comes to sex and affection as a whole, so it always shocks me when those with intimacy issues can be so intimate. The problem is that it made me feel special. It made me feel like I was important to Patrick, because I personally can only do such a thing when my heart is involved too. I can only rub someone's arm for ten minutes, or make love to someone if I care about them, or am very attracted to them. And, unfortunately, I tend to think that others' feel the same way about that stuff as I do, which is a problem I have always had.

He didn't really answer my question, he just sort of laughed as if to say, "What do you mean? I'm always nice." But he did say a few minutes later how good it felt to lie around with me, and to just be with each other. And I agreed wholeheartedly.

Another problem I have when I'm enjoying a situation is that I can't help but think about when I can enjoy that situation *again*. I have a hard time staying in that moment, and in the present. But surprisingly, I actually didn't have a hard time with it when I was with Patrick. I was able to think about how much I have wanted this, and how much I appreciated it happening. I smiled and thought to myself, *This feels so nice, and I want to enjoy every moment of it.* Every time I was with him I would think about it possibly being the last time, and I was just glad I was living it . . . even if only for one more day.

I was able to be a little vulnerable, and I told Patrick how much I was going to miss him, and miss *this.* He made it sound like it was no big deal, and that we would likely have more of these days, since he was still supposed to be moving to Atlanta at some point. I explained that my husband doesn't go out of the country often, so it would likely be our last time. That's when I told him that I hoped having sex didn't ruin our friendship, because being able to text him anytime and having him care about me, was way more important than having sex with him again. Don't get me wrong . . . I wanted him again, but I wanted his friendship more. He looked me right in the eyes and assured me that I didn't have to worry about that. "We will always be friends, no matter what," he said. I believed him, but now I wish I wouldn't have.

We both fell asleep, and were awakened by my phone ringing. I had to always keep my phone on because of my special-needs child. It's twenty-four-hour intensive care with him, so I could never turn off my phone when I wasn't with him. I looked at the caller ID and it was my husband. I was kind of surprised because it was about 5:00 p.m. my time, and 3:00 a.m. his time. I was also surprised because he usually just sent me a text via What's App when he was in India, but he was physically calling instead. I turned to Patrick and told him that I had to answer it, because I was a little concerned. Patrick was actually cool about it, and said he was going downstairs to get a sandwich, and would give me some privacy. I thought that was nice, because I'm not sure I could've done the same thing if the situation was reversed.

I answered the phone while Patrick slipped out the door. My husband sounded upset, and the connection was bad. He said something about someone dying, and I couldn't hear the rest. When the connection got a little clearer, I was able to piece together that his grandfather had died.

I was so devastated for him. One of the reasons he was going to India was to visit his grandfather, who had been ill for some time, so he knew he didn't have much longer. And, unfortunately, he died right before my hubby got there. He wasn't actually in his home town yet, and was calling me from Delhi while waiting for his connecting flight. I told him I was so sorry, and if only he knew how sorry I really was.

I felt terrible, and like I had something to do with his death. I mean, I know I didn't kill his grandfather, but I felt somehow responsible. I guess that's what guilt does to you. I felt like I was being punished for my bad behavior. I had only met the man once, but my husband was very close to his grandfather. I felt an overwhelming sense of sadness for my husband. Here I was having sex with someone while he was burying his grandfather. I knew right then and there that I would be going straight to hell.

I got out of bed and put on my clothes. I don't know why I was so determined to get out of there, because I wasn't going to be able to go to India anyway. I had to stay with Jack, due to his inability to make a seventeen hour flight. Autism would not allow it. I guess I just felt like lightning was going to strike if I stayed in that hotel room any longer, like everything was going to go to hell in a handbasket the longer I stayed in the *sin room.*

When I finished going to the bathroom, Patrick walked in the door with a big smile on his face. I could tell he had gone to the coffee shop in the hotel, and stocked up on sandwiches, pastries, and coffee for both of us. His smile disappeared immediately when he saw my face, and the fact that I was fully dressed. I wasn't crying, nor had I been. But I was probably gray and peaked from the news I had just gotten, and the guilt that came over my entire being.

I told Patrick what happened, and he appeared sincere with his apologies. He likely felt a tinge guilty as well, even though he didn't know the man, or my husband. But I know if the tables were turned, and his wife's family member just died after we had sex, I would feel like a shitty-ass person who was only thinking of herself. I didn't want him to think of himself that way, but I was definitely feeling that way about me . . . a shitty-ass, selfish, horrible human.

I told him I had to go in case hubby needed to talk to me further about anything, or if I had to take care of some arrangements. He acted like he completely understood, and called me a taxi. We kissed again outside of the car, but it was more like a *slightly-more-than-friends* kiss. Very understandable, though, due to the circumstances.

Chapter 17

Having My Cake

The next month was busy for me without hubs, and being the only caretaker for Jack, besides the occasional babysitter help. Hubby had to stay in India for almost an entire month, due to the Hindu rituals after someone dies. Luckily there wasn't much to be done in the US for the funeral, so most of the work hubby and his family were able to do in India. Therefore, I was able to focus all of my attention on Jack.

I texted Patrick every once in a while just to check-in where and how he was, and he did the same with me. We kept the texts very PG. I knew his living arrangements were up in the air, plus he was continuing to travel a lot. And if this is possible, seeing him again was both the first thing on my mind AND the last. I craved it, especially with the added stress that I was having being a single parent for those few weeks. Patrick was my escape from reality, and I needed it even more than I had in the past. But I had to push the thoughts out of my mind, because I did have so much other stuff to focus on. Plus, I pushed the thoughts aside because every time I thought about him, especially intimately, the guilt would take over. And to make matters worse, I felt guilty that I didn't feel MORE guilty than I did. I know that sounds weird, but I still felt like I deserved to feel as amazing as I did those few days with Patrick, even if it was wrong. That's how strong my desire continued to be. I didn't really care about the ramifications if it meant being that happy for another day.

I wasn't planning on telling hubby anything, especially with this added stress he had. But my small guilty conscience wanted to tell him the truth at some point in the near future. I didn't think I could keep it in due to my own guilty feelings, but I also didn't want to tell him for my own selfish reasons. I truly didn't want to hurt him, and I also didn't want a divorce. I knew if he found out, he would divorce me faster than I could say "no." And it wasn't as if Patrick wanted to be with me, nor did I think it would be possible to be with him. So, if divorce was going to be an option, it was going to be because I wanted a divorce. Not because I wanted to be with somebody else. However, the fact that I wanted to spend most of my free time with someone else made me question exactly what it was I truly wanted.

I went out to dinner with Elizabeth one night. She was the only one I could talk to about Patrick, and while we were eating, she asked me a very important and relevant question. She said, "If you could have your way, and have exactly what you want, what would that look like? Even if it's unrealistic." This stumped me for a minute, because I wanted my life just as it was. But, I wanted Patrick WHEN I wanted him. That was selfish, I knew. I was being more than honest when I answered, "I want my cake, and to eat it too." I wanted exactly what I had right then and there. I wanted to be married, and to have the united front that hubby and I had for our son. I wanted to be able to have my best friend living with me, so we could be there to help each other through the hard autism times. And, Jesus, there were so many of those. But I wanted to be able to have Patrick whenever I needed some affection, or wanted to smile.

Even though I was anxiously awaiting the day I could be in Patrick's arms again, I figured I would let the universe decide again when that would be. I planned on living my life as is, and if we happened to see each other again, then that would be a bonus. But I was done forcing the issue. I knew that I was the one who pushed us together over the last six months, and I was okay with that. Why? Because I made it all freakin' happen, that's why. I got what I wanted. Well, again, not the "O," but Piper can't have everything. I was the instigator in all of this, and I knew he was just a willing participant. I didn't know if he wasn't doing any of the initiating because I was married, or because he didn't even like me at the end of the day. But during the times that I was doing all of the initiating, I didn't care why. I wanted him, and I got him. It's funny because before my self-titled "#BestYearEver2017," I would have told myself, "Girl, why the hell are you wasting your time on Patrick . . . he doesn't give a shit about you." But my newfound "you only live once" mentality told me, "Girl, why the fuck not! Life is way too short! Go after what you want!" And I guess what I was telling myself now was, "Girl, you got it. Now what?"

I made plans to go home to Texas for Thanksgiving, since my brother, Parker, was also coming into town from Portland. I hadn't talked to Patrick about it, and figured if he happened to be there, fantastic. But I wasn't going to make it happen like I had in the past. He was going to have to do some of the initiating this time around. But I was just excited to get away from autism for a few days, and relish in the comforts of home and good food from mom.

I ran across a funny meme on Facebomb, and had to send it to Patrick. It was a picture of Leonardo DiCaprio on one side toasting a wine glass outside in the sunshine. The other side of the picture had Kate Winslet from Titanic, dripping with water and ice, freezing on the floating thing at the end of the movie. At the top of the meme, it said: "When he turns down the thermostat." This was such an inside joke with us, since both encounters in the hotel included a battle between him turning down the thermostat, and me turning it up. He responded rather quickly after I texted it.

Jimmy:
November 20, 5:52 p.m.
Ha!! Good one.
Check out the new spot, I'm sweating right now.

Attached to this text was a picture of his big dog sitting on a porch, with a beautiful pond and dock in the background.

Me:
November 20, 6:04 p.m.
Wow! Where are you? Is that your place? Looks
so nice and relaxing.

Jimmy:
November 20, 6:22 p.m.
Yep, right in the middle of the city, if you can believe
it. Any cute pics of you that u want to share w/ me?
Need cheering up today. U taking any trips soon?

I think this was the first time that he had ever asked for a picture of me, besides the infamous gold chain pic. I wasn't much into selfies, but I figured I could find a decent one to send. I hope he wasn't referring to a tit pic, or booty pic. I know I definitely didn't have any of those. But the thought of my face making him feel better was a nice feeling. And since he asked if I had any trips coming up, this was the perfect opportunity to tell him about my Texas trip. And if the pic he just sent was his new place, and he would be in town for Thanksgiving, that may work out in my favor.

Me:
November 20, 6:40 p.m.
I'm going home for Thanksgiving in a few days,
but other than that, not much. Hope to go
somewhere warm soon—already sick of the cold.

Jimmy:
November 20, 6:45 p.m.
Home as in Texas?

Me:
November 20, 6:51 p.m.
Yep

Jimmy:
November 20, 6:59 p.m.
Will you be able to get away for a minute and
come see the place?

Me:
November 20, 7:14 p.m.
Absolutely. More than a minute. I'll be there
Friday thru Tuesday, although my flight is at
6 a.m. Tuesday . . . so freakin early!

Jimmy:
November 20, 7:28 p.m.
Prrrfect. I can take you to the airport.

Me:
November 20, 7:47 p.m.
You sure? 3 a.m.?

Jimmy:
November 20, 8:09 p.m.
Of course. Maybe we'll go do something fun in
the city Monday night and stay close, or not.
Either way, I'll get you to the airport.

Me:
November 20, 9:36 p.m.
Sounds good. Can't wait.

Okay, now this is what I meant by initiating. I told him I would be there, and he did the rest. I wanted him to show me that he wanted to see me, and these texts confirmed that for me. Now I couldn't wait for the trip even more. I attached a picture of me with a good friend of mine. It wasn't the best picture, but it was the only decent one of me that was easily and quickly accessible. It wasn't sexy, but I looked aight. I was just hoping it was good enough for touching himself. Ha!

I figured this would be the last of our text exchanges for the evening. It was not only getting late, but it was his MO to end texts, so I was surprised when I heard from him again before I went to bed.

Jimmy:
November 20, 10:10 p.m.
You're beautiful. Even prettier on inside & cool
as shit to boot.

Here's another example of a compliment that may sound weird to others, because it's not as though "shit" is actually "cool." But to me, this is probably the best thing Patrick could've said at this point. I felt like Patrick knew me, and liked me for *me*. I'm glad he thought I was beautiful too, but looks fade. And you can tell people all day long how good-looking they are, but to like someone's insides is what's most important. I didn't really know what to say, and I didn't want to ignore such a sweet text, so I just sent a kissy face emoji.

I only had three more days to prep for my trip, and it was kind of hard with Jack being out of school for the whole Thanksgiving week. I wasn't going to text Patrick until I got there, which was going to be after Thanksgiving anyway. I made plans with some friends while I was there, too, since I didn't want to spend my whole vacation with Patrick. As wonderful as that sounded, it was unrealistic on so many levels. I would be staying with my parents, and as cool as they are, it would be kind of hard to explain why I was having a sleepover with a friend at the age of forty-three. And as much as I don't mind omitting information, I'm not a good liar.

I got to Texas the day after turkey day. I couldn't leave until after Thanksgiving day because my husband had to work, and then he took off the remaining days to take care of Jack so I could have this break. He knew how bad I needed a break from my mundane autism-life. Since he was gone for almost a month, I had been sleep deprived with Jack's sleep disorder. Usually hubs and I take turns with the monitor, so at least one of us can get a good night sleep. But when there's only one adult in the house, it's all on that one person. Night, after night, after night. There are some nights that Jack only sleeps five or six hours, which means we only get about four or five hours, since it's impossible to go to sleep the second he does. When Jack finally goes to sleep is when I have the alone time I need to get things done around the house. I knew I wasn't going to be able to actually catch up on my sleep while I was in Texas, but at least I would be relaxing.

Parker and my parents came to pick me up at the airport, and

I spent the day with them. We went to the movies, then out to dinner, and it felt like the old times when it was just us four growing up. That night, Parker wanted to go to the local bar, because they had a live band playing. I went with him to catch up on our lives. I was close to my brother, but we didn't see each other, or talk often. So, it was fun to catch up, and hear about all of his single life shenanigans. Just like Patrick, he is almost in his midforties, never been married, and no kids. I told him what had been going on with Patrick, and I was surprised that he was more than understanding. He knew Patrick a little from high school, but they were not friends, or hung in the same crowd. And just like Elizabeth, he completely understood my need for escape, and my desire to get a release from autism-land. He had visited Atlanta a few times, and saw first-hand how hard Jack really was. Jack is a great kid, but a handful is an understatement. Parker told me that he had no idea how I did what I did, and that he didn't want to have kids because he was afraid of a similar outcome. I loved my son more than life itself, but the struggles were real, and I appreciated that Parker could see that.

Parker is also not one to be completely faithful to his girlfriends, so there was definitely no judgement from him. I love sharing my issues with not only those I can trust to stay quiet, but those who don't judge me. To be honest, I would judge the shit out of my own actions before a year ago. I never understood affairs, and those who cheated. But I felt like this was different. It really wasn't different, but I felt like it sort of was because it was only this one person that I wanted to be with. I didn't find some random dude on the side to have sex with. This was a man who had been living in the back of my head for almost thirty years, so what did that mean, exactly? Regardless of what it meant, it was just as bad as any affair at the end of the day.

I had been in town for almost a whole day and hadn't texted Patrick. I was proud of myself, until the alcohol that Parker and I consumed broke my control.

Me:
November 25, 12:54 a.m.
Please tell me Angie's saloon isn't the best hangout
in the city! This place leaves a lot to be desired.

I know it was after midnight, but he *was* a single man. And if he was out at the bar down the street, I didn't want to miss my opportunity to see him. I didn't hear back from him that night, so I assumed he was in bed asleep. I did, however, finally get a text the next afternoon.

Jimmy:
November 25, 1:51 p.m.
Hi, I was there right before you last night.
Whatcha up to?

And before I could even respond, I got this . . .

Jimmy:
November 25, 1:53 p.m.
Can't wait to see you!! That's not wrong is it?

Well, just as the saying goes . . . if it's wrong, then I don't want to be right! I didn't answer with this cheesy quote, of course, but it was definitely the first thing I thought of. And this was one of my other favorite texts from Patrick. He actually wanted to see me, and I couldn't be happier. Literally! I was hanging with my parents and twin brother, who I love with all of my heart, eating my favorite "home" foods. Plus, I was getting ready to spend the weekend with some good friends, and hopefully some with Patrick. My life seriously could not have been any better than that very moment. Besides getting Jack to talk, there was nothing else I would have wished for right then and there!

Me:
November 25, 2:09 p.m.
Not wrong at all! What are your plans tonight?
I'm going out with Dianna and Parker later but
I better see you soon.

Jimmy:
November 25, 3:02 p.m.
When do I get u to myself?

Now we're talking. If he only knew how bad I wanted him all to myself. That is exactly what I had been waiting for since I left the hotel in Atlanta two months prior.

Me:
November 25, 3:09 p.m.
Any time after that. I'm pretty free till Tuesday morning. And FYI—you don't have to take me to the airport early, or at all . . . I got a later flight out Tuesday instead.

Jimmy:
November 25, 3:12 p.m.
Gotcha! I'm taking u to the airport. 100% xo

And just like typical Patrick, I never heard back from him until I texted him at 9:45 p.m. that night, slightly inebriated. He knew I was going to be with Dianna and Parker, but I was hoping I could squeeze him in sometime soon. I still hadn't seen his new place, and I was so tempted to just drive my ass over there and show up on his porch.

Me:
November 25, 9:45 p.m.
Whatcha up to?

Jimmy:
November 25, 9:59 p.m.
Honky Tonking . . . wishing I was at the Hammond Regency with you. About to head over to Frankie's Feast. Where are you?

Attached to Patrick's text was a picture of a seedy bar with a small live band on a make-shift stage, definitely "*honky tonk*" looking. I loved his Hammond reference, since I just realized right then that both of the hotels that we had sex at were Hammond's, just in two different parts of the city. And I was happy that he wanted to be there with me.

Luckily, we were already at the Frankie's Feast that night, so I didn't have to chase him around town. And this made me go right back to my earlier inference regarding the "Why is everything falling into place for me?" Why did Patrick happen to be in town when I was, and we didn't even plan it? Why were we going to be at the same bar, coincidentally, when there were at least ten other bars in the area? That whole fate concept was rearing its pretty head again, and I couldn't help but think there must be some reason why shit was working out so perfectly.

Me:
November 25, 10:05 p.m.
That's where we are. See you soon.

At that point, I told Dianna and Parker that Patrick was coming to meet me in a little bit. Dianna looked at me kind of weird, because she had no idea about us. I acted very nonchalant, and told her that we had been in contact recently. She was still looking at me weird as I was trying my best to hide my guilty face. She was aware of our past, and my long-time obsession, so she knew something was up when I acted like Patrick meeting us at the bar was no big deal.

Patrick and his friend, Stephen, walked in the door together. I knew Stephen from high school, and knew that he and Patrick were still close, but didn't realize he was going to be with him. I'm not a big fan of Stephen, at least, not the old Stephen. He was always kind of an asshole, but he knew he was, so I respected the fact that he didn't try to hide it. I was hoping that after twenty-plus years, he was a better dude. He seemed to be when Patrick introduced us, and Stephen smiled at me, and asked how I was doing. I honestly don't think he has ever smiled at me, let alone smiled at all. At least, not in my company. So, it was nice to see.

I was pretty drunk by the time Patrick and Stephen met us at the bar. I always love being intoxicated, since it makes me happy, and lose my inhibitions. But the problem is that I also tend to be so happy that I can't focus, and I forget all the good stuff. I don't black out or anything, I just forget the specifics of conversations. And on that particular night, I really wish I remembered all the details of our talk, but I don't.

One thing I do remember is when Patrick told me that Stephen was staying with him, and that he had told Stephen earlier that day about me, and about us. I honestly didn't care if Stephen knew about us, even the juicy details. He never seemed like someone who would gossip, because he was always too involved with his own shit. I guess I was so drunk that it took a while to register that Stephen would be in Patrick's house, and therefore, I might not be able to have any kind of sexual encounter while he was staying there. This kind of bummed me out, but I figured Patrick had his own room, so it may work itself out after all. I didn't know at the time, unfortunately, that Patrick had a studio with no bedroom at all.

The other thing I vaguely remember, but so wish I remembered better, was something Patrick said after he told me about his conversation with Stephen. I was trying to press him for more details, like finding out exactly what he had said to Stephen. Patrick mumbled something about how he had been "thinking of me a lot," which made my ears perk up, but my brain stayed muffled with alcohol effects. Hearing that he actually thought about me had me all kinds of excited, so I continued to push him for details. Patrick turned to me, looked me right in the eyes and said, "I like you, Piper." But the way he said it gave me all the good feels. He wasn't just telling me that he liked me, he was emphasizing the word "like." It was almost as if he was saying that he really liked me, but didn't want to. It was the first time I felt like Patrick was finally falling for me. Maybe he wasn't, but it felt like it in that very moment. Or maybe it was the alcohol leading me to believe that, but I felt as if he was letting his guard down a little, and I loved seeing him a bit vulnerable.

Or maybe I didn't like the vulnerability after all, because the next thing I knew, I was so busy talking to my brother that I didn't notice that Patrick left. I think I might have freaked out a little after Patrick told me that he liked me, because I got up from the table and sat at the bar with my brother to hang with him. After noticing that Patrick was nowhere in the bar, I went to the bathroom to break the seal that was destined to be broke. Sitting on the toilet, I heard my phone ring. It was weird for anyone to call me, let alone at 1:00 a.m. I'm a texter, and my peeps know that. So, I was a little confused while I rifled through my purse to get my ringing phone. It said "Jimmy" was calling, so I answered it. But I think I answered it, "Where the hell are you?" I wasn't mad, I was just drunk and confused. He told me that Stephen was tired and wanted to go to bed, so they left. Patrick told me that Stephen was sleeping on his couch, and that he would see me on Monday. This kind of made me mad, because I felt low on his priority list. I knew he was super close to Stephen, so I didn't care about their bromance. I just cared that it interfered with my sexual needs. I figured Patrick might have picked up on my freak-out after he told me that he liked me, and maybe that's why he left so quickly. Regardless, I still couldn't wait to see him again.

Chapter 18

All That Glitters Isn't Grills

I spent all day Sunday doing nothing, and loved every minute of it. I lay on the couch literally all day, only getting up to eat or pee. I watched at least four *Lifetime* movies, and an Adam Sandler movie in the middle there somewhere. I never get days like this, so I reveled in the wonderful relaxation. By Monday morning, I had no idea what the plan was, but I just knew that the plans better involve Patrick, or I was not going to be happy. I thought about not texting him and waiting to see if he texted me, but I went back to my previous mindset of *you only live once.* I wanted to spend my last night at home with him, so I was going to make it happen. And sometimes in order to make things happen, YOU gotta make them happen.

Me:

November 27, 12:14 p.m.

Hey! Just wondering what the plans are . . . didn't know if I should pack up my stuff today before we hang tonight, or just pick me up tomorrow? Let me know.

At least I gave him a huge out if he didn't want to see me. He could very easily have just said he would pick me up and take me to the airport tomorrow. But, luckily, he didn't say that.

Jimmy:
November 27, 12:38 p.m.
Hell yes we're hanging out tonight and I'll take u
to airport too. I'm taking Stephen now.

Me:
November 27, 12:52 p.m.
Cool. Hopping in shower now . . . will be free after.
Text me with plans.

And just like always, I started worrying he wouldn't text me back. Or that he would ignore me until I bothered him again around 9:00 p.m. Like I said before, he truly made my sixteen-year-old self come alive. I don't mean my occasional happy and relaxed sixteen-year-old self, I mean the unconfident, self-conscious, uncertain, unassertive, and inhibited sixteen-year-old version of me. Luckily he didn't make me feel that version for long, but he did have me sweatin' for a couple of hours.

Jimmy:
November 27, 2:49 p.m.
On my way back. Whatcha up to?

Me:
November 27, 3:02 p.m.
Just got done having lunch with the parents.
What are we doing?

Jimmy:
November 27, 3:19 p.m.
Don't have any set plans. Any wants or suggestions?

I guess now was my chance to tell him that I really just wanted to come over, check out his place, have sex, and lay in bed together all night and into the next morning. But I thought that might be too forward. Why can't we all just be forward like that? It would be so nice if in the early stages of dating we could just be upfront and honest about what we want and feel. Not that Patrick and I were dating, but it felt like that. I felt like I had to be careful with what I said because I didn't want to be too forward, but also didn't want to be not forward enough. Everybody seems to always worry about what the other person might think or feel, but isn't honesty the only thing that will make any relationship work? And again, not that we were in a relationship, but I guess we were in our own right. So, I thought I would just be direct, and tell him what we were going to do instead of beating around the bush.

Me:
November 27, 3:26 p.m.
I got my mom's car. I'll come over to your place
around 5:00 and we can figure it out from there.

I spent the next hour freshening up. Yes, it took me an hour . . . so what? A natural beauty I am not. Or any kind of beauty, for that matter. But I had a pretty good feeling that I would be having sex that night, and I wanted to be as sexy as my unsexy body and face would allow.

When I got to his place, it was kind of weird. It wasn't the being around him that was weird, necessarily, just his place. He didn't tell me that he was basically renting out a room in a house. It wasn't just a room, but more like a studio apartment in one of the wings of the house. At least it had a bed, couch, a kitchen (sort of), and a bathroom, but it was all in one room. Well, the bathroom had its own room, but it was the size of a New York hotel's bathroom. And if you haven't seen one of those, take my word for it . . . they are very small. I'm not high maintenance, and I'm definitely not one to care about how big or beautiful your house is, but I couldn't help but laugh inside that he made it sound like his house was the best house in the city. Don't get me wrong, it was kind of cool, it just wasn't the best, and wasn't technically *his* house either. Oh well, I was assuming the bed was still able to be used, so that's really all I cared about. And an added bonus was that the place was quite clean.

We just sat around and talked, like we usually do, for what

seemed like thirty minutes, but was probably more like two hours. He mentioned he was hungry and wanted a steak. I told him I didn't mind going with him, but I would just get a dessert, since I was still full from a late lunch with the parents. I had to pee, so I used the tiny bathroom before we left. As I was sitting on the toilet, something sparkly on one of the small shelves caught my eye. After washing my hands, I looked closer at the glitter covered object and realized that it was a grill. Like, a mouth grill. Like, a rappers teeth grill. Like, there was seriously a fucking glittery grill sitting on the bathroom shelf. Like, similar to an orthodontic retainer to straighten teeth but clearly wasn't that type of grill. Like, Lil Wayne must have been in Patrick's bathroom at some point in the last twenty-four hours kind of grill.

Then, all of a sudden, I remembered his text from a long time ago that said he "should have brought his grill," and realized he was dead serious. I never mentioned the grill to Patrick. I figured he must have wanted me to see it, or else he would have hidden it before I came over. I didn't want to feed into his childish behaviors, so I acted as though everyone has a glittery grill sitting on their bathroom shelf, and I never said a thing.

When we got to the restaurant, I was hoping we wouldn't run into anyone we both knew, which was highly possible in a town that size that we both grew up in. We mainly talked about his up-in-the-air decisions on where he was going to live. He had about six options, and was torn on all of them. Since Georgia was one of those options, I blatantly told him that I would love for him to move to Atlanta, but I didn't know if it was the best idea. As much as I would love him close by, I know I would go crazy wanting to see him all the time. I didn't say that exactly, but kind of. It was hard to completely open up, because I wasn't really able to. I didn't want to leave my marriage, and I didn't want to give him the impression that I would. I wanted him to know I was crazy about him, but that we didn't really have a future.

When we got back to his place, we had sex, of course. I guess I shouldn't sound presumptuous and say "of course," but y'all know that's what I came for. But, unfortunately, STILL NO ORGASM.

I realized afterward that I still didn't know what all this meant. Was I wanting a relationship with him? Or did I just get my rocks off, and now I don't need him anymore? Or did I just want a sex thing on the side? I ruled that one out because I didn't just want to have sex. Not because it was bad, or anything, but because I knew I *did* care a little more than sex. Or was I in love with him, and wanted to be with him forever? Doubtful, but who knows at this point. I sure didn't.

We enjoyed each other's company for another few hours, and it was as perfect as always. Not that we were perfect, but our "hanging out" always felt perfect. At least, I thought so anyway. We always had something to talk about, and we always seemed to care what the other had to say. I also could kiss that man for eternity, and that's a fact.

Chapter 19

No Regrets

The holidays were hard for me, as usual. Hubby had to work the entire Christmas break, and Jack was out of school, so we were stuck in the house all day because it was too cold to do anything else. That's one of the many reasons I hate winter. We are stuck inside, and Jack goes a little stir-crazy, which then causes me to go a little nuts. It's next to impossible to travel with a severely autistic child, so we are unable to visit any family or friends during that time. It's a little easier to visit people during the summer, because if there is a pool in the general vicinity, Jack is a happy camper. And so is mom and dad, since that is pretty much the only time you can leave Jack unattended for a short period of time. I know it sounds crazy that my child is safer when in a large body of water than when out, but it's the truth. Jack is a phenomenal swimmer, and keeps himself very occupied and happy when in the water. It's when he's out of the water that you have to worry about him grabbing people's towels or sunglasses and throwing them in the pool, or running out of the gate and into the street. So, the holidays were spent watching a lot of Dory and Nemo, along with some Buzz Lightyear in between.

I still didn't know when I would see Patrick again, but I was trying not to think about it. Well, it was impossible not to think about Patrick at all, but I was trying to let the cards fall where they may. I did that before Thanksgiving, and it worked. So if the universe wanted us to be together again, the universe would make that happen.

But then I reminded myself that I was the one that manifested every single thing from the beginning of the year. Me and only me did this! I had not only reconnected with Patrick, but I successfully completed the sexual fantasy with him. Minus the big "O," of course, but there was still time for that. I also reconnected with old girlfriends, and strengthened my relationship with current friends, like Elizabeth. Plus, I made a point to see my parents and brother, whom I rarely got to see. I'm the one who did all of this, and I was happy I did it. I proved that happiness was not only a choice, but one we sometimes have to create. And I loved my new creation.

The night before New Year's, I sat back and pondered everything I had done since January. I realized then that 2017 was by far my *BEST YEAR EVER*! Don't get me wrong, I still had marriage struggles and autism challenges, but I felt like I was at a place where I accepted what is, and was better prepared for the battles. I felt like 2017 just made me an overall happier person. I felt more desired, I felt good about my looks and my self-worth. I felt like I had a purpose for the first time ever, and that was educating anyone and everyone I could on autism. I wanted to help people see the individual, not the diagnosis. Autism had defeated me over the last five years, but I fought back in 2017 . . . and won!

I owed a lot of this newfound happiness to Patrick. Not that a person can actually make you happy, but I felt more willing to take risks, and wasn't scared about consequences. And the risk I took on possible blows to my self-esteem when I reached out to Patrick showed me that the gamble can be worth it. I didn't regret one thing about 2017!

Patrick and I went a little over a month without a text from one another, between January and February. I knew I would be going back to Texas for a family reunion in March, but didn't know if Patrick would still be living there after the way he talked about moving sooner rather than later. This "Patrick-free" month also happened to be a rough time for me on the work front. I had been at the same job for over fifteen years, and actually really liked my job. Since I was unable to work full time, or part time for that matter, they happily worked around my schedule, and were very flexible with my availability. Having a severely autistic child made it difficult for me to work, since the income as a social worker is lower than it would cost an experienced person to babysit my son. It just didn't make sense for me to work full time, and make less than what we would pay someone else to take care of Jack. So, luckily, I just worked weekends when hubby could take care of him, or some weekdays here and there while Jack was in school.

I was starting to notice all of my full- and part-time coworkers getting raises. I was considered PRN, which means "as needed," so therefore I was not eligible for a raise. I had not received a raise in over eight years, so I felt like I deserved to be an exception. When I approached my supervisor about a raise, with whom I dearly loved, she actually agreed. She told me that she had already noticed my hourly wage, and asked human resources about the possibility of giving me a raise. I knew she would work hard to help me, so I was pretty content with the response. I knew she couldn't work miracles, but I also knew she would fight for me. I'm not an entitled person, and I definitely didn't think I deserved a raise just because everybody else was getting one, but I knew I was worth way more than what I was getting. I would like to have considered myself a valuable asset to a company with whom I had given a lot of myself for over fifteen years. I helped out when I could, and I always worked hard for the few hours I was there.

I had to wait a few weeks for a response about the raise. During those three weeks, I felt a little depressed. I was sad because I had to wait so long to see if they would actually give me that raise, but I was also sad that I hadn't heard much from Patrick for over a month. I realized then that he was the perfect escape for me, both from autism and work. Work used to sort of be my escape, since I didn't have to think about Jack, or autism, or the challenges that it all presented. But Patrick was a much better escape than work, even if I wasn't getting paid to be with him. But I wasn't getting paid much to work, either, and that was the problem.

Unfortunately, I carried this frustration into work with me one day, which just happened to be the wrong day to fuck with Piper. However, one of the mental health assistants, who obviously had no idea who I was, decided that, in fact, it was the perfect day to fuck with Piper. Again, I'm not entitled, but usually when people know I've been there for over fifteen years, I tend to get a lot more respect than the average social worker. Which is only natural, in my opinion. It pisses me off when people aren't treated equal no matter what, but I do enjoy utilizing that seniority at times.

The interaction between me and this particular individual was one of those scenarios that's difficult to explain, or put into words on paper. But I can say this much . . . Whatever she said was enough to piss me off so much that I threw my keys and badge of fifteen years on my supervisor's floor, and told her I don't get paid enough to put up with this shit.

Now, I am not an impulsive person whatsoever, as I'm sure I have already stated. So, the fact that I quit my job of over fifteen years had to be a pretty freaking big deal. I'm one of those kinds of people that can handle one, or two, or maybe three stressful events at once, but when it starts to pile on my emotions, I kind of lose it. And I lost it that day. I think I was just upset about the fact that I hadn't heard whether I was getting my raise, and then being treated like a piece of shit by that bitch just triggered the fact that I was also missing Patrick, or at least missing my escape. Or maybe I was just downright sexually repressed. I hadn't had sex since I last saw Patrick, and I guess another trigger to my breakdown was not knowing when, or if, I was ever going to see him again.

My supervisor called me the day after my work meltdown. She was really cool about it, and said they would look at the video and talk to the employee. I was a little put off by that, though, since there wasn't much to see on the video without hearing what went down. The cameras didn't have audio, so it would look like a normal brief discussion between the assistant and myself, until I ran out of the unit and into my supervisors office, which luckily was not on tape. I don't think anything was done to the employee, unfortunately, but my supervisor did give me the raise. She then told me to take a couple of months off before coming back, if I wanted to come back. Which I did. My work was my other escape, so I wasn't ready to get rid of it, no matter how much someone there pissed me off. So, I used that time off to relax as much as possible, and to plan my March trip to Texas.

So far, my 2018 was nowhere near my 2017, but I wasn't surprised. It was going to be very difficult to beat the perfection that was 2017, and I knew it would be. I think my expectations would be way too high if I thought I could even have a comparable year, but I was going to try.

Regardless, though, still no regrets.

Chapter 20

That There Pioneer Woman
(in a Southern Accent)

I was at an autism conference in Philadelphia one weekend when I finally heard something from Patrick. Luckily I wasn't speaking at the conference, just attending and learning, so I could somewhat relax while there.

Jimmy:
February 24, 12:29 p.m.
Hi Piper, how ya doing?

Me:
February 24, 12:58 p.m.
Hey you! I'm ok. At an autism conference in Philly. How are you?

Jimmy:
February 24, 1:10 p.m.
I'm good. Bet you are smarter than everyone else there . . . or at least prettier. I'm in Georgia today, leaving tomorrow, but will be back around soon.

Me:
February 24, 1:27 p.m.
I'll be in Texas next week . . . Thurs thru Sun. Let me know if you will be there.

Jimmy:
February 24, 1:34 p.m.
I will be in TX next week too. Yeah!!

And that right there was enough to make my weekend so much happier. Part of me was pissed that I was out of town when he was in Georgia, but I knew I likely couldn't see him if I was there anyway. Now I only had to wait five more days to see him again, and it was still too long. Hubs and Jack were staying home while I was in Texas, both to give me quality time with the family, and also because Jack is impossible to travel with, as stated before. So, I knew I could squeeze some quality time in there somewhere with Patrick. I didn't want to ask him if I could stay at his place because I honestly didn't even know my plans. I had a hotel room reserved, and some events were already scheduled, but the rest was playing by ear. Also, I had no idea if Patrick had a girlfriend, or someone that may be staying with him. Or maybe he just didn't want some married chick all up in his grill (pun definitely intended). Ironically, I was staying at a Hammond, which I couldn't help but think of as another sign, since that was kind of "our thing." I texted him the day before I left in hopes to see him right after I got there.

Me:
February 28, 5:15 p.m.
What are your plans tomorrow? I get into AUS around noon so I will text you sometime after that to see what you're up to. I'm staying at the Hammond Regency Austin. Is there anything fun going on in town tomorrow night?

Jimmy:
February 28, 5:53 p.m.
Wet T-shirt contest at the Butt Hut for a free carton of camel lights and $50 gift card for Tricky Ricky's bail bonds. Other than that, naw.

This particular text was one of the many reasons that I was so glad we were friends again. It may be a stupid, silly response, but he always made me giggle. Where he comes up with this shit, I have no idea. I knew there was no Butt Hut, or a Tricky Ricky's bail bonds, but I also knew that the next night would consist of numerous laughs, and I couldn't wait. However, I was kind of disappointed that there wasn't a response regarding our ritualistic Hammond hotel stay.

Right after I landed, I had lunch with Dianna, then was able to check into my hotel a little early. Most of my family was flying in the next day, so I had all night free. About five minutes after I texted Patrick to tell him I was leaving Austin and on my way to his house, he called me. Here I was thinking the same thing I always think when I'm anxiously awaiting to see Patrick. The fact that he was calling me instead of texting back with a "Great, see you soon" type of response made me worried he was calling to say he was not home and wouldn't be able to see me, or that he had to go out of town unexpectedly. But even though those sixteen-year-old insecure girl thoughts took over for a minute, they were quickly squelched when I answered the phone. Patrick was just checking on the time frame, because he did have a quick errand to run, but wanted to be home by the time I got there.

When I got to his house, it was so good to see his face. He was like the old cliché of a "breath of fresh air" for me. It was like all of my stress just dissipated when I was around him, and I was pretty positive that he was the only person in the world who did that for me. I wasn't sure if it was just that escape from reality that I loved about him, or something more. All I know is that I had to enjoy every minute of that feeling of freedom and happiness. So, I made a mental note right then and there, sitting on his couch with his dog in my lap, that I was happy. REALLY happy. And that I was going to appreciate every moment of the evening I was hopefully going to spend with him. I didn't bring anything to stay, so I knew I wouldn't be sleeping overnight, but I was still hoping to spend the majority of the night with him and only him.

We did our usual talking and laughing, and catching each other up on our lives. There was no kissing or sex yet, and I was okay with that. It made me wonder if he had a girlfriend or something, since being intimate with me appeared to be the last thing on his mind. But I truly didn't care. I could just sit and talk with him all night. However, I *was* locked and loaded, and ready for some action.

Patrick asked if I was hungry, which I was, so he took a shower and we headed out to dinner at about 7:00 p.m. Still no touching or kissing, but I was enjoying myself, nonetheless. On our way to the restaurant, I began smelling a really horrible smell. For a second I thought he may have passed some gas, so I didn't want to say anything to make him embarrassed. After a couple of minutes, the smell grew even worse, and I could tell it likely wasn't gas from a person, but more like natural gas coming from somewhere outside. I finally said something because I was not only worried we were going to blow up, but I also didn't want him to think that it was MY body emanating such a horrible smell. If he thought it was me, I was pretty sure I wasn't getting laid, and I can't say I would've blamed him.

When I mentioned the horrible smell, he told me that he actually did think it was me. I hoped he was joking, but I never knew with him. When we pulled into the parking spot outside the restaurant, I told him to drive back by the smelly area, mainly to prove to him that it wasn't my insides that were causing the entire city to reek of gas. And sure enough, when we drove back through the same neighborhood, the smell got worse. When we rolled down the window, the horribleness smacked us in the face as if we were sticking our nose up someone's ass crack.

I still don't know what we were smelling, and luckily the city didn't blow up, but there was definitely a gas leak of some sort. When we pulled back into the parking spot at the restaurant, Patrick stopped the car, looked at me and hesitated, then said, "I love you for doing that," with the biggest grin on his face. I was confused as to what he was referring to until he explained that he thought it was so funny and awesome that I made him go back, just to show him it wasn't my farts. It was kind of a weird moment to remember, and weird that he loved that about me. But it was also one of the few times that the look on his face told me a lot. The smile, hesitation, and compliment told me that he admired me, in some sort of way. I knew he didn't mean "love" as in the true-love form, but more like the *Patrick-love form*, and you know I take what I can get. And even if it was for something related to farts, I was just glad he liked me for something.

We sat down at the bar inside the restaurant, and ordered some appetizers and drinks. As we were waiting for our food, I looked across the bar and saw someone that I graduated high school with. It wasn't someone I hung out with, or was necessarily friends with, but we definitely hung in the same crowd, so I was pretty positive he would remember me. I even remembered his name, which was Joe. I couldn't believe that, since I seem to have forgotten everything about my high school days. Not because they were bad, but just because they weren't that good.

I quickly had to think about my mannerisms when we walked in. Like, was I holding Patrick's hand, or was I touching him when we sat down? It was so natural for us to be slightly touchy-feely, and I guess I felt a little more free to do that being in a different state. But I forgot that people in this state know both me *and* Patrick. And they also know, thanks to social media, that I'm married, but not to Patrick.

I continued to act like I didn't see Joe, and resumed my conversation with Patrick, all the while being super conscious about not touching him or kissing him, which I honestly could not wait to do. A woman and two teenage girls sat at the bar next to us. Since Patrick has never met a stranger, he struck up a conversation quite quickly with the ladies. After introductions, I realized they were a mom, her daughter, and her daughters friend. They explained they were just getting home from a mini vacation in Oklahoma, and tried to have Patrick guess what it is they did while visiting the panhandle state. Patrick started guessing some things, but after answering "no" every time, the mom turned to me and said, "You are a woman, you should know why we were in Pawhuska, Oklahoma." I honestly could not guess why a woman and two teenage girls were visiting small town Oklahoma, but I was glad for the distraction, and the reason to continue being oblivious to Joe sitting right across from us.

After approximately five incorrect guesses as to where the ladies went for their vacation, they finally revealed to us that they went to visit The Pioneer Woman. For those who don't know who The Pioneer Woman is, you must be living under a rock. Or, you never shop at Walmart, since she seems to be on every product they sell there. She is a famous food blogger who also sells cookbooks and cooking paraphernalia. Along with having her own TV cooking show, she has a line of dog food as well. But what made the girls even more excited than their recent tour of The Pioneer Woman Mercantile was the fact I personally knew The Pioneer Woman. Or as I know her, Ann Marie "Ree" Drummond. My brother dated Ree's younger sister for about two years. It wasn't like we were BFFs, but I definitely knew Ree on a somewhat personal level, so the mom and two girls immediately began treating us like we were celebrities. They thought I was so cool because I knew her, and she knew me. Well, I was pretty sure Ree knew me, or at least my name, not only because her sister dated my brother, but because I recently found out that Ree actually read my autism blog.

A girlfriend of mine had met Ree at a food blog conference, and asked her if she remembered me. My friend was a huge fan of Ree, so I told her before she left for the conference that she could mention my name if she wanted a reason to try to small talk with Ree. I was thinking and hoping that she would likely remember my name, or at the very least, my brother's name. Needless to say, she not only told my friend that she knew exactly who I was, but that she read every one of my blogs. That was huge for me. Here was this uber-famous woman who had achieved so much, and I was very flattered and surprised that she was taking time out of her busy schedule to read about autism from me. My blog is nowhere near popular, so I'm pretty sure her sister told her about it, or else the odds of her running across it on a normal day are pretty slim. But regardless of how and why, I was just honored that she did.

As I continued to talk everything Ree with the ladies, Joe began walking in our direction. He stopped next to my chair and said, "Hi, Piper," then turned to Patrick and said, "Hey, Patrick." Well, he definitely remembered both of us, and likely knew we were not a couple, and were not supposed to be "together" in that sense. Joe and I did the usual catching up on the past twenty-five years of our lives, which always ends up being a very abbreviated version, since twenty-five years is a long time to fit into a five-minute discussion. Joe talked briefly about his kids and his divorce, and I talked about my new epiphany of reaching out to old friends, and making the best of life. I made a point to say something about that so that he wouldn't think anything more between Patrick and I, besides old friends catching up. He seemed to be content with our answers, and we said our casual goodbyes to Joe as he left the bar.

I hadn't noticed that while I was busy talking to Joe, Patrick was busy talking to the ladies next to us about his glory days of being a famous college football player, with pictures included. I began rolling my eyes, making fun of Patrick bragging about his nineteen-year-old self, and the fact he had twenty-eight-year-old pictures in his phone to show people. The mom saw me rolling my eyes at the ridiculousness of Patrick's bragging, and asked us if we were married . . . to each other. I realized then that I had my wedding ring on, as usual, so I could see why she would think that. Plus, I knew how amazing our chemistry was together, so I could see why people would think that Patrick and I were a couple. After the mom asked us that, we looked at each other and weren't quite sure what to say, so I just blurted out that we were cousins. However, when I said this, I started laughing. I quickly explained, sort of, what we were to each other as best I could without both lying *and* telling the whole truth. I said we dated many, many years ago, but that Patrick thought he was too cool, and didn't want to be my boyfriend. And now we were just old friends catching up. I couldn't help but laugh even harder when mom concluded, "So, shouldn't it be the other way around now . . . YOU are too good for *him*?" looking at me while she said it. I knew she was completely joking, but I think that was her indirect way of saying that Patrick should have never thought he was better than me, and that he was a damn fool for letting me go. Well, I think she meant something like that, anyway. That's the way I took it, but all in good fun.

I guess it didn't hurt Patrick's feelings too bad, since he ended up buying all three ladies their entire dinner and drinks. As they walked out of the bar, they all gave Patrick a huge hug, as though they were so happy to meet a "football celebrity."

And I continued to roll my eyes.

Luckily, the hideous stench had dissipated by the time we got back to the car. And it didn't appear as though anything blew up, thank God. When we got into the car, Patrick said, "I love hanging out with you, and telling them that we were cousins, it was priceless." It was a fun AND funny moment, and I knew Patrick would get the humor in it. However, it was then that I realized something that I didn't want to realize. I realized that I might be a "cock-blocker" to Patrick, for lack of a better phrase, and that spending time with me might stop him from getting into a relationship. Don't get me wrong . . . I didn't actually want him to be in a relationship, but I know he wanted one, and not one with a married woman and an autistic child. I didn't want him to feel like spending time with me was just delaying his opportunity to get a girlfriend. Not that we were hanging out all the time, but what if he was wanting to talk to that mom in the bar, or the hot waitress, and being with me stopped him? I didn't want to be the reason that Patrick couldn't go on to bigger and better things. I knew he deserved someone available, not just perfect for him.

I was silent for a minute or two while I pondered the cock-blocking issue, then I said, "You know, the day you call me and tell me that you are getting married, or that you got some chick pregnant, I'm probably going to vomit. But after I vomit, I'm going to tell you that I'm happy for you. It's going to kill me, but I realize I'm married, and I have no right to stop you from moving on with your life, and getting everything you've ever wanted."

Patrick paused for a brief moment, then said, "Well, you will never hear me say that I got some chick pregnant." After I looked at him a little weird, he clarified, "Not that I can't get anyone pregnant, to my knowledge, but that's not who I am anymore."

I wasn't sure what to say after that. I got a little nauseous just thinking about Patrick getting married, or getting some chick pregnant. But I also knew I really didn't have the right to care. I realized that no matter how much *I* wanted to be the one marrying Patrick, it would never happen. I wondered what exactly he meant by his "that's not who I am anymore" comment. I'm assuming that he meant he wasn't some dude who went around fucking anyone and everyone, kind of like he did in college, and I'm guessing the majority of his twenties and thirties as well.

I also realized, in that very moment, that Patrick must care a little about me after all. Because if he didn't go around fucking every female with a vagina anymore, I must be a little more than a vagina. I knew he cared, but it was nice to think he might have a tiny bit of feelings for me. But Patrick confirmed my feelings when he said, "Unfortunately, Piper, you have set the bar pretty high, and finding anyone as awesome as you is going to be a tall order. But it doesn't matter anyway, because there are no more good and single ones out there anymore."

I'm not sure why I decided to be Team Patrick Needs a Girlfriend, but I told him, "Trust me, there are plenty of good ones. But you probably wouldn't even notice a good one if it bit you in the ass. You have to give the decent ones a chance."

What the fuck was I doing? I was urging him to look for a good one, and hold on to her. This statement is definitely the only thing I have ever regretted saying to Patrick. Less than a year after I told him this, trust me when I say that I was kicking my own ass for being his cheerleader that night.

I knew we were likely going to have sex that night. I also knew that I was still on a mission for an orgasm. And because I preferred the good ol' missionary position, I figured I might try something new, since that position was obviously not doing the job. I mean, it was doing the job, because it was pretty phenomenal every time, but it wasn't doing "*THE* JOB."

We began kissing the minute we walked into his house. My purse wasn't even removed from my shoulder yet before his hands were up my shirt, and my fingers were unbuttoning his pants. I know I've said this before, but Patrick was the only human that has ever caused me to lose all sense of control. I wanted to feel his naked body on me the split second his lips touched mine . . . every time!

After removing Patrick's pants, I pushed him onto his bed. I ripped off my shirt, along with the bra that he had already unhooked. I pulled my pants off in record time, and then I was on top of him, kissing his entire body. I realized then that I actually wanted to give him a blow job. This was new for me, since I had a pretty bad gag reflex. But remember, Patrick was the only man that made me lose all sanity, and definitely the only human that I wouldn't mind gagging for. However, even though I was surprised at how much I wanted his erection in my mouth, my selfish body was not willing to wait. I straddled him, and inserted his hard dick inside of me.

As I began slowly moving back and forth, and then even slower up and down, I opened my eyes to look at his face. Besides being the most beautiful human on the planet, as always, I saw something in his eyes that I hadn't seen before. The look resembled that of pure ecstasy, like he didn't want to be anywhere but where he was right then and there, and I know I felt the exact same way. It's so easy to have sex with your significant other while thinking about all of the errands you have to run the next day, or the lunch you forgot to pack for your child, because life gets in the way. No matter how much you want to focus on the sex, it can be difficult at times. But tonight I was focused on him and him only. And for the first time, it was almost as if he could sense that from me, and I think he liked it.

I continued to look into his eyes while making love to him. I could tell that he seemed to be enjoying the process a little more than he had in the past, which made sense, since he wasn't doing all of the work this time. However, in true Piper form, I got tired. I'm not gonna lie, I typically hate being on top because I am profusely out of shape. I thought my adrenaline would keep me going, but no matter how much I wanted to stay on top, my muscles were starting to shake from doing shit they are not used to doing. Like, ever. I had to roll off, but luckily Patrick wasn't done. He immediately got on top of me and finished. And as magical and perfect as it was, there was still no "O."

We fell asleep in each other's arms. When I woke up to Patrick's incessant snoring, it was 3:00 a.m. I was quickly reminded of another huge reason why we couldn't be together . . . he snored like a fucking freight train. I knew I had to get back to the hotel because all of my stuff was there, and my family would be slowly trickling in soon. I grabbed the closest T-shirt I could find, then finished getting dressed. I kissed Patrick's cheek, and quietly told him goodbye. I'm not positive about what his response was exactly, but it sounded something like, "Please stay, this is the best part."

That made me smile.

Another thing that made me smile was the fact that I had a freakin' fantastic time with my entire family, and definitely drank a little too much. Luckily I didn't make too much of a fool of myself. When I was packing up to head to the airport, I realized I couldn't find one of my favorite pair of earrings. I traced my steps to the last time I had them on, and realized it was when I was with Patrick three nights before.

Me:
March 4, 11:21 a.m.
Hi! I'm packing up to head home and realized I must've left my earrings at your house? Let me know so I know they aren't lost somewhere. Hope you are having a good time in Dallas!

I knew that he was heading to Dallas for a work trade show the day after I left his place, so I wasn't sure if he would be too busy to respond any time soon. I was pleasantly surprised when I heard his text about four minutes later.

Jimmy:
March 4, 11:25 a.m.
They're there. I will send to ya. Did you have fun with your family? I really hope this is my last trade show for a while. Hate'm.

Attached to the text was a picture of my earrings. I was a bit confused because I was pretty sure he was in Dallas, but I wasn't sure why he would've taken my earrings with him. But since I know some tricks of the trade, I saved the picture from his text into my photos. I don't know if many people are aware that if a picture is taken on a phone, and the recipient of that picture also has a phone, you can see when and where the picture was taken. Well, the older phone versions did it, anyway. Screenshots don't work, but actual pictures taken with the camera on the phone will register that information, which you can then see at the top of the picture when saved into your phone. I'm not sure if it works anymore, what with all of the constant updates. But anyway, I looked at the picture information above my earrings, and he had taken it at 7:50 p.m. on Friday, March 2. It was currently 11:00 a.m. on the fourth, so now I was even more confused why he would've taken the picture on Friday, and not let me know then that he had my earrings. Better yet, why would he have taken the picture of my earrings at all?

Me:
March 4, 11:37 a.m.
Don't worry about sending them. It'll be a reason to see you again. Let me know next time you are in Atlanta.

Jimmy:
March 4, 11:46 a.m.
Of course.

When I got to the airport, I sat and scanned my social media accounts, as usual. I came across one of those long quotes with no author. I don't know where some of them come from, but sometimes they hit hard, in good and bad ways. This one hit in a really good way, and made me happy about my relationship with Patrick, whatever that relationship actually was.

"Sometimes you meet someone, and it's so clear that the two of you, on some level, belong together. As lovers, or as friends, or as family, or as something entirely different. You just work, whether you understand one another or you're in love or you're partners in crime. You meet these people throughout your life, out of nowhere, under the strangest of circumstances, and they help you feel alive. I don't know if that makes me believe in coincidence, or fate, or sheer blind luck, but it definitely makes me believe in something."

I couldn't have said it better myself.

Chapter 21

Tore Up from the Floor Up

I got back to my reality, and quickly missed my fantasy world. I had no idea when or if I would be seeing Patrick again, so I had to appreciate my reality whether I wanted to or not. And the reality was that I was married to a good man, and I had an amazing kid that I not only worshiped, but enjoyed being around more times than not. And I had to be okay with that. At the end of the day, I was okay with that. But it was the other times of the day, like when I had to drive my son to and from school for three hours total every day, or when my husband would come home from a business trip and ignore me because of his anger, or when I had to pull dangerous objects from my son's mouth . . . those were the times when I wasn't okay with my reality. Unfortunately there were so many of those times. But, I had to be okay with my reality. I didn't have a choice. Patrick was merely an escape for me. A beautiful, sexy, funny, and amazing one at that. And even though I knew it wasn't the best choice for my escape, it was by far my favorite one.

I went back to work, and decided to focus on that for the time being. I also decided to start my licensure process for my LMFT (Licensed Marriage and Family Therapist). It was a licensure that I had been eligible for many years ago, but I hadn't felt like it was important to have until now. As evidenced in my story, autism can cause undue stress and chaos in families, and I wanted to help others with similar stressors. Autism parenting can make you feel very alone, and not many people can relate. I would be able to empathize on a level that would hopefully be beneficial for my clients. However, I started second-guessing myself, and thought that maybe I wasn't quite ready for this licensure, since I was not displaying the most appropriate coping skills and self-care ideas in my own life. But most therapists don't practice what they preach anyway, so at least I knew what I was *supposed* to say to my clients.

I tried really hard to focus on that part of my life, but I couldn't help but occasionally stray to the fantasies. They were fuel for me. Even just the thoughts of the past few times with Patrick were enough to get me through the tiring days when Jack refused to sleep, or while sitting in boring supervision groups. I felt like a sixteen-year-old again, getting through life with unrealistic sexual fantasies. But unlike my sixteen-year-old fantasies, which involved me being a backup dancer for New Kids on the Block, and having both Jonathan Knight and Joey McIntyre fall in love with me, my forty-four-year-old fantasies actually happened. I was just reliving them in my head. And knowing they really did happen, I wanted them to happen again. I mean, if I couldn't convert Jonathan Knight to a straight man and fall in love with me, at least I could get Patrick to want me. Now if only I could get him to fall in love with me. But why on earth would I want that? I didn't need more drama in my life. I guess I wanted to turn the tables to make him feel what I felt when the girl answered his door twenty-five years ago. But feeling desired by Patrick Barnes didn't seem to be enough for me. Don't get me wrong, it was amazing. But, just like most people, when I get something I want, I sometimes want more. And even though I knew we would never be together, I still wanted him to wish we could be.

One day after getting my hair did, I realized it had been a minute since I touched base with Patrick. While trying to figure out what to text him, "our" song started playing on the OG station. It was the same song from our past that was playing in the airport when I texted him the year before, so once again, I knew it had to be a sign. I took a picture of my dash that displayed the name of the song and artist, and texted only the picture to Patrick. He quickly texted back.

Jimmy:
March 22, 4:04 p.m.
Hey there, how's it going? Crazy 4 me but that's good I guess.

Me:
March 22, 4:12 p.m.
Where you at these days?

Jimmy:
March 22, 5:01 p.m.
In Nashville now. Looks like I'll be moving to Atlanta 4/1.

You would think I would be jumping up and down at the thought of Patrick being a quick car ride away from my house. But, there were two reasons why I wasn't getting overly excited quite yet. One, he had told me the same thing before, and it never happened. Two, the thought of having such easy access to Patrick scared the shit out of me. I never responded to Patrick's last text because I was afraid I would say one of the two reasons just listed.

One afternoon in mid-April, Elizabeth called and asked if I wanted to finally do our downtown ATL hotel weekend that we could not seem to accomplish no matter how hard we tried. It was always either sick kids, or sitter issues, but I was going to make sure it would happen this time. I didn't realize she was talking about the weekend coming up in four days, but I desperately needed the break! I said yes before I even knew the details, and figured I would work out childcare issues later. Elizabeth told me that she was asking last minute because she originally planned on going with her husband. He had gotten some concert tickets through work for one of his new favorite singers who was going to be playing at the City Winery. However, her husband couldn't go anymore due to a work commitment, but they had already arranged the hotel. She didn't have the concert tickets anymore, since they were given to another coworker of his, but I figured Elizabeth and I could still find something fun to do in the city. I didn't know who Johnny Burken was anyway, so not having the concert tickets anymore was no big deal for us.

When I got off the phone and looked at the calendar, I immediately yelled, "Shit!" Luckily, Jack was not in earshot. I forgot that my hubs was leaving for a long business trip on Friday afternoon, and Elizabeth had the hotel for Friday night only, so I wasn't sure if this was going to work out after all. But, I was leaving fate in the *Moral Gods'* hands once again, so I figured if it didn't work out, it wasn't meant to be. However, in true "everything seems to work out with Patrick and I for some fucking odd reason" form, the sitter texted back in record time to say she could watch Jack for the night, and even the whole weekend if I wanted her to.

But, as excited as I was to know that babysitting issues were taken care of, I had no idea whether Patrick was even going to be in Atlanta. Oh well, once again, the *Moral Gods* would decide what was supposed to happen. But I also texted Patrick to see if he was going to be around. I had to know whether I needed to stop eating for the rest of the week, in order to fit into my sexy new jeans that I purposely bought one size too small.

Me:
April 16, 8:08 p.m.
Hey there! Are you "home" in Georgia yet?

Jimmy:
April 16, 8:15 p.m.
Not yet. In TX currently. Driving there Wednesday.

Me:
April 16, 8:22 p.m.
Awesome! Well, I will be downtown Friday night.
Elizabeth and I have a hotel room. Drive safe,
and hope I get to see you.

I never heard back from Patrick that night. Like always, I wasn't surprised. It is funny, though, because as I go back and look at all the texts that I have sent to Patrick with no response, I realize how anyone could clearly see that Patrick didn't give a shit about me. Honestly, I think I knew this, but I didn't care. I knew he liked me in his own special way of liking people, whatever that meant. But usually when you text someone and say that you hope to see them, and they don't respond with *anything*, that likely means they don't hope to see *you*. Regardless of whether this was just me making excuses, I did always remind myself that I was married, and I could totally understand why I had to do all the work, and why he always hesitated to say he wanted to see me too. But I also knew that even if he didn't want to see me, I wanted to see him, and I was going to make it happen, just like all the other times. You see, I have a good sense of self-worth. I'm far from conceited, and I'm able to see how far from perfect I actually am, especially with the whole committing adultery thing. But, I didn't need someone to tell me they wanted to see me too. I would rather people be honest and not say anything than say something they didn't mean. And I really didn't give a shit at that point in time about anything but getting my escape, and my fantasies fulfilled. At least, that's what I thought.

Elizabeth and I made it to our hotel on Friday around 4:00 p.m. Traffic was a bitch, so it took a little longer than expected, but since we didn't have any set plans, it didn't really matter. I still hadn't heard anything from Patrick since I texted him four days before, so I waited a couple of hours to text him with my fingers crossed, in hopes to see him at some point in the evening.

Me:
April 20, 6:09 p.m.
We just checked in to our hotel . . . are you in
the ATL? Anything fun going on tonight?

I fucking flipped my lid when I read the text that quickly came from him in return.

Jimmy:
April 20, 6:15 p.m.
Johnny Burken at the City Winery ... ever
heard of him?

It was way too much of a coincidence that Johnny Burken was indirectly the reason we were there. Unfortunately, we didn't have tickets to the show anymore, but I assumed Patrick's text meant that he was in town, and would be at the concert. I had seen something that afternoon about the concert being sold out, so now I was bummed that we didn't get to keep the tickets after all.

Me:
April 20, 6:24 p.m.
So funny you say that ... he is sort of the reason
we are here, but we don't have the tickets anymore.

Jimmy:
April 20, 6:29 p.m.
Funny u say that ... we just got done playing golf
Together ... we're related.

Attached to Patrick's text was a picture of him and some long-bearded dude, which I could only assume was this Johnny guy, but I had no idea what he looked like. I then searched Johnny Burken on the internet so I could see a picture of him, and low and behold, it was exactly who Patrick was standing next to in his picture. Now Elizabeth's husband was going to hate us because we know someone who knew Johnny personally, and her husband was supposed to be the one going to the concert, not us. But we were likely not going to the show anyway, due to it being sold out. But then I thought, *Wait, if they are related, I'm sure he could hook a sister up.*

Me:
April 20, 6:42 p.m.
I saw that he was sold out, so if you could swing
us some tickets since you got the in with the
relation, we're there. If not, that's cool too. NP

I figured why not. I wouldn't normally be so pushy and make him feel weird about getting us tickets, but since I just saw a picture of them playing golf together, I thought it was likely not a problem on his end. If it was a problem, he would just tell me, and he knows I would still love him anyway. I mean, I wasn't pimpin' myself out for some backstage passes, or anything. But I would sleep with Patrick for them, if necessary. Sometimes you gotta take one for the team!

Jimmy:
April 20, 7:11 p.m.
I'm meeting him bout 9. Shouldn't be a problem.

Me:
April 20, 7:47 p.m.
Just let me know when and where, and we will be there.

Jimmy:
April 20, 8:46 p.m.
These are yours . . .

Attached to his text was a picture of two tickets, but they looked more like VIP passes. They didn't say VIP, they just said "GA," for General Admission. But they resembled passes, not concert tickets.

I know I should've been happy that I was getting into a sold out concert for free, which I was happy about, but I really just wanted to see Patrick. Elizabeth immediately called her husband to rub it in, and I could hear him screaming through the phone. Not necessarily an anger scream, just a "I'm so fucking jealous of you right now" scream. She didn't give too many details to him about from whom and how she got them, so as not to give away any clues about my adulterous shenanigans.

We met Patrick at a bar across the street from the venue. I guess I was also super excited for Elizabeth to finally meet Patrick. I had actually talked to her about him probably five years prior, which was three years before we even reconnected. Elizabeth and I were out one night talking about old flames, and ones we still carried a small torch for, and he was the only one I thought of. So, now she would finally meet the mystery man.

We greeted each other with our signature hug, plus the innocent peck on the cheek. It had only been less than two months since I last saw him, but because I never know when and if I will see him again, it made my heart happy when I did. And my va-jay-jay happy too.

Elizabeth and Patrick hit it off just fine, which I knew they would because they are both so easy to get along with. We walked into the venue shortly before the show started. One of the band members, which we didn't know was a band member, began talking to Elizabeth. He jokingly asked her if she wanted to watch the show from the stage, since she was all of four feet nine inches tall, and because we were all the way in the back behind the crowd. She just laughed, not having a clue who he was, but appreciated that he acknowledged her height limitations. When he walked through the crowd and got onto the stage to check the equipment and instruments, Elizabeth kicked herself for not following him. We realized then that he was the keyboard player for Johnny Burken, and that he was probably serious about letting her go on the stage to watch the whole concert. But then she was kind of happy she didn't, since her husband would never let her live it down.

I don't even remember much about the concert, because I was having so much fun catching up with Patrick, as usual. Right when the show started, a friend that Patrick stayed with whenever he visited Atlanta, joined us. I loved Jamie immediately. He was a little younger than us, but very cool and fun, and easy to talk to. Which wasn't surprising, since Patrick was the same way. Patrick told me that they had been good friends for a while, and that he appreciated Jamie letting him stay every time he was in town. I figured if he put up with Patrick staying in his house for long periods of time, he had to be pretty awesome. I love a lot of people, but I don't necessarily want them staying in my house. So, kudos to Jamie.

I know Patrick was trying to enjoy the concert, since he was obviously a fan of Johnny Burken, but I couldn't help but want to catch up. Luckily, he didn't seem too bothered by my incessant questions, and reciprocated the conversation, even though we had to scream at each other over the music. One of the first questions that I asked Patrick was how he and Johnny Burken were related. Not too surprisingly, he admitted that he was just joking, and that there wasn't any blood bond between the two. But Patrick did say they had become friends through Jamie, which was still cool.

As usual, I had been drinking, so I don't remember many details of our conversations. But I always remember those few times when he says something very important and meaningful to me, and luckily one of those times happened. We were talking about the last time we had seen each other, and the fun night that we spent together. He laughed about our interaction with the girls at the bar, and the smell that took over the entire city. Out of nowhere he brought up the sex, and the fact that I was on top that night. He rolled his eyes and said to me, "When your beautiful naked body was on top of me, I felt like the luckiest man in the world." I think the eye roll was because he knew he was going to be vulnerable in what he was about to say, and I don't think he was used to letting his guard down so much. He always complimented me, but this one insinuated that I made him happy. Or, at least my out of shape, naked body made him happy for a brief moment that night. I was so content with the words that came out of his mouth that all I could do was look into his eyes, and give him the biggest smile that I had probably ever given anyone.

After the show, we walked to a bar around the corner, and the four of us sat down together at the bar. While we sipped our drinks, Jamie asked me how I knew Patrick. I wasn't sure what Jamie already knew about me, but figured I would give him the abbreviated version. I said, "Well, we have known each other since high school, and we sort of dated in college, but he was a player and too cool for me, so he didn't want to date just me."

Jamie's response made me laugh when he said, "Oh, he just THOUGHT he was cool, I'm pretty sure it was just in his head." I laughed, but regardless, I have always felt like I wasn't good enough for Patrick. Don't get me wrong, I know I am good enough! Period! But I have never felt like I was good enough in Patrick's eyes. However, his comment earlier about feeling like the luckiest man in the world made me question that. Maybe he did think I was good enough after all.

Somehow we all got on the hot topic of politics, and Elizabeth and Jamie got into a heated discussion. Luckily, not an argument, just emphatically agreeing on the present political situation. Since I tend to avoid any politics when in a social setting, I just turned to Patrick and smiled. He looked at me, shook his head, then looked away. Of course that made me wonder what he was thinking, and if he was also not in the political mood, so I asked him, "What was the head shake for?" At first, he just said, "Nothing." But we all know that saying "nothing" after a head shake never actually means nothing, so I asked him what he was thinking. He looked down, and quietly said, "God, I just want to tear you up right now," through clenched teeth. Luckily he didn't say this too loud, and the others didn't hear it. The only thing I could say in return was the first thing that popped in my head, which was, "Do it, then."

I think I got instantly wet when he said that. I quickly imagined him actually tearing me up, which in layman's terms is basically ripping off my clothes, throwing me down on the bed, and fucking me. And I was more than ready for a good teardown. However, I wasn't quite sure how this was going to go. I was sharing a hotel room with Elizabeth, and I know for a fact that she wouldn't really appreciate hearing me moan and scream in excitement from the other bed just inches from her head. I also had no idea if Patrick had his own room, or slept on the couch when he stayed with Jamie. But I could hear the desperation in his voice, so I was going to make it happen no matter what. I did a good job of keeping the desperation out of *my* voice, but the desperation was definitely emanating from my va-jay-jay.

Elizabeth must have picked up on my desperate, emanating va-jay-jay, because she quickly said she was going to head back to the hotel to go to bed. She took a ride share, and the three of us continued with one more drink. I think Jamie must have also sensed my desperately emitting va-jay-jay because he insisted that I join them back at his place. Even if I didn't get the opportunity to get "tore up," I still wasn't ready to say goodnight to Patrick, so I joined them in a ride share back to Jamie's, hoping and praying the whole way that Patrick had his own room.

I was pleasantly surprised when we walked in the door, and Patrick immediately escorted me to *his* room. The house was big enough for a couple more rooms, so I was pretty sure he wasn't sharing this one with anybody. My excitement quickly lessened when I looked on the dresser, and saw a plate with a short line of coke. Not soda, obviously, but cocaine. Now, I have never actually seen real coke on a plate, because I have never personally done it. But I've seen enough movies, and I was pretty sure that's what it was. I didn't really care about other people using drugs, and I definitely never judged others for doing what they wanted, I was just personally not a fan of anything illegal. Even though I never had an intense conversation about drugs with Patrick, he did know that drugs weren't my thing, and I did know that sometimes they were his thing. And I never gave him shit for it. But when he realized that I saw the plate, he denied that it was his, and said Jamie must have left it there, even before I could say anything. I'm pretty sure it was Patrick's, but I honestly didn't care. If anything, I was hoping it would just enhance his performance.

Patrick yelled to Jamie over the loud music that we were going to bed, and he shut the bedroom door. I tilted my head and looked at Patrick as if to say . . . "Wait, isn't he going to wonder why you are going to bed with a married woman?" Jamie knew I was married, since it was brought up in conversation at the bar. I didn't necessarily care if Jamie knew that I was fucking his friends' brains out in his guest bedroom, but he didn't know me at all. I didn't want him to think terribly of me after meeting me for the first time, even though I was doing terrible things. I was hoping Patrick would clarify our relationship, and not make me sound too much like a whore, even though I was starting to feel like one.

As much as I wanted to rip his clothes off, I was waiting for Patrick to initiate. We lay on the bed and talked for at least an hour. I got some kissing in there, but we were clothed, for the most part. Oh, I did have my shirt on but no bra, because I forgot to mention the first thing he did when we got on the bed. Patrick got this crazy, probably cocaine-induced, idea that he would put the two Johnny Burken show passes on both of my breasts, covering my nipples only, then take a picture. I could actually see his vision, plus I was almost wasted, so I agreed to this. If my face wasn't in it, nobody would know they were *my* tits. There were only a limited number of people who have seen my boobs, so I wasn't worried about anyone knowing they were mine if they saw the picture. Plus, Patrick did say that he wouldn't go around showing it, because he didn't want other people seeing my boobs. I thought that was kind of sweet and territorial, and I liked it.

But anyway, a problem with the "pass over the tits" idea arose when Patrick could only find *my* pass, but not his. This left only one pass, which is kind of hard to cover two 34DD breasts. So, Patrick put the one pass in the middle of both of my boobs, covered my face with a pillow, and took a picture of my tits. It actually ended up being a pretty cool picture, if I can say so myself. I was a little hesitant to let him show it to Johnny, but I figured he would be the only person who I wouldn't mind seeing it, since he's never met me. I told Patrick that if I ever saw my tits on an album cover, that I better get some proceeds. Patrick texted the picture to Johnny that night, at 2:30 a.m. As of this writing, I have never seen my tits on a T-shirt or album cover, so I should be good.

I was ready and willing to be "tore up" that night, but I wasn't. Instead, I was gently caressed, and softly kissed, and made love to. And I was more than okay with that. It was beautiful, and intimate, and just *really* nice. It lasted longer than usual, so maybe the cocaine helped. Ha ha! I just took it all in, every second, and every inch of him. I acted as though it was going to be the last time I would ever be able to make love to Patrick. For all I knew, it was. Something had to give sooner or later. Either my husband was going to find out, or I would want to work on my marriage and stop all contact with Patrick, or, heaven forbid, Patrick got a girlfriend. I knew our ending was inevitable, I just didn't know when it would be. And I definitely didn't realize how *hard* it would be when that day finally came.

I know you all are wondering about the orgasm, but no. Still no "O." But honestly, I loved making love to Patrick, I didn't need an orgasm. His body on mine, his dick inside me, and his lips all over my lips and breasts were the only "Os" I needed. There was a euphoric feeling that can only be felt and not described every time I was with him, clothed or naked, but especially naked. I hope everyone gets their "Patrick" at least once in their lives. Even for that brief moment, it's everything!

When I got back home the next day, I had to quickly take over Jack duties, and return to autism-land. Even on a little less than four hours of sleep, I was ready and prepared to be autism mom all by myself for the next week. It was amazing how one fantastic night could tide me over for a while, both physically and emotionally. But, I also knew that in about two to three weeks, I was going to start having Patrick withdrawals.

Right after the sitter left, I texted Patrick just to let him know I made it home safe and sound.

Me:
April 21, 4:01 p.m.
I just wanted you to know that I made it home,
and that I had a great time. I LOVED Jamie, btw.
Thanks for including us.

Jimmy:
April 21, 5:23 p.m.
Ur my BFF. He loved u too.
And this is from another chick who loves
people who snore . . .

Attached to the text was the picture he took of my tits. Hey, you never know when you might need a picture of your own tits, so I saved it in my phone. And luckily, this particular picture was actually kind of cool. I knew he was probably still bitter about me leaving in the middle of the night, and he also likely knew that I left because of his snoring, hence the snore comment.

I loved the fact that he called me his "BFF." That was just confirmation for me that at the end of the day, we were friends. And I did cherish that. But, I had to know if Johnny had responded about the tit pic yet.

Me:
April 21, 5:43 p.m.
Did Johnny say anything about the pic? Like, is
it going to be on the next album cover? I want
the proceeds.

I was busy being autism mom, so I didn't even know if Patrick had responded until the next morning when I saw he texted late at night.

Jimmy:
April 22, 12:18 a.m.
Burn that picture now, I erased it too . . .
Yesterday was one of the best nights ever.
It will make the book. Johnny fortunately
thought the pic was sexy and funny AF. When
I saw he was calling me this afternoon I thought,
oh shit, might have been overstepping my new
bromance . . . then he asked me to make a
T-shirt and hoodie for his tour merch. Yay!
Hope ur having a good night.

Me:
April 22, 9:08 a.m.
That's awesome! As long as the T-shirts and
hoodies don't have my tits on 'em.
And I hope I had a little something to do with
it being one of your best nights.

Jimmy:
April 22, 9:13 a.m.
Of course u did.

Chapter 22

Where's Jimmy?

For the next month, Patrick and I had an occasional text exchange. And surprisingly, a few of them initiated by him. Most of the time they were pictures of some kind of inside joke between us, or an article regarding something we talked about. It was getting to the point where every little thing I saw reminded me of him, and that freaked me out. It had me questioning if I was in love, or if I was just thoroughly enjoying having my friend back in my life, or if I was starting to rely a little too much on my next escape to get through the day. I kept wondering why we would have so many little inside jokes, and similar likes and dislikes. Don't get me wrong, there definitely was a lot that we didn't necessarily agree on, but we both saw the humor and happiness in very similar things. But, what did it mean? I was always trying to figure out why almost every detail continued to fall into place when it came to Patrick.

During that month, I also went on vacation with my husband for a week. We went to Miami, and had a great time together. It made me realize how good I actually had it. Granted, I felt like I was still having my cake and eating it, but I felt like just having the proverbial cake, which in this case hubby, was enough. He was a wonderful, caring, loving person who always put his family first. That was the number one priority, and I knew enough about Patrick to know that he would never compare as a husband and father. There was nothing to compare. Hubs was the best. But I still couldn't get Patrick out of my mind, for some odd fucking reason.

One morning I was eating breakfast at a local breakfast place, waiting to pick up my son from school for an early morning speech therapy appointment, when Facebomb had to remind me that one year ago that day, I was in LA. There were no memories on there of Patrick, since I didn't post anything then. But there was a memory check in post from the restaurant that Heather and I went to. So of course, as always, it made me think of Patrick, and how I texted him for the first time from that very restaurant. The memories made me suddenly realize how much the last year had most definitely, without a doubt, been my best year ever. Not necessarily because of Patrick, even though he was definitely part of the "best" of the year. But, I wouldn't have even reached out to him in the first place if I wasn't already feeling good from starting my life-changing skincare, which did just that, and losing some unexpected but much needed weight. So, the fact that I was feeling good about myself already made it easier to reach out. Plus, in early 2017, Jack had gotten into the best and only school I had wanted him in since he was diagnosed with autism. That in and of itself was enough to render 2017 my #BestYearEver. Then to add Patrick, plus numerous and amazing girls trips, plus quality family time to top the year off, there's really not much that could have made it better.

I felt it was important to let Patrick know how happy I was that we were friends again. I was so worried about losing *that* part, in the mix of all this physical stuff. I remembered how he promised me that first night in the Hammond that we would be friends no matter what happened between the sheets. But now, I'm kind of mad that I believed him.

Me:
May 18, 10:18 a.m.
Happy 1 year anniversary. Ha! But seriously, Facebomb reminded me that I was in LA 1 yr ago today. I'm so glad I texted you that day, and so happy we are friends again.

Jimmy:
May 18, 10:26 a.m.
We're not friends. I tolerate you!
Jk. You're my favorite friend that's a female.
Stephen has the other title.
I go back to China Sunday so say a rittle prayer
for my safe return prease.

There he goes again, indicating that I'm his BFF, in female form, anyway. And, there he goes again making a joke about our friendship at first. It was so his MO to start texts with a somewhat insulting joke. But it was who he was, and most of the time, it made me laugh. And lastly, there he goes again, making some racial slur with the insult of the way Asians say their "l's." That characteristic of Patrick's I could definitely do without.

Me:
May 18, 10:47 a.m.
Safe travels. When are you getting back?
And when are you coming this way again?

Jimmy:
May 18, 10:52 a.m.
5/28 & never

Great, he wasn't coming back to Georgia. Well, he says that now, but who knows what he will say next week. He seemed to change his mind about his living arrangements every time the wind blew.

Me:
May 18, 11:29 a.m.
Well, that kinda sucks!

Jimmy:
May 18, 11:38 a.m.
Guess you'll have to follow me on Instapic

What? That was kind of a weird retort. What does following him on Instapic have anything to do with seeing him? I guess he was insinuating that since we likely wouldn't see each other again, Instapic would be the only way to catch up on his life. I did start following him that night, but there wasn't much on there. It had an occasional post of a product from his company, or a rare picture of him and a friend with some of his clothing line "gear" on.

It looked like this might be the last of Patrick, and I hated it. I had to think of what my life would be like without such a fun escape. My life kind of sucked, on average, so I had to find another outlet, another fantasy that I could make come true. Not only is it my fear in life, but it is practically a guarantee that I will have to take care of Jack until the day I take my last breath. Just let that sink in a little bit. Not very many people in this world know that the rest of their life is going to be spent taking care of somebody else. And I mean "taking care of" in every description possible from bathing, dressing, and meal preparation to driving around to various therapy appointments all day every day. I saw a meme the other day that said something about how autism moms can't die, even of old age. But as much as you and I might laugh at that, it's very accurate. There's nobody left to take care of our babies, and I know Jack is going to need all the help he can get. So, it's not an option for me to be there for him as long as I physically, spiritually, and emotionally can.

And that little tidbit of information was just given to reiterate the fact that . . . I needed a fucking escape! I needed something to look forward to! I had no trips planned, or any future plans to see Patrick. And right as I was stressing out about that fact, my phone rang. It was Dianna in Texas calling to invite me to her mother's seventieth birthday party. I was very close to her and her family in junior high and high school, so I was excited that they invited me.

I made my travel arrangements for June, and luckily my parents would be there, so I could stay at their house instead of a hotel. Barbara, Dianna's mom, didn't know that I was coming, so I couldn't wait to surprise her. At least now I had something fun to focus on. Not that a seventieth birthday party was going to give me the same kind of feels that Patrick would (pun intended), but it was still a fun trip to plan. I had other friends that I loved catching up with every time I went to Texas, so I texted them all and made lunch and dinner plans for most of my time there.

I knew Patrick was in China, so I didn't bother to text him. I had no idea what time it was there, or if he could even get texts. I hadn't been out of the country for over six years, and I was pretty sure technology had improved since then, but figured I would just wait to see if I ever heard from him. Luckily, I didn't have to wait very long.

Jimmy:
May 26, 10:28 a.m.
Guess where Jimmy's at . . .

Attached to Patrick's text was a picture of him standing in front of a billboard with Chinese writing all over it. Well, I don't know Chinese, so I'm assuming that's what it was. I was actually quite shocked that he was texting me, especially from a different country. I mean, he barely texted me when he was in the fucking US, so why do it from across the world? I guess I should just be happy he texted at all.

Me:
May 26, 10:35 a.m.
I'm guessing somewhere in China? Hong Kong?

Jimmy:
May 26, 10:52 a.m.
Nope. Heaven!

Me:
May 26, 11:12 a.m.
I'm glad you are enjoying the trip. Surprised, but glad. So, I guess you are never coming home?

After I sent this text, my husband and I went to eat brunch at our favorite restaurant. We had a sitter for a few hours, so we were taking advantage of it. After we ordered our food, the sitter sent us a cute video of Jack playing at the park she had taken with her phone. I handed my phone to hubs so that he could watch the video while I went to the restroom. As I was sitting on the toilet, I got a weird feeling. I began to freak out, worried that Patrick would text me back while my husband was watching the video on my phone. I had face recognition to unlock the phone, so he couldn't read any text if my phone was closed. But, it was open for the video, and he could read a text that came through, or could go to my app and read my texts while my phone was already open. But then I figured there was no way in hell Patrick would likely respond anyway. And even if he did, it wouldn't be anything incriminating, so nothing to worry about. Right?

I got back to the table, hoping the whole way that my weird "on the toilet" feeling was all in my head. Hubs acted normal, and we talked about the video of Jack. Whew! Thank God I dodged that bullet. When the food came, I was midway opening my mouth to eat my yummy egg sandwich when hubby asks, "Who's Jimmy?"

For one split second, I had no idea what he was talking about. I didn't know a Jimmy, so I didn't know who and in what context he was referring to. And literally one millisecond later, I figured it out. And can I just say, I don't do stupid well, and I can never tell a lie. I tried to be all nonchalant, acting like I was trying really hard to think of a Jimmy. And the only thing I could come up with was, "Jimmy? I don't know. Why?" And yes, it probably sounded exactly like you would think a guilty person sounded. Hubs then said, "Jimmy texted you when you were in the bathroom, and it said something about getting you to come with him."

Now I was even more confused. Not only was I surprised that Patrick texted me back at all, I was more surprised that he was coming to get me, since he was in China. Luckily, my confusion probably helped me look a little more innocent.

I then figured the best thing to do was to tell most of the truth, leaving all of the other *stuff* out. So, I said, "Oh, Jimmy! That's my old friend from high school. He was probably joking about something . . . he always jokes around."

I was hoping and praying that I was pulling this somewhat of a lie off. Everything that I just told him was 100 percent accurate, I just left out that "Jimmy" was actually Patrick, who was actually in China. And, of course, I left out all of the other unnecessary juicy details for obvious reasons. I figured I would look less guilty if I actually checked the text, since I was supposed to have no idea why he was texting. So, I picked up my phone and looked at it.

> **Jimmy:**
> May 26 12:15 p.m.
> I'm coming home, but only to get you to come back with me.

Of all the fucking texts that my husband had to see. I guess I should be happy that it didn't say anything naughty, and it didn't say anything about him being in China, so it could've been referencing any place for him to take me. But just the fact that he was going to pick me up and take me anywhere was a little hard to explain. Then I realized that he was just joking anyway, because there's no way that he would actually come and get me and take me to China. Therefore, I didn't have to lie when I said, "Oh yeah, that's just Jimmy being Jimmy." Because it actually was just that. And I guess I was convincing, since the topic of Jimmy wasn't brought up again.

After the shock of hubs seeing the text wore off, I realized what the text actually said. It made me very happy inside that even though Patrick was joking around, he was joking around about getting me and taking me to China. So, joking or not, at least the thought crossed his mind. And I will always take what I can get.

Chapter 23

That Damn Thumbs-Up Emoji!

One morning, after a no-sleep evening with Jack, I decided I needed a little break. Since Patrick didn't seem to be an option anymore, I had to settle for a "vacation" with Jack. I put vacation in quotes, because any trip with Jack is FAR from a vacation. Any trip with any kid is unlikely relaxing, but vacationing with one autistic kid is probably equivalent to taking about ten little kids to a third world country. Outside of our limited world, Jack's need for constant attention is even more than when at home, since our home is slightly "autism-proof." But most other houses and hotels have picture frames, and candles, and little trinkets here and there, which is guaranteed to end up in Jack's mouth, or thrown on the floor within minutes of eyeballing it. Unfortunately, orally is how Jack explores his environment, as the occupational therapist once explained to me. While us neurotypicals use our hands and eyes, which are much less intrusive, he uses his mouth as the sensory mode. He has a "chewy" attached to him at all times, which helps some. And no, he's not a dog, but it is similar to a dog chewy. And until you have a severely autistic child with oral issues, you have zero right to say I'm a terrible mom because I give my child a chew toy. Trust me, people say things, and I've heard this one a few times. All the more reason why I needed a fucking escape. "Autism-momming" can be really hard, and sometimes it feels like you are being kicked in the gut while you are already on the ground, barely breathing. It's a tough journey, and stupid people have a tendency to make it worse.

So, Jack and I went to stay at our friends' house in Hilton Head. Since Jack likes to swim, and they have a pool, I knew we would be good, for the most part. The only area we struggled with was sleep, which was only surprising because he was swimming for numerous hours a day. Normally, no sleep for Jack is quite common. But the child was swimming for ten straight hours on some days, or at least in the pool for that long. Any normal human would sleep good after a day like that, or at least get a decent night's sleep. But no, not Jack. At about day three, I was barely hanging on with only four hours of sleep a night, on average. I couldn't nap because someone had to watch Jack at all times while he was in the pool, or watch his oral fixations when he was in the house, and I didn't want to put that responsibility on my friends. It's tough to literally chase him around just to make sure he's not jumping off the balcony, or eating the remote control, which can happen in a matter of seconds with Jack.

After a brief rain shower one day, a beautiful rainbow appeared in the sky. I'm not big on rainbows, but it was really pretty, so I took a picture and texted it to Patrick, using the same concept he did when he was in China. I wanted him to guess where I was, because I hadn't told him.

Me:
May 30, 2:53 p.m.
Where's Piper? Tell me something good . . .
I'm close to miserable. Did you make it home?

Jimmy:
May 30, 3:00 p.m.
I did. I wish I could, but all good news is business based. All else is miserable. Mizz ya.
U in Hawaii?

Me:
May 30, 3:09 p.m.
I wish! Friend's house in Hilton Head. Jack isn't

letting me sleep, so I'm running on fumes. Glad business is good.

Jimmy:
May 30, 3:15 p.m.
Poor thing . . . sorry. When's ur next alone vacation time?

I was surprised and happy that he wanted to know my next vacation time, because the question felt like he was hoping to see me during my next break. Maybe that's not at all what he was insinuating, but I was hoping. I was eager to tell him that I was going to be in Texas in a few weeks, and had my fingers crossed that he would be too.

Me:
May 30, 3:22 p.m.
My friends mom is having a surprise birthday party in Austin next month, so I'll be in TX for a few days. Other than that, no big vacate in the near future.

Jimmy:
May 30, 3:25 p.m.
Fk yes!

I assumed this meant that he was going to be there as well, and was excited to see me, but I had to make sure. There are many things that can be construed from a "Fk yes."

Me:
May 30, 3:27 p.m.
Will you be there?

Jimmy:
May 30, 3:31 p.m.
I will be now. What days?

Wow! He was actually excited to see me? I don't remember a time that he appeared this eager to see me, and I loved it. And I definitely don't remember a time that he actually wanted to know the dates to make sure he was available. Hell, when I told him I was going to be in a hotel in downtown Atlanta, he didn't even give me a fucking thumbs-up emoji, let alone any response whatsoever. So, this was kind of a new Patrick, and I couldn't wait to see it to believe it.

> **Me:**
> May 30, 3:52 p.m.
> I don't remember the party date, but I'll be there June 20–24.

Jimmy:
May 30, 3:56 p.m.
#metoo. I can pick you up from the airport.
The pool is full and feels amazing.

Cool! From the sound of it, he not only wanted to see me, but wanted to spend some quality time with me. This made me internally jump up and down! I couldn't actually jump up and down because my friends and Jack were nearby, but Lord, I wanted to.

> **Me:**
> May 30, 4:02 p.m.
> Yay! Because I don't think my parents pool will be ready by then.

Jimmy:
May 30, 4:12 p.m.
Probably should just stay here then. There is a bad ass show on the 20th at Broken Wheel, let's go!

> **Me:**
> May 30, 4:15 p.m.
> I'll check what time I land, but that sounds fun.

O.M.G. He really did want to see me, and even offered for me to stay with him. Because I know Patrick, I know he was partly kidding. But I'm sure if I said, "Okay, I'll stay with you," he likely wouldn't argue. I remembered that when I was in Texas last, he told me that the next time I was in town, I could stay at his place whether he was there or not. So, maybe he was a little serious. I thought it was weird when he told me this back in March, so I told him I would never expect to be able to stay at his place. First of all, he was just renting, and I think month to month, so he could be out of there any day. Also, I told him that I can't assume that he wouldn't have a girlfriend, which I would be imposing on. He just rolled his eyes when I said that. But that was the reality of the situation, even if I hated the thought.

I figured that was the last of our text exchange, for a while at least, until two hours later when he texted again.

> **Jimmy:**
> May 30, 6:42 p.m.
> Send me a pic. A good one . . .

This made me literally laugh out loud . . . and smile. Even if he just wanted it to jack off, I was more than okay with that. As long as he thought about me when he did it, I was going to send him a sexy one. But then I realized he already had a picture of my tits, what else did he want? I definitely was not going to send a pic of my va-jay-jay, so I just sent him a recent decent selfie. No bikini or underwear, but he could use his imagination. I was in the middle of fixing Jack his dinner, so it took a while to text him back with the picture. I also included a little inside joke between us about masturbation in the shower . . .

> **Me:**
> May 30, 7:49 p.m.
> Sorry for the delay . . . I was feeding Jack. I hope you weren't waiting in the shower.

> **Jimmy:**
> May 30, 7:54 p.m.
> I was in the pool. Ur a great mom, really. I think ur patience is sexy af. I mean it. I know I clown a lot but I love your pace in life.

His text took me by surprise. I didn't talk much about Jack, or parenting for that matter, when I was around Patrick. When in his presence was the only time I didn't have to be responsible for anything or anyone. It was like my world stood still for those hours that I felt like I could do anything, and be happy without worrying about life. Every time I hung out with Patrick, I would laugh so hard and get lost in the moment so much that I forgot all about autism, and the shit that comes with it. So, the fact that he acknowledged my parenting was very touching.

I also must put on a good show for him, because my pace can actually be quite crazy. But I guess when he only sees the good and happy Piper, he thinks I'm always like that. I wanted to tell him how that wasn't my normal persona . . . that I'm normally a train wreck, and hate autism some days, and cry a lot. But he did see my best side, so I was going to let him continue to think that was the real me. I *was* real every time I was with him, but that was because he made me feel happy and free. And as cliché as it sounds, he brought out the best in me, which is a side that I hadn't seen for many years.

The next two weeks were spent finishing out our "vacation," and starting my REAL vacation while Jack was in summer camp. I loved when he was in summer camp, for so many reasons. The main reason being that it was located about two miles from my house, so it was a breath of fresh air, compared to the three hour total commute per day in the car that I spend during the school year.

One summer day I went shopping, which was actually quite rare for me, and bought two new swimsuits. Swimsuit shopping day is probably the least favorite day for most women, and I was no exception. But I had lost a few pounds, and I wanted to show it off for the first time ever. I actually bought a bikini, which I don't think I had done since high school or early college, when I was at least fifteen pounds lighter. I was so excited about Patrick's pool, and I fantasized all day every day about both of us lying around his pool, talking, and doing other things. Just basically relaxing, which I rarely got to do. I did get some relaxation while Jack was in camp, but I always had to get back in the car at some point and pick him up to take him to occupational therapy, or speech therapy, or a swim lesson. And I wanted an actual vacation that didn't involve a schedule, or a limited time frame to get everything done. I wanted a vacation where I didn't have to make any food for anyone, or for myself. Not that I was a big cook, but cutting up that corn dog in just the right size circles can be exhausting work, let alone getting it out of the microwave fast enough before a meltdown occurs. And, I wanted a vacation where I could literally sleep, eat food made by someone else, drink some alcohol here and there, and just laugh and talk with friends and family. I couldn't wait.

I realized I hadn't heard from Patrick in a couple of weeks, so I wanted to make sure he was still able to pick me up from the airport. He always followed through with what he said he was going to do, but you know how insecure I was when it came to him. And I knew from my parents that they'd had some pretty fierce storms in his area, so I was hoping and checking that all was still a go.

Me:
June 14, 6:55 p.m.
I hope your pool is still good to go after the storms y'all had cuz I have some new swim suits. You still picking me up next Wednesday?

I had to work for the next three days, so it wasn't until Sunday afternoon that I realized Patrick had never texted me back. Not that I hadn't thought about it at all, but it hadn't bothered me until then. My trip was only three days away, so if he wasn't going to be there to get me, someone had to be. I had plenty of friends and family that could and would do it, but I wanted Patrick to. He's the one who offered, and I wanted to spend any time I could with him. I thought it was kind of weird and unlike him to not respond at all to a question. Not responding to a basic text, yes, but not an actual question about picking me up. But, he was pretty good at follow through, so I don't know why I was fretting. I decided to text again just to make my sixteen-year-old, insecure self happy.

Me:
June 17, 12:27 p.m.
I realized I never heard back from you after my
last text . . . let me know if you can still pick me
up Wednesday 10:45.

I still had five more hours at work, and I put my phone in my pocket so that I could feel the vibration when he texted me back. However, when I still hadn't heard from him around 4:00 p.m., I started to get a little anxious. He usually didn't blow me off this long, especially when it involved seeing each other. It definitely made me wonder about some things, but I wasn't going to let my anxiety and insecurities win. Even if he didn't text me back, I had plenty of people who loved me, and would come and get me in a heartbeat. In moments like this, I did wonder why I was so eager to spend time with someone who didn't make me a priority.

I texted Elizabeth from work around 5:00 p.m., stressing to her about his lack of response. She basically said the same thing I was thinking . . . *If he wants to spend time with you, he will.* Simple, right? Elizabeth once asked me why I was so adamant about spending time with Patrick, when he rarely went out of his way to spend time with me. And for the most part, she was correct. I was doing most of the work, but that is when I always started giving myself the excuse that I was married, and pursuing anything with me was not possible anyway. I also made the excuse around the fact that I wasn't trying to pursue a relationship with Patrick, so why did it matter if he wanted to be with me or not? I didn't really have to worry about coming on too strong, or not strong enough. I didn't have to play the dating games that I hated so much when I was single. I had a husband, and a good one at that. But I did love my fantasy man too. And I wasn't willing to give him up just yet if he was still willing to spend that fantasy time with me. And until that moment, sitting at my desk at work waiting for his response, I had always believed he wanted the same thing I did.

And finally at 5:16 p.m., I got a text from Patrick. However . . . just a fucking thumbs-up emoji.

Chapter 24

Rosé All F*cking Day

Since I assumed the thumbs-up emoji meant that we were still on for airport pickup, I never texted Patrick back. I was going to wait until I got to the airport that night to give him the details about my late night flight. However, Wednesday afternoon, I got a text . . .

Jimmy:
Jun 20, 2:04 p.m.
What's ur plans? The show I told you about is tonight. When you get a free minute give me a shout.

Okay, what did he mean, "What are my plans?" I'm flying into Austin and you are picking my ass up at 10:45 p.m., just like you have offered, and just like we fucking planned! I don't know what time they usually do concerts in Texas, but around Atlanta, they rarely have a concert start after 11:00 p.m., so was he blowing me off? Was this his way of saying, "I'm going to the concert, maybe I'll see you later?" Unfortunately, I couldn't call Patrick back for a couple of hours, due to autism. Jack has a tendency to scream non-stop when I'm on the phone, and I was not wanting Patrick to have to endure the incessant annoyance in the background. Plus, I had a feeling Patrick might piss me off, so I wanted to be as far away from Jack as possible, since he picks up on my feelings so strongly.

When I called Patrick during Jack's swim lesson, he informed me that he was going to the concert, but would still be picking me up. I basically told him that wasn't possible, since I was landing at 10:45 p.m., so he would have to leave the show early. He actually sounded a little perturbed, and a bit inconvenienced. So, this pissed me off, just as I thought he might. He had never done this before. Why did he offer to pick me up in the first place if he wanted to go to the concert? I was still confused when we ended the call, and all he said was that he would be there when my plane landed. I guess I should've just been happy that he was picking me up. But honestly, I wanted him to WANT to pick me up. I wanted to be a choice over a concert, and I didn't feel like I was. I sensed as though he thought I was a nuisance. It had been two months since we last saw each other, so I wanted him to want me. But for the first time in a year, I didn't feel like he did.

I was really hoping it was just my hormones making me feel so insecure. It was going to be my time of the month the following week, and sometimes that week before can make me a bit moody. I was also worried that these new insecurities were based on the fact that I might have stronger feelings for Patrick after all. It was as if I was feeling needy, and that is so not like me. I have never *needed* anything or anyone, but Patrick was definitely something that I wanted . . . really bad.

And then all my insecurities faded away when I received this text about ten minutes later.

Jimmy:
June 20, 4:25 p.m.
I was able to trade my tonight's tix for 2 tomorrow night . . . sweet. Be there at 10:45. And you can use my car if needed this wkend. And you're staying here tonight . . . no parents.

And just like that . . . all was fine in Piper's world. Not only was he letting me borrow his car, but he wanted me to stay with him. Neither was likely going to happen, but the thought finally put a smile on my face.

And the smile quickly dissipated when I got to the airport and found out that my flight was delayed. Shit . . . now Patrick was going to be pissed that he could have gone to the show, since I was now landing around midnight. Oh well, hopefully my face was going to make up for the disappointment, or my body would, at least. He was likely getting laid, so hopefully that was going to be better than a concert. It would be in my opinion. Well, maybe not a NKOTB concert, but probably any other performer. Or maybe not Justin Timberlake, but possibly.

We finally boarded the plane about two hours later than originally scheduled. This put me landing around 12:45 a.m., instead of 10:45 p.m. I texted Patrick and asked if that was too late, and if he wanted me to get someone else to pick me up. And luckily, he insisted on doing it, and acted like it was no big deal. But then, in Piper vs the *Moral Gods*, right before takeoff, the flight attendant came over the loudspeaker and stated that there was a problem with the plane. We would all have to get off, and onto yet another plane. I guess those *Moral Gods* were doing everything they could to sabotage my evening. I can't say that I blame them, since I was going to be committing adultery, and I know how they are about that. But come on, my last two months had been filled with stress and anxiety, and I needed a release. I know those *Moral Gods* would make exceptions on occasion, but not tonight, I guess.

But when I texted Patrick with an update on the new arrival time, he still acted like it was no problem at all. Whew! When we all got situated on the new airplane, I texted Patrick with my new ETA, which was now around 1:45 a.m. central time. I told him I was shutting off my phone, and would see his face in two hours.

About an hour and a half into the flight, the flight attendant came over the speaker to say we were landing in approximately fifteen minutes. This put me getting into Austin about fifteen minutes earlier than I had told Patrick. I hoped that he was checking the flight status, as he told me he was going to, and would see our new arrival time.

After landing, I texted Patrick to let him know that we had

landed early. I was hoping he might immediately text me back to say he was already there and waiting, but I didn't get a response until I was pulling my suitcase off the baggage carousel. My phone began vibrating incessantly in my pocket, so I realized he was calling instead of texting. This, of course, made me worried he was calling to say he wasn't coming. My insecurities rearing their ugly head once again. And because I am used to people blowing me off, I quickly tried to figure out who would come and get me at such a ridiculous hour. It was about 1:30 a.m. local time when I answered the phone. Luckily, it was Patrick, and he was on his way. However, he had just left, and was still about forty-five minutes from the airport.

Okay . . . so this is where you will see how absolutely different I tend to be with Patrick than with anyone else on earth. If this was anyone besides Patrick, and especially if it was hubby, I would have cursed that mother fucker out for making me wait for forty-five minutes outside of the airport at 2:00 in the morning.

I think my flight was the last one that landed for the night, so after everyone got their luggage and left, I was honestly the only sole sitting on the bench outside waiting for a ride. And to make it worse, I looked kind of hot. I mean, I just had jeans and a tank top on, since it was hot as shit outside. But I was looking "Patrick ready," until the humidity took over my entire being while sitting outside waiting. And anyone could have come along and killed me, or kidnapped me, or robbed me. After about fifteen minutes of waiting outside, there was not a sole in sight, so nobody would have seen the "demise of Piper," if that was to be my final night on earth.

I actually sat outside on that bench for forty-five minutes with a fucking legit smile on my face. Looking back now, I can't believe I wasn't pissed as hell. So again, why was I a completely different person when I was with Patrick? Was it because I was just happy for my reward when we got back to his place? Or was it more? I constantly asked myself this question, and I think I was getting sick of asking it.

When Patrick finally pulled up almost forty-five minutes after I had sat down on that bench outside, it was kind of weird between us for the first time ever. He got out of the car to open the trunk for me, but he didn't even hug me or kiss me on the cheek like he always did on our initial interactions. After I put the suitcase in the back, and we got into the car, I leaned over to kiss him on the cheek. He reciprocated a quick peck and smiled, but I was hoping that the slightly less excited affect was because it was 2:15 a.m.

After some signature chit-chatting, Patrick asked if I wanted him to take me straight to my parents' house, or go back to his place. Because my body was still on Eastern time zone, and was feeling every bit of the 3:15 a.m. body clock, I was tempted to tell him to take me straight to my parents' house for my comfy childhood bed. But who was I kidding? After the fucking long night I just had, I was going to top it off with something good. He told me adamantly that he was not going to be driving me to my parents' house after we got to his house, and said I could drive his car home if I didn't want to stay. He knew staying with him was not an option, both with his ridiculous snoring, and also to avoid my parents worrying about me.

When we were about fifteen minutes from his house, Patrick turned to me, somewhat excitedly, and said, "Hey, I saw someone wearing a shirt the other day that said 'rosé all day' and I immediately thought of you." He gave me a huge smile as if to say, *Isn't that sweet that I thought of you?* But in that moment, all I could do was keep looking at him, somewhat dumbfoundedly, waiting on the punchline. I answered truthfully, "Why would you think of me? I've never had rosé in my life. You must have me confused with your other girlfriend."

Sorry, but the look on his face was worth the forty-five minute wait on that bench outside the airport, in the hot June heat, in the middle of the night. He truly did get me confused with another girl, and as much as I hated it, I loved it. That guilty face of his said it all. For someone who considers themselves having the "memory of an elephant," he obviously had been putting his trunk on other trunks, besides mine. But, I couldn't give him too much shit for it. I was the married one, and was surprised that I wasn't getting him confused myself. He was entitled to do what he wanted, but I would be lying if I said I wasn't a little taken aback with his confusion. Even though he was a single man, I thought I was the only one currently in his life. Obviously, I was wrong.

When we got to Patrick's house, it was about 3:00 a.m. local time. It was way past my bedtime, but whenever I was with Patrick, I didn't seem to need sleep. I was always happily charged up and ready for anything. We didn't jump right into bed like we have in the past, and I was hoping his lack of affection was due to the long and late night. We did lie in bed while watching our signature reality TV shows, and just talked and cuddled for a while, fully clothed. I felt a little distance, and again was just hoping it was the exhausting night.

After almost an hour, we finally started kissing. And JESUS, did I miss those lips. I knew they must have been kissing someone else, but tonight they were kissing me, and that's all I cared about. I may not be his "rosé" girl, but tonight I was all his, and he was all mine. And I was exactly where I wanted to be.

Without giving any details about the sex like I sometimes do, I will say this . . . (Drumroll, please) . . . I finally got my orgasm! And it was just as amazing as I knew it would be, and well worth the wait. Well, maybe not the entire year worth the wait, but it was pretty damn great, nonetheless.

Very shortly after the big "O," I got dressed and left. It wasn't like a "hit it and quit it" type of situation, but it was 4:30 a.m. local time, and 5:30 a.m. by my body clock eastern time, so sleep was imminent. I took Patrick's car home to my parents' house, per his request, and promised to bring it back whenever he needed it the next day. My parents left the back door unlocked for me, and I went straight to the bed that I'd had since I was in high school, and slept like a baby.

The next morning, I had that brief feeling that you have when you wake up somewhere that's not your bedroom, and for that split second, you don't know where you are. Then I immediately looked over at my four-foot-tall stuffed Smurf that I've had since I was eight years old, and remembered exactly where I was. Yes, I was the faithful one who held onto that Smurf all these years, and still remembered the happiness I felt when I opened that huge present on Christmas morning. It was very similar to the giddiness that I felt this very moment, thinking about where I had been just seven hours before. Instead of pinching myself to make sure I wasn't dreaming, I looked out the window at Patrick's black BMW sitting in the driveway, and smiled. If someone would have told my ugly, insecure, sixteen-year-old, NKOTB-lovin' self, while staring at the most beautiful boy in the football stadium seats, that his car would be in my parents driveway exactly twenty-eight years later, I would not have believed a word of it. But looking out at that car, I was overwrought with emotions of all kinds, from happiness, to sadness, to guilt and shame, and every emotion in-between. It was almost as if I knew our time together was ending soon, and I needed to savor each and every last moment.

It must have been the nostalgia in combination with the mixed emotions, but I suddenly remembered something that my ex-husband once told me. Shortly before he realized he didn't love me, never loved me, and wanted a divorce, he and I were out to dinner one night. Somehow the topic of exes was brought up, and he began telling me a story about how he walked in on his ex-girlfriend with another man, which made me think of the time I walked in on Patrick and his female friend. I reciprocated with telling him my experience, along with the fact that Patrick and I still dated a little bit even after this incident, and how he lived in California, and that I would probably never see him again. After I got done telling my story, there was complete silence for at least ten minutes while we ate our dinner. I wasn't sure about the reason for the complete shutdown on his end, until I asked him if everything was okay. My husband at the time looked up from his last bits of food, and said, "The look that you had in your eyes just now when you were talking about that Patrick guy . . . you have never looked at *me* like that." I said nothing in return. There wasn't anything to say. He was right.

My ex-husband left me about three months after that conversation, but I still have never regretted a thing.

Chapter 25

Plot Twist

After finally getting out of bed, I texted Patrick to see when he needed his car back.

Me:
June 21, 1:06 p.m.
Good morning sunshine! Let me know when you want your car. My parents' pool is up and running after all, so I'm headin' to swim.

Jimmy:
June 21, 1:16 p.m.
I'm just knocking out some emails etc. so anytime you want to come by. If need me to take ya anywhere I sure can, or ur welcome to come here and float in the pond. ha.

Well, I guess it was good that he wasn't in a hurry to get his car, because I wanted to get my tan on! And he even offered to take me somewhere, which I thought was so sweet, since he already knew I could drive my mom's car if needed. But that was just confirmation that he still wanted to spend some time with me, and that was all I needed to hear. We had briefly discussed the concert that evening, and Patrick told me he wanted me to join him, so I knew I would be spending another evening with him, and I couldn't be more excited.

I returned Patrick's car to him later that afternoon, and at around 7:00 p.m. I headed back over to his house in my mom's car so I could drive myself home whenever I wanted after the concert. I was a little stressed that I was going to be late getting to his house, because I know how excited he was about this damn concert, which had been somewhat of a sore subject after the ticket/airport pickup conflict. It was a country singer that I had never heard of, which wasn't that odd since I rarely listened to country. I swear I heard more country in the past year with Patrick than I listened to in my entire life. I guess that was also a sign of how crazy I was about Patrick. He and only him could make me listen to a genre that I hated! But, of course, I loved it when I was with him, and didn't mind listening to it if it meant I could be with him while I did it.

Now, here comes the plot twist . . .

Patrick was definitely quieter than usual on the forty-five-minute drive to the venue. But just like the night before, I initially blamed it on the lack of sleep, or possibly sun overexposure. Tired, cranky, and distant would have been a good description used to explain Patrick's mood that night. I initially didn't think much about it, to be honest. I, too, get cranky at times, and there's not always an explanation. And truthfully, I was actually happy that he knew he could be himself around me, even if his tonight's self was "grumpy old man" mood.

It was very crowded when we first got there, and Patrick held my hand as we maneuvered through the people. We got our alcoholic beverages, and found a good spot to stand in the general admission standing room only area. Once the music started, I put my arm around Patrick's waist, and continued to drink my vodka tonic with the other hand. It took me a minute to realize that Patrick was doing all he could to avoid touching me whatsoever. I noticed that he had one hand holding his beer, while the other hand was tucked into his pocket. When I tried talking to him over the music, which was kind of hard with the volume, Patrick wouldn't even look at me. He answered my questions, and was polite enough, but didn't even make eye contact with me. Again,

I just thought he was in a bad mood about something, and I was trying to lighten his mood and make him feel better, but it obviously wasn't working.

For a second, I thought maybe he just didn't like PDA, which I'm not a fan of either. Or maybe he was trying to be respectful, in case we saw someone we knew, and didn't want them to see us together. It wouldn't be the first time it happened with us, but the odds were definitely smaller here. But then I remembered our slightly touchy-feely moments out in public at past events, so this was definitely different. Usually, our chemistry made it hard not to touch each other, using some form of our bodies or limbs. Or, at least, it was ALWAYS hard for me. So, I found myself questioning whether he had always been like this and I just never noticed, or if this was a new, guarded version of Patrick. But I quickly realized it was definitely a new guarded Patrick, and I had no idea why.

I asked him if he was okay, and he just smiled and said, "Yeah!" like in an "of course" kind of way. Then I thought *grumpy old man* was finally disappearing when he said, "Oh guess what . . . Derrick is coming into town this weekend, and I'm sure he will want to see you!" I was very happy to hear this. Not only because I hadn't seen Derrick in years and couldn't wait to see him, but because Patrick seemed to be coming around with his mood. And if anything, it was another opportunity to see Patrick at least one more time before I headed back to reality.

I told him I absolutely wanted to see Derrick, and to let me know when they were out so I could join them. But unfortunately, after this brief conversation, *grumpy old man* came back, and all was not well. After only a few songs in, Patrick quickly turned to me and said, "Let's go!"

So, now I was even more confused. Why was he in such a bad mood, and why did he want to leave a concert early that he had been talking about for over a month? But I wasn't going to argue, since I wasn't feelin' the music anyway.

Once we got outside, Patrick told me that he didn't feel well.

Now things were starting to make sense. That explained his behavior and his actions toward me, or so I thought. But why didn't he tell me this when I asked him if he was okay? We headed back home, and stopped halfway at a gas station where Patrick got a snack. Quickly after that, he told me he was feeling much better, and all was right in our world again.

Maybe.

I followed Patrick into his house when we got there. We hadn't discussed whether I was coming in, or going straight home. But at this point, it was almost a given that we would spend some sort of quality bed time together, sex or not. I just loved his intimacy more than anything, even fully clothed. Although, another "O" would've been pretty awesome too.

I had to pee something fierce, and when I walked out of Patrick's bathroom he was fast asleep, snoring away on his bed. It was like in those movies where the woman comes out of her bathroom with sexy lingerie, ready to get it on, and the man is passed out. Well, there goes "O #2" I guess. I kissed Patrick on the cheek, and he mumbled something about seeing me later. I was pretty exhausted too, so I didn't mind going home and going straight to bed myself. I figured we would just pick this up again next time.

But there wasn't a next time.

Chapter 26

Recovery Mode

I woke up feeling invigorated. I got a great, long nights rest, and was ready to spend more time with Patrick. Barbara's birthday party wasn't until the next evening, so I was hoping to hang out with Patrick and Derrick later, if he was already in town. I was assuming that Patrick slept great as well, and would be back to his happy mood by now. I had lunch plans with an old girlfriend, and it was really nice catching up. I still had not heard from Patrick after lunch, so I thought I would text to see what was going on.

Me:
June 22, 3:44 p.m.
I hope you slept as well as I did, and that you are feeling better. What r ur plans today/tonight? Is Derrick in town yet?

I decided to go visit Dianna, and hang out with her for the night. I knew I was going to see her the following night at her mom's surprise party, but I wanted some one-on-one time with her. I figured that if Patrick wanted to see me, or if he was with Derrick, I could make it an early night with her and join them later. I was never one to wait at home for a text, so why start now. Of course I wanted to see Patrick, but I also wanted to see my friends, and was more than happy to do so. If he wanted to see me, he would text me.

About three hours after I sent the text to Patrick, he finally responded while I was driving to Dianna's house.

Jimmy:
June 22, 6:45 p.m.
Golf'd and now grabbing food with Derrick
and family

Okay. I guess I'm glad he texted back, but there was no mention of seeing Derrick, or him for that matter. I figured they had been drinking and having a blast golfing all afternoon, per his text, so I understood the delay in response. But was I going to have to beg at this point? Because I wasn't too proud to.

I had so much fun with Dianna, but it was hard not to tell her anything about Patrick. Dianna was one of my best friends, but she knew Patrick personally, or at least the old Patrick. I trusted her, but the fewer people who knew, the better. And honestly, she was smart enough to know something was going on, and wise enough to not ask.

A few hours after Patrick's last text, and after I had a few drinks too many, I texted him back.

Me:
June 22, 10:45 p.m.
Tell Derrick hi and I hope I get to see him

I figured there wasn't much else to say. He knew what I wanted, and now the ball was in his court.

It wasn't until the following day that I realized it was going to be a little tight to try to squeeze in Patrick or Derrick, because I had the birthday party to attend that evening. But I guess it didn't really matter, since I hadn't heard back from Patrick yet anyway. I was starting to get a little pissed because I really did want to see Derrick, and Patrick was almost ignoring me. Well, he was periodically responding, but ignoring anything related to making plans. And he hadn't responded at all to my text from last night.

Derrick and I share the exact same birthday, so when we were in college, we would go to lunch on our birthday and get a free milkshake. I hadn't seen him since college, and I really wanted to. I didn't have his number, so I had to rely on Patrick to arrange it. But so far, it wasn't happening.

Before hopping in the shower, I remembered that I was supposed to grab some compression sleeves that Patrick's company made, but I forgot about them the last time I was at his house. I had overheard Jack's therapist talking about how a tight sleeve might help the kids with letter boarding at school. Sometimes putting pressure on muscles and joints can help the body focus on the task, and autistics tend to highly benefit from this pressure. I told Alexis that I could get her some to try, since I knew Patrick's company made them. That way she didn't have to buy some and waste money if they weren't going to be helpful. Patrick was more than willing to give me some for free, since this was the same therapist that thought he was hot. In fact, I think his exact words were, "Anything for a girl who thinks I'm hot."

I decided to be as direct as I possibly could. I'm not a phone talker, plus I thought I might be pissed if I tried to call Patrick and he didn't answer, so I gave one more plea in a text. That way he wouldn't feel pressured, but would know that I really wanted to see them both. And that I still needed to get those sleeves.

Me:
June 23, 3:15 p.m.
Any fun plans today/tonight? Let me know when
I can see you and Derrick before I leave tomorrow
night. And I still have to get those sleeves.

I mean, how much more direct and descriptive could I get? But, unfortunately, he wasn't quite as descriptive but WAY more direct with *his* response . . .

Jimmy:
June 23, 3:38 p.m.
Recovery mode now.

Okay, so, he's hungover again. But still no plans. What happened to "You can borrow my car all weekend" bullshit? Or the "Stay with me the whole time" nonsense? Or the "Derrick wants to see you" bologna? I was so confused about how he went from wanting to spend the weekend together, to nothing.

Me:
June 23, 4:02 p.m.
Well, must've been a good night : I'm heading to the city in a few, can I swing by and get the sleeves? Or let me know a good time tomorrow?

And his response?
Nothing.
Radio silence.
No return text at all.
A.k.a., ghosting.

Chapter 27

WTF?!

I landed in Atlanta around 9:00 p.m. on Sunday night. When I got home, Jack and hubby were still up and at 'em. It was after Jack's bedtime, so I was curious what exactly was going on. Hubs informed me that he forgot to pick up Jack's sleep medicine, and the pharmacy had already closed by the time he remembered. My initial thought process was, *Oh shit, this is going to be a long night.* But then I remembered that we hadn't forgotten Jack's sleep medicine for over four years, so it might be a good time to test if he actually still needed it to sleep.

And the consensus was . . . Yup, he definitely still needed it!

Truth be told, Jack was up the entire night. Like, literally the entire night! Like, he didn't actually go to sleep until 8:30 p.m. the FOLLOWING MONDAY NIGHT! Most people don't believe me when I tell this story, but it's 100 percent true. Jack was awake for an entire thirty-seven hours straight. Just let that sink in a little bit. All three of us were up the entire night without one minute of sleep. Well, I think my husband might have gotten an hour, since he's the one who had to work the next day. And I got about five minutes, while I lay with Jack to attempt sleep on his end, to no avail. But thankfully, I did get a little nap the next day, while Jack was at camp. And yes, he still went to camp, participated in his equine horse therapy all morning, then went on a hike with them in the afternoon. And he was perfectly and autistically fine all day. That's the amazing thing about autistics' brains and bodies . . .

they do whatever the hell they want to do. And, unfortunately, they don't have much control over themselves either. So it's hard to get mad at them, but easy to want to bang your head against a wall . . . over and over and over again. It was in this moment that I remembered something I saw amongst all my autism research. I had read an article about the stress levels of autism parents, and the study concluded that autism moms have stress levels equivalent to combat veterans. I am not a combat veteran, nor would I have any idea what their stress level was like. But I knew what I felt in those types of hopeless and helpless moments as an autism mom, so I can only assume they were similar emotions and stress levels. Hence, the reason once again for my need for escape.

As I lay there with Jack the entire night trying to get him to calm down enough to sleep, all I could think about was how this was my punishment, and how much I deserved it. I had been having sex with another man just four nights before, so this was exactly what I deserved. And thinking about the fact that Patrick didn't have enough respect for me to tell me the truth, whatever that "truth" was, made me feel like a big piece of trash. I knew I wasn't that, but his ability to just toss me aside made me feel like a cheating whore. And at the end of the day, that's exactly what I was.

By 5:00 a.m., I had lain in Jack's bed crying for a good two hours off and on, while he vocally stimmed, and jumped up and down occasionally. I was crying for numerous reasons, but mainly because I was so fucking tired. But I also cried because I knew my escape, which was Patrick in this case, was now gone. And I kept crying because not only was it gone, I had no idea why. Where did it go? Where did *he* go? What exactly happened? What did I miss? And what made me continue crying was the fact that I not only lost my escape, but I think I lost my friend too. I had finally gotten him back, and now he was gone again. Not only had I gotten him back, but I got him back right where I wanted him, which was basically wanting *me*! For the most part, Patrick had wanted me over the last year, and now I questioned that. I knew he didn't want to BE with me, but I pretty much thought it was because he couldn't, because I was married and because it didn't fit for us. But whatever it was that we were doing was working for me, but I guess it wasn't for him anymore. But why did I not get an explanation?

Did he owe me an explanation? That was the main question that kept spinning around and around in my head, along with all of the other questions I had. I was married and we weren't exclusive, so did he owe me any kind of an explanation? This made me think about the girl answering Patrick's door twenty-six years earlier. We weren't exclusive then, or "boyfriend and girlfriend" as we called it back in the day. And we weren't this time either. But it still hurt. And in a way, it hurt a lot worse than it did twenty-six years ago. You would think it wouldn't be as painful, since I was now older and much more prone to disappointments. But I thought we had matured. Why didn't he just have the balls to tell me there was someone else, or that he just didn't feel it with me anymore? Maybe he didn't know either. But something would have been better than nothing. And nothing is what I got.

But was there an actual issue after all? I mean, just because he had been ignoring me for a few days didn't mean that much in Patrick's world. He had done it to me many times before, but I would like to think this time was different. I mean, we had planned to spend the weekend together. Not exactly, but in a way. Didn't we? That's the feeling I got anyway. Or was I just completely off base? I had no idea what the fuck happened, if anything actually did. So, I was just going to wait it out.

But the waiting was torturous! I felt like he was playing games. I know I could've easily just texted and been like, "WTF?" But besides my ego, I felt like I shouldn't have to. He knew I wanted to see him, and he chose not to see me. That should have been explanation enough.

About a week after I got home, I still had not heard from Patrick, and Jesus I missed that escape. Patrick was the place I went to in my head when I was trying incessantly to get Jack to go to sleep every night, or when my husband was away on a long business trip, or when I had to sit through an emotional family session at work, or when my son wasn't invited to a party because of his autism, or when we had yet another emergency room trip due to Jack's possible seizure-like episode. Those were the times that I would allow my thoughts to go to another place entirely, just to get away from life. Because let's face it, my life sucked. And honestly, the problem was that there wasn't anything else I'd rather fantasize about, and no other fantasy that I wanted to come true. Maybe the ability to use my hall pass on Donnie Wahlberg, but other than that, none.

I have always been grateful for what I have, and that has never changed. But having a special needs child is extremely hard in all arenas. And until Patrick came back into my life, I didn't have something that made me feel good, or to look forward to, or to make me smile, or to fantasize about, since my son's diagnosis. I was stuck doing the same thing, over and over and over again. And even though I was still doing all of the stressful autism stuff over and over again for that year that I was intermittently with Patrick, I was able to dream about good stuff, then make it a reality. I made everything that I wanted come true. So, what was I whining about? I realized I should just be happy that it happened, and happy that I actually made something so amazing happen . . . to ME! But I was selfish, and I wanted it again. I liked the way he made me feel. He made me feel sexy again, and I wanted that back. He made me feel desired and admired, and I'm not sure I ever felt like it to that extent before. He made me feel like I could actually make my dreams come true. And I wasn't ready to give that up yet. But it looked like I was going to have to.

Two weeks later, I got a phone call from one of my friends in Texas asking me for a favor. She wasn't one to ask for favors, so I figured it was important. She explained that one of her friends, whom I didn't know, was part of a small conference they were having in Austin, and autism was one of the topics. She knew about my Autism Specialist Certification, and my desire to help educate everything autism, so she asked if I wanted to be one of the speakers. I didn't even hesitate, and told her yes before I even knew the details.

I was glad that I had an excuse to fly out and hang with some of my friends again, but I was a little stressed about possibly being in the same city as Patrick, and not being able to see him. I made my travel arrangements as soon as she gave me the details, and I flew out on July 18. However, shortly after my parents picked me up from the airport, I got a call from one of the organizers for the conference. She went over the specifics that she wanted me to touch on during my presentation. I already had my entire PowerPoint set, and wasn't prepared to add more, but I was willing to listen to her requests.

During this brief conversation with the organizer, I realized that every topic she wanted me to focus on was involving "cures" for autism. As much as I would love to "cure" autism some days when my son is struggling, my focus of the presentation was on the abilities and strengths of autism, and not how to fix it. I mentioned my concerns, and what I was actually planning on discussing at the conference, but she wasn't liking what I was telling her. She told me that she wanted me to discuss vaccines at some point during my presentation, and how they play a role in the cause of autism. Since I don't believe vaccines play a direct role in autism, I told her to find somebody else to talk about that, and I hung up. I didn't want to be mean, but I will not let someone tell me what to think and feel about something that I have done years of research on. And I'm definitely not going to present information that is untrue or fabricated. And fabrication is exactly why Andrew Wakefield, the man who started the "vaccines cause autism" movement, was barred from practicing medicine after he was found guilty of falsifying a correlation between the two.

As eager as I was to speak at the conference, their focus was not on what I felt people should know about autism. It felt like a negative underlying vibe, and I wasn't down with that. So, I decided to cancel my presentation, and spend the next three days relaxing again with family and friends. Even if it was only one month after my last "vacation," I like any relaxation I can get. I already had dinner plans set up with friends for the next two evenings, so I could be easily distracted from my stress when thinking about Patrick, along with the conference that was no longer happening.

On the second day of my vacation, I woke up to the smell of my favorite bread. Every time I came home, my mom made her signature banana bread, and I loved waking up to that smell. I would have preferred to wake up with Patrick's car in the driveway, like last month, but I was happy to feel the comforts of home again.

I know that the sense of smell tends to be closely linked with memory, so I'm assuming that was why I couldn't seem to get Patrick out of my head. The last two trips that I had spent in this room, I had come from Patrick's house, which made my bed smell just like him. And the flooding memories brought back even more of those feelings of *why*. What exactly happened to completely end the friendship? And was it the end? Even though it was a friendship with "benefits," and every relationship with those is always a bit complicated, I was still confused as to why the end of "us" was so abrupt. I know we had gone a month without talking or texting before, but it felt different this time. And I wanted to know if I was just feeling insecure, or whether I was accurate in my assumption of the end.

I got a wild hair up my ass and decided to just text him. I wasn't sure what exactly to say, because I wasn't sure what exactly was going on. I felt like I needed some sort of closure, even though I hate that word. I was likely in the same town as he was, depending on his work travel schedule, so I was hoping that we would have an opportunity to talk about it in person. I decided to go with a nonaccusatory approach, since I know how much men love being accused of shit. (Ha!)

Me:
July 19, 12:18 p.m.
Hey! You alive? I'm in Texas . . . not sure if you
are. Also not sure about the ghosting. All OK?
In your fame and fortune, don't forget about us
little people.

I was almost positive that he would pick up on my sarcasm with the "fame and fortune" part of my text, since he always talked about how rich he was hoping to get when his business took off. I figured if I didn't get a response at all, that would most definitely be my closure. Well, not that it would explain anything, but it would definitely be a slap in the face. However, I wasn't prepared for the response I *did* get, and sort of wished for the slap in the face instead.

Jimmy:
July 19, 1:52 p.m.
My dad is in hospital. My care or concern for
anything or anyone else is nonexistent.

Boy did this response cause a huge chaos of emotions for me. At first, I felt sorry for Patrick, which I think is a common immediate feeling you have when someone you care about is hurting. I wondered if this explained everything. Had his dad been sick this entire month of ghosting? Even if that was the case, it still didn't explain no text AT ALL. You can still text people from a hospital. Not that we texted every day, but he told me that I was his BFF on numerous occasions. And as much as I know that he was partly joking about the actual phrase of the best friends forever concept, I knew we were friends at the very least. Well, until one month ago, anyway.

This *"concern for Patrick"* feeling inside of me quickly turned into a pity party for myself. I totally understood where he was coming from, since I would likely feel the same way if my dad was in the hospital. But I didn't deserve that response. I didn't deserve to be treated like a nuisance, or like someone he didn't have time for. I understand being worried about your dad, but I feel like it could have been done in a better way. I would never treat a "friend" like that, regardless of the pain or concern I was experiencing. But I might say that to someone that I didn't give two shits about. So, maybe that was the answer to my closure.

But now how the hell was I going to respond? I had half of me worried about my friend, and the other half of me feeling like he was casting me aside like an inconvenience.

> **Me:**
> July 19, 3:05 p.m.
> I'm sorry. I had no idea, obviously, but I figured something might be wrong. I wasn't asking for your care or concern, but I know you are hurting. Just know I'm here if you need anything.

I thought I did a good job of not only being a friend, even though he hurt my feelings, but also calling him out on being an asshole. When shitty things are going on, it doesn't give you an excuse to be a dick. But being the social worker that I am, I wanted to let him know that I understood how people tend to act out when they are scared or upset. So, I gave him an out, both for why he was mean AND for why he had been ignoring me, even if neither was true.

I actually thought at this point I would hear nothing from him. Like, ever. He had already been completely ignoring me, and now he had an excuse to never talk to me again. But, I was wrong.

Jimmy:
July 19, 3:40 p.m.
Thank u. Stressful time in all aspects of life currently. Staying positive & focused. It's hot af here, huh!

Positive? In what way, shape, or form was his prior text anywhere near positive? I guess I should just be glad he actually responded, and to a text that didn't call for a response. Maybe he felt bad after all, and realized I was just being a friend. I did appreciate that he threw the heat comment in there, knowing how much I love the heat, because it showed he remembered one of my likes. And this time I wasn't the "rosé all day girl," and he actually *was* accurate in the memory of my adoration of summertime. But the current temperature outside was 109 degrees. And that wasn't heat index, that was Fahrenheit. Therefore, I was loving the pool way more than the heat at this point in the day.

I initially wasn't going to respond, since I knew he had enough going on, but I didn't necessarily want things to end in that manner. Plus, he was indirectly apologizing for being a dick, in his own Patrick way. The social worker in me wanted to acknowledge and validate his stress.

> **Me:**
> July 19, 4:02 p.m.
> You know I am loving this heat, but appreciating my air conditioner more. I'm sorry to hear about the current stresses, and I really do hope your dad's going to be OK.

I guess this was going to be it. This was maybe how we would leave things? I totally understood why he wouldn't suggest seeing each other while I was in town, since he was occupied with his family. But I didn't know when I would ever get the opportunity to see him again. I guess every time I was with him I had no idea when and if I would see him again, but this time felt more final.

Ironically, Dianna and I ran into Brad that evening. Brad was our mutual friend who originally gave me Patrick's number just one year before when I was heading to California. The funny thing is, or maybe it's not so funny, Brad informed me that Patrick's dad went into the hospital that same morning. Therefore, explaining the extreme and immediate concern for his dad, but NOT explaining the month of ghosting. His dad's health problems hadn't even been an issue until that morning. I guess it was something completely different that had caused his distance the past month. If I only knew.

The next day was still a heat stroke waiting to happen, so I spent all morning and afternoon in the pool again, talking with my mom as we floated on our rafts. When I finally went inside to pee, I looked at my phone and shockingly saw a text from Patrick.

Jimmy:
July 20, 2:39 p.m.
U been enjoying yourself? Things are really good right now other than my dad. Just stressed about one of our products that's about to hit the market & could change my life for the better. Need some luck. U seeing Dianna while here?

The only thing I could think about when I read his text was the emoji of the woman shrugging her shoulders like, "I don't know." I mean . . . WTF?! First of all, I'm super surprised he even texted me. Second, it sounds like he only texted to brag about his business. Third, why would he care anymore who I spent my time with while I was in town, since he obviously wasn't offering his time to me? And fourth, I thought he just said yesterday how stressful life was, and now he's saying that things are "good?" Again . . . WTF?

We had a couple more back-and-forth texts. Most of them were him updating me on his dad's status, or me telling him what I had planned with Dianna that night. Nothing exciting, and no offering to see each other. So, at this point, I knew whatever the hell we had was over, but I STILL didn't know why. And that drove me crazy. I guess I'm more of a control freak than I thought, because the not knowing was driving me batshit nuts. I just thought we had something special, even if it was just friends with benefits. I thought he had enough respect for me to talk to me about what he was thinking, since he surprisingly had been pretty good at that most of the time we were together.

The next morning, I was a little hung over, thanks to the all night partying with Dianna. It was fun, though, and I definitely needed it. I realized it was highly unlikely that I would be seeing Patrick, but I remembered that I still needed to get those sleeves from him before I headed back home. Alexis had texted me about them a few days before I left, and I told her I would try my best to get them. I figured Patrick was probably staying put at the hospital, so I made my text request as painless as possible.

Me:
July 21, 9:24 a.m.
Do you still have those sleeves for me? I know you got a lot going on with your dad, but if there's any way I could get them, that would be awesome! You can put them in your mailbox or on the porch if it's easier. I can pick them up today or tomorrow morning. Thanks!

Jimmy:
July 21, 1:01 p.m.
I gotcha covered. I'll be done at the hospital at 3 today and home tomorrow til 2, so anytime you want to come by you can if you want.

So, this was kind of surprising. Not only did I think I wouldn't get a response at all, I figured he would have zero interest in seeing me. I thought for sure the stuff would be left outside. But now I was a little torn. Part of me was hoping we could talk through some things, but the other part of me just wanted to see his face and enjoy his brief company without stress, which I'm sure he had plenty of already.

I texted him back with my ETA, but I was running a little late. I had dinner plans in Austin with two girlfriends from college, so it only left about ten minutes max at Patrick's house. Luckily, or unluckily, I knew there would be no time for sex. As much as I wanted to feel his body on top of mine again, I knew today would not be that day. But I was curious to see his demeanor toward me, or if he mentioned anything about "us."

It was really nice to see his face again. We did our usual innocent signature hug and kiss on the cheek, but kept it PG. It was hard to focus on our interaction, since my girlfriend kept texting me asking a million questions, including but not limited to what I was going to wear that night, and if I would be staying at her house. But the distraction was also kind of nice.

I thought it was a bit strange that he didn't even have the sleeves set out and ready for me. I assumed he would have them already organized to hand over, so he could get rid of me sooner. Instead, he rummaged through a big box of them while I was standing there, making sure he got different sizes for various aged kids.

As Patrick was putting the sleeves in one large bag for me, I was playing with his dog. I absolutely adore his dog, but despise the hair he leaves on me! Unfortunately, I was wearing a little black dress. Well, fortunately I looked pretty hot in it, but it was now covered in dog hair. I asked Patrick if he had a lint roller. He looked at me and honestly asked, "Why would I have a lint roller?"

Gee, I don't know, maybe because you have a dog that sheds everywhere? I didn't actually say this out loud, but as I thought it, the look on my face had to be screaming it. He did help me brush off the dog hair that stuck to the back of my dress, which I appreciated. I also wanted him to feel my awesome ass just one more time, while he used his hands to wipe off the hair. I guess he was thinking the same thing, since he smacked me hard on my right butt cheek. Now, we were never the S&M type folk, so the *Fifty Shades of Grey* spanking was not part of our sexual repertoire. But I have to admit, that slap felt kind of sexy coming from Patrick. However, I gave him a dirty look as if to say, "Don't start what you can't finish, my friend." And I think my "Don't tease me if there's not going to be any follow through" look must have been successful. He held up his hands in a "don't shoot" type of manner and said, "Hashtag, me too."

As we said our extremely platonic goodbyes, I had an overwhelmingly uncomfortable feeling that I would never see his face again.

Unfortunately, I was right.

Chapter 28

#puzzlepieces

Coming back to reality once again was another hard adjustment. And this time, I didn't have my release that I had always turned to over the last year. In the past, I always had a gut feeling that I would see Patrick again at some point in the near or far future, but not this time. And I was still pissed about it, because I still didn't know why, or how, or what, or who. I struggled with the idea of just saying "fuck it," and texting him to ask what the hell was going on, but I was hesitant for two reasons. One, it kind of backfired the last time I tried that. And two, I felt like we left as friends, and that was always the most important thing for me through all of this. I didn't want to ruin the good part we still had left, whatever that good part was.

I knew I had to move on. I knew I had to accept that my life would continue on without Patrick. Now, don't get me wrong . . . I was never the delicate flower, wilting away until Patrick watered me and provided sunshine to bring me back to life. But that's kind of what he did. He brought me back to *me.* He took the thick and pointy cactus of my shell and made me into a beautiful bouquet of flowers, without even realizing he did it. He made me see how happy I could be again, and for that one year, I completely forgot all about the sleepless autism nights over the past five years. I had forgotten that life is always going to be what you make it, and he indirectly reminded me of that. Even though he was far from my lifeline, he did provide the "phone a friend" concept for me. But, I'm going to stop using stupid analogies and metaphors. Even though one definition of a "lifeline" that I found online said, "a thing which provides a means of escape from a difficult situation," I knew I could definitely live without him. But I still didn't want to.

For the next four months, I tried so hard to find another escape, or outlet. I worked hard on my licensure, getting into weekly supervision, and getting my letters of recommendation sent to the appropriate people. I updated my website, and pushed my educating autism agenda. I also got invited to present at three different organizations, all before the end of the year. So, I was busy with my power points, which luckily kept my mind off things.

Another issue that did help get my mind off of things was Jack. But this time, it wasn't the happy escape that Patrick had provided me, but rather a stress-consumed autism escape. Jack had two more seizure-like episodes before the end of the year, which prompted us to get an EEG, EKG, and a sleep study done. You can only imagine how difficult any of these things are on any child, but for an autistic child, these types of procedures are absolute hell! Both for the child *and* the parents. No child enjoys having fifty leads stuck to their head with an odd sticky substance, but for a child with sensory issues, this can be pure torture. It's probably equivalent to having fifty needles stuck in the head of a neurotypical kid. Autistics can have sensory systems that are so acute that any touch can be overwhelming, especially when it's a weird textured substance that's being stuck to your already extra sensitive head. Or when you have sticky leads, which you later find out cause an allergic reaction on your skin, stuck all over your body, and in places you can't reach so you can't rip them off. And these examples are just the tip of the iceberg for how difficult these things can be for my poor baby Jack.

Luckily, my sweet Jack ended up being okay. He had to get some of these procedures under anesthesia, which was in and of itself a fucking nightmare. Well, it was good that he was unconscious for some of the procedures, so he didn't have to experience the pain and trauma related to it. But, waking up from the drugs, and not knowing what the fuck was going on was quite painful to watch. I know how miserable I am when I wake up from those drugs, and I feel like I want to die. Literally. I hated watching him suffer, and not able to verbalize to me what he was feeling, or if he was hurting somewhere.

It was while sitting in the hospital on those long, excruciating days that I wanted my escape. I wanted something to completely take me away, but I didn't have any fun sex fantasies that I could make come true anymore. And the hardest part *still* was the not knowing what the hell happened with Patrick. I missed the days I could grab my phone and hide somewhere and text him, just so I could feel better when he responded, if even for just five minutes. He always said something that would make me laugh. And, Jesus, did I need a laugh at this point in my life.

As the new year approached, I thought about the entirety of 2018, and how different it was from the previous year. The first part of the year was okay, but after June, it was all downhill. And not just because of Patrick, but because of Jack stress, and not having any fun escape during those stressful times. It was even more evident that 2017 *was* by far my best year ever, and that 2018 was quite a disappointment.

When January came, I thought for sure I would be way past caring about Patrick, but I wasn't. I think I needed some form of closure, and I didn't get any form of it. At least, that's what I was hoping would help me get through this mourning period, for lack of a better description. I was confused because in all my past life events that brought temporary pain, I was always able to focus on something good. I was able to put the negativity aside, and focus on everything I had that was positive. And sometimes, those hurtful events in the past even pushed me to be a better person. I found that I occasionally strive when I'm hurting, because it pushes me out of my comfort zone. But it wasn't doing any of that this time. I felt stagnant, like I couldn't move past this. And that made me hate myself for the first time ever. I hated that I cared so much. I hated that I couldn't just say to myself, *Piper, what the fuck is wrong with you? You know better. You are stronger than this. You should just move the fuck on.* But I couldn't. And I hated the fact that I didn't hate myself for cheating, but I hated myself for not being able to get over him.

I figured Patrick must have a girlfriend, or why else would I be nothing to him anymore. But then I thought, *What? Your text app doesn't work on your phone anymore when you get a girlfriend?* I mean, a simple and innocent text wasn't going to kill anyone. I wished he had just told me if he had a girlfriend, so at least I wouldn't be thinking *I* did something wrong. Or if he did have someone special, I felt like knowing that information might be the ammo I needed to move on. I know that sounds weird, but sometimes pain can help me process, and get over things faster. At least then I would have an explanation, and maybe the "closure" process would start. So, I thought.

I occasionally checked Patrick's Instapic, or "IP" as the cool kids call it, but it never showed a girl, or any indication that he wasn't single anymore. It was always just business stuff. Since Patrick wasn't on Facebomb anymore, I had to stalk his IP occasionally, just to check up on his life. I didn't follow him, though, because I didn't want to give him the satisfaction. But I really did want to see what was going on with him, and luckily his account was public, so anyone could see it. I thought my stalking might answer some questions, but it never did. So, I was still left wondering what went wrong. Until one not so fine day when it finally made sense, but didn't . . . all at the same time.

I was actually on my own Instapic page, trying to figure out how to post a new picture. Yes, I felt like my grandma trying to figure out how to use a cell phone. I realized that this was why I always stuck to Facebomb. This IP bullshit was way too millennial for my liking. But, it did provide some entertainment, so I played around with it periodically.

On this particular afternoon, while trying to figure out how to hashtag my own photo, I thought I would check and see if Patrick had any new posts. When I clicked on his page, I saw he posted a new picture just two hours before. It was just a picture of some shirts with different sports teams that his company was getting ready to launch. I saw that he had a few comments on the picture already, so I thought I would see what kinds of bullshit he was getting from everyone about how awesome he was, and how cool the merchandise was, like his conceited ass needed more people to tell him how great he was. And of course, there were friends telling him how proud they were of his success, and couldn't wait to be able to buy all of the products . . . yadda, yadda, yadda. Then, the last comment was from a girl whose name I didn't recognize that said, "You are amazing, my love. 2019 is going to be the best year ever!"

When I clicked on the woman's profile, the twelve most recent pictures that were displayed on her profile page answered all my questions. It was a barrage of pictures that consisted of only her and Patrick. I was so utterly dumbfounded that for one split second, I honestly didn't believe what I was seeing. At first, I thought maybe the woman was Patrick's sister, since I had never met or seen pictures of her. Then I realized right away that there was no way in hell that his sister would have an obsessive amount of pictures with the two of them together, and in very close proximity to one another, and pretty much nobody else on her IP *but* the two of them.

As I swiped through all the pictures, I think my heart literally stopped beating for a minute. Each picture got more and more difficult to consume all at once. In one post, there was a collection of pictures from Christmas, and it was evident in each one that they were living together. One picture had two matching stockings hanging next to each other on the fireplace . . . one with the name "Patrick," and the other, "Abby." My body shook uncontrollably as I realized that Abby was the girlfriend, and the reason for everything . . . the reason for the ghosting, the reason for the emotional distance, the reason he couldn't text, the reason he was an asshole, and the reason that I didn't seem to matter anymore.

I wasn't actually surprised that Patrick had a girlfriend, since I always thought that was the only logical explanation for everything. However, I *was* surprised that he was living with her. It had only been about seven months since we last slept together, and that was quite a short period of time to meet someone and move in together. It suddenly hit me that just the year before, **I** was the one having the time of my life with Patrick. I felt like it wasn't fair that this year, she got to be the one. And from the looks of it, she got ALL of him, which explained why nothing was left for me. As relieved as I was that I was finally getting the closure that I desperately wanted, the shock of every detail all at once was almost too much to bear.

Even though my emotions were doing crazy things, I felt like a lightbulb turned on above my head. Everything finally made sense. And as I continued to torture myself, scanning every picture for more of an explanation, I stopped on one that began to put all of the Patrick puzzle pieces together. It was a picture of Patrick and Abby, of course, toasting to each other with glasses of wine. At the bottom of the picture was a series of hashtags, such as #tous and #cheers, along with a couple others. But the last one surprisingly made me smile.

#roseallday

I finally knew who the "rosé all day girl" was, and suddenly that entire last weekend Patrick and I spent together came rushing back. It was almost as if each instance that left me wondering WTF that weekend was being put together in its final pieces of the proverbial puzzle. And I must enjoy torturing myself, because I continued to look at all of her pictures, and read all the comments that she put at the bottom of each post. I honestly didn't know how much more I could take, but it was like staring at a bad car accident. You don't want to, but you almost have to. Some of the comments and hashtags felt like a stab in the heart. One of the painful posts had #loveofmylife, and I'm pretty sure she was talking about Patrick, since he was the only other person in the picture. Another had a comment from him telling her that he loved her, and couldn't wait for their future together. That one killed me. But, the last picture that I looked at had a hashtag that felt like the final dagger in my heart. It was Abby's most recent post, talking about the new year, and how amazing it was going to be. It was a collage of various pictures from the last year, and 90 percent of them were of her and Patrick. At the bottom she had written #2018 to indicate all her favorite pictures from the entire year. And the last hashtag on the collage was the last of the torture that I could handle for one day.

#BestYearEver

Chapter 29

Only in My Dreams, Take Two

The next morning, I woke up feeling surprisingly fresh. Even after the emotional rollercoaster the day before, I felt like I had some closure. Not only closure with Patrick, but a different form of closure with my husband. I rolled over to look at him while he slept, and as much as I wanted to punch him in the face because he was snoring louder than a fucking freight train, I knew I loved him. I knew that he would never do what Patrick did to me. Ever! He was an honest, loving, caring, and pure individual. He deserved to be loved fiercely. He deserved to be the only one for me.

Don't get me wrong, the guilt made me feel like he deserved better than me . . . a better wife who didn't think about another man for the last two years, every day, for the majority of each day. But, I also knew in that moment, I would never think of Patrick the same way again, nor my husband. But this time, the situations were reversed. I had so much adoration for hubs, and whether he knew about the last two years or not, he loved me through it.

It was almost like a wake-up call . . . like I had to have an affair to realize what was important to me. I had to get my heart broken by the same person twice to realize that he was definitely not the one for me. And the only one for me was still there. Through all the shitty autism struggles and life stress, hubs was still there. And I knew, without a doubt that morning, that he always would be. I was so thankful and grateful that I didn't have to lose him to figure that out.

As guilty as I felt, I also realized that morning that I deserved to have someone who loved *me* fiercely too. I deserved to have someone who put me as a priority, and not only when it was convenient for them. And as much as I loved feeling sexy again, that part sometimes diminishes, or goes away over time. But loyalty and love can stay forever. And I had that with Paul, my husband. I can finally say his name, and not feel like a cheating whore.

But Patrick actually did teach me a lot. My favorite was the fact that he showed me it was okay to be vulnerable. I hate letting my guard down with the best of them, but I did that and survived, and learned, and grew. He put me so far out of my comfort zone, and I enjoyed every minute of it, even the hard ending. But most importantly, he showed me that I actually can make my dreams come true.

Our wake-up alarm on the phone went off, and I got out of bed to brush my teeth. Paul came in the bathroom shortly after to brush his teeth and take a shower. Before hopping in the shower he said, "Let's do Thai tonight when the babysitter comes . . . and I can't wait to hear all about the cruise!"

I stopped the toothbrush mid-clean and turned around to look at him, with an evidently dumbfounded affect, but he had already gotten in the shower. The cruise? What cruise was he talking about? Did I miss something?

As I finished brushing my teeth, I had a weird feeling that something was off. I secretly pinched myself to make sure I wasn't dreaming. Luckily, Paul was too busy in the shower to notice my overwhelming confusion. I immediately ran to my phone to check the date. I hadn't been on a cruise for over two years, so I didn't know what the hell hubs was referring to.

I began to internally shake a little bit when the date on my phone said November 2. It didn't show the year on my phone, but yesterday was January 12, 2019, so I thought. I clicked open the calendar app which indicated that, in fact, it was not only November 2, but it was the year 2016.

Okay, now I was beyond confused. I turned on the TV, just in case my phone was acting weird. I never watched anything besides *General Hospital,* so the TV was always set to ABC, and it wasn't showing the date. Hey, make fun of me all you want, but remember, this is a woman who goes on New Kids on the Block cruises at the age of forty-two. So, the fact that I have watched almost every episode of *General Hospital* for the past thirty-five years of my life, thanks to my mother, should not be that surprising. I anxiously searched for a news or weather station that indicated what the actual date was. I finally came upon CNN, which was discussing the probable outcome for the next presidential election. I wasn't too weirded out at first, because they were discussing the odds of Trump winning the election. But then I realized that they weren't discussing his reelection, but rather his win. As I verbally told the TV that Trump was already president, Paul came around the corner and said, "Wow, you are watching CNN? I can't believe it," knowing I never watched anything related to politics. He continued. "And wow, I can't believe you just said you wanted Trump to win."

I quickly turned to Paul and exclaimed, "No I didn't want Trump to win, but he did!" Paul cocked his head a little, and looked at me funny. He said, "You never know," in a sing-songy voice, and walked back into the bathroom.

Now what the fuck do I do? Not only do I have no idea what the actual date is, I have no idea what fucking year it is. I picked up my phone again to look up Patrick's Instapic account, but I couldn't find it. I tried searching under numerous names, and even reluctantly tried looking up Abby, dreading the thought of seeing her face again. But I found nothing.

Okay, this is too much . . .this doesn't make sense, I thought to myself. So, after searching Instapic with no success, I went into my past texts. Even though I hadn't gotten a text from Patrick in over six months, I had kept every single one he ever sent. But as I searched "Jimmy," nothing came up.

I stood in the middle of the bedroom, with the remote in one hand and my phone in the other, not knowing what to do next . . .

not knowing what was real and what wasn't. I began realizing what my psychotic patients must feel like when they are having delusions and hallucinations. Sometimes they are able to tell me that they know something is not real, but it appears more than real to them. It was like everything that happened with Patrick over the last two years didn't happen, but it did. I know it did! Didn't it? I mean, the sex, the kissing, the conversations . . . I remember every detail like it happened yesterday. And I guess, in a way, it must have.

I looked over on the bedroom floor and saw my suitcase, with the Carnival tags still attached. I suddenly remembered how I threw down my suitcase when I got home super late the night before, and instead of going to "my bed," I crawled into hubby's bed while he was sleeping. I hadn't done that for a while, thanks to autism. But I remembered how exhausted I was after driving all day from New Orleans. I must have slept so hard that I dreamed the last two years.

Now the puzzle pieces were coming together, but this time, the pieces fit much better. My fantasy that became reality was actually a fantasy after all. The *Moral Gods* were definitely in the house that morning to remind me that fun stuff like that doesn't happen to Piper. It just doesn't. I never get the man of my dreams. But morally, thank God I really didn't. Because maybe I already had him.

I told myself that it all had to be a dream, because I had too much self-respect and admiration for myself to allow some asshole to rule my emotions and feelings for two years. There was no way that I would be a "only when it's convenient girl" for anyone. I deserved to be number one, and I was to Paul. I'm also not a cheater, and I knew there was no way I could actually cheat on my husband, no matter what obsession I had. Well, maybe Joey McIntyre, but that's for another book.

I went back into the bathroom and got dressed, ready to take Jack to school. As I was putting on my shoes, Paul came back in to kiss me goodbye. The kiss was warmer and longer than it had been in years. It was like we had a whole new connection, a stronger connection. It felt not only more loving, but more liking. I liked and loved Paul, and in that moment, I was so glad that everything was just a dream. I realized that my fantasy world was actually right here, at home, and maybe I already had the man of my dreams after all. I reminded myself right then and there that life is what you make it, and even though you might not always get everything you want, you can make it what you want, and have a fucking fantastic time doing it.

Paul told me he would meet me at our favorite Thai restaurant at 7:30, and walked out of the bathroom. As I was brushing my hair, he quickly peeked back in and said, "Oh, by the way, who's Patrick?"

Acknowledgments

First, I want to thank Laura because without you, none of this would be possible. I also want to give a shout out to my girl, Rachel, for reading along as I wrote it and cheering me on the whole way. Thanks also to Fat Booty for giving me the motivation and determination to do this. Thanks to Amy for indirectly finding my publisher. BIG thanks to my parents for always believing in me, and supporting me every step of the way . . . I love you more than words can say. And last but definitely not least, thanks to my hubby . . . just for being the amazing person you are!

About the Author

Karli Cook has been a hospital social worker for over seventeen years. She currently lives in Atlanta, Georgia, with her husband and nine-year-old autistic son. You can follow Karli's autism mom truths at autismmomthebomb.com, or go to spectrumisms.com for autism resources and to book Karli as a speaker for your next event.